L

Also by Zoë Barnes

Bumps
Hitched
Hot Property
Bouncing Back
Ex-Appeal

Love Bug

Zoë Barnes

LONDON NEW YORK SYDNEY TORONTO

This edition published 2002
by BCA
by arrangement with Judy Piatkus (Publishers) Ltd

CN 107241

Set in Times by
Phoenix Photosetting, Chatham, Kent
Printed and bound in Germany by
GGP Media, Pössneck

Acknowledgements

Grateful thanks to Gillian, Judy and Emma for their support, encouragement and completely heroic patience. And to Jupiter, who test-licked every page.

To every princess who's sick of kissing frogs.

Prologue: Cheltenham, one Monday morning in spring

There was no putting it off any longer.

Laurel Page stood in St Thaddeus Place, a lone fixed point in a two-way stream of people disgorged from buses and cars. Her second-best work suit itched horribly; all the little hairs in the woollen fabric seemed to have worked their way through her tights already, and it was only eight-thirty. But it was too late to go home and change.

Setting down her briefcase, she felt for the bunch of keys in her pocket – a brand-new set, cold and unfamiliar to the touch – and took a good hard look at the brass plate on the door in front of her. It read: DOVECOTE & MARSH MARRIAGE BUREAU (est. 1856). The very sight of that old-fashioned, mock-wood-grained door made her smile, sandwiched as it was between the Day-Glo-fronted One-Stop Copy Shop and The Happy Nappy: it looked for all the world like the portal to some other, more leisurely dimension.

And anyway, who in their right mind would run something that called itself a marriage bureau, in this day and age?

Me, she thought: that's who. And the concept felt crazier than ever. What on earth are you doing, Laurel? she asked herself for the umpteenth time. You of all people, running a dating agency! Not to mention that by some odd quirk or another the job also included acting as agony aunt for the local rag, when frankly she could have used one herself right now, the way she was feeling. Not that she'd know what to say if one did pop up like a genie from a bottle.

She imagined a quill pen scratching across vellum. *Dear Auntie Laurel, Today I'm starting my new job. Lucky me.* No, scrub the cheap sarcasm. *The thing is, it's all so embarrassing. I'm thirty-two years old and I feel like a four-year-old on my first day at nursery school. And I keep wondering if I'm making this really big mistake, you know, setting myself up for another fall. After all, I did promise myself I'd never be in charge of anything again after ...'* Her mouth dried at the memory. *After you-know-what. But this is hardly some massive multinational, is it? It's just a cute little old marriage bureau. Surely nothing can go wrong this time.*

She swallowed hard. 'Can it?'

A tiny shiver ran up and down her spine. And then the quill pen raced to the bottom of the page.

Yours sincerely, Laurel Page, spinster of this parish.

2

'Right,' she said out loud, determinedly ramming the key into the lock. Time to see the whites of their eyes.

Chapter 1

Laurel sat down in her squeaky leather armchair, behind her monolithic mahogany desk, and revelled in her splendid new office. Not that the word 'new' could really be applied to anything at Dovecote & Marsh, where even the franking machine had Queen Anne legs: it was like walking into a Charles Dickens theme park. What with the converted gas lamps and the etched glass windows, it felt as though a gang of street urchins might pop up from behind the aspidistra at any moment and break into 'Consider Yourself'.

I could really get to like this, she thought, and directed another beaming smile at Miss Gemma Brodie, her very first client. This matchmaking lark was turning out much easier than she'd thought; and better than that, it was fun. 'Well, I'm sure we can help you,' she said brightly, tucking a strand of collar-length blonde hair behind her ear. 'As our brochure says, there's someone for everyone at D&M.'

Miss Brodie's impressive chest heaved with pleasure, and the giant panda on her rather tight T-shirt suddenly looked several dinners better off. 'You really think so?'

Laurel ran a thoughtful finger round the rim of her teacup as her eyes darted around the five open files on her desk. No computer matchmaking here; everything at D&M seemed to live in pink cardboard folders, with an ad hoc filing system that had even colonised a cardboard box in the lavatory. It was certainly a change from the dot com company where she'd looked after publicity. Not that that was necessarily a bad thing.

Laurel's gaze lighted on one file in particular, and she smiled. 'Yes. As a matter of fact I really do.'

'Oh, thank you!' Gemma gushed, grasping Laurel's hand. 'Thank you so much!'

Somewhat embarrassed by this excess of gratitude, Laurel gently extricated her fingers. 'Don't mention it. It's what we're here for.'

'Yes I know that, but old Mr Case – you know, the one that was here before you – well, he just didn't seem to understand. I could talk and talk and talk, but it didn't make the slightest difference what I said, he just kept staring at me.' Gemma leaned forward and her chest spread out alarmingly across the desktop. 'I'm sure his mind wasn't on the job.'

Laurel could see why. 'Oh, I'm sure that wasn't the . . . er . . . case.' She winced at her own terrible pun. 'The important thing is that you're here now and we're going to introduce you to lots of suitable people. In fact,' she confided, 'I think I may have just the man for you right here.'

It was perfectly true. Laurel couldn't think of anyone

6

easier to find a match for than this voluptuous pocket Venus.

Miss Brodie's eyes widened in delight. 'Oh, how lovely!'

'In fact if you're comfortable with the idea, there's someone in the waiting room now I'd love you to meet.'

Miss Brodie grinned broadly. 'Really? That would be wonderful.'

Laurel mentally rubbed her hands together, and placed a tick in an invisible box. Job done. That nice Mr Coxon was in for a real treat.

Flushed with success, Laurel sauntered into her secretary's office with the empty teacups. 'Well! Are they all that easy?'

Connie Stanway looked up from stabbing at her aged typewriter with a pair of scissors. There was ribbon ink all over her bitten fingernails, and a blob of Tipp-Ex on her pale pink cardigan. 'Sorry?'

'Miss Brodie.' Laurel lowered her voice. 'The one with the chest.'

Connie's face acquired a couple of extra frown lines. At forty-three it was still a pretty face, but one that didn't smile quite as much as it ought. 'Ah. That Miss Brodie.'

'So, are they all that easy to match up?'

'Match up?' A hint of concern appeared in the cloud-grey eyes. 'Actually, I meant to tell you about—'

Laurel wasn't really listening; she was too busy basking in the afterglow. 'Easy as anything.' She bounced up and perched on the edge of her secretary's desk. 'As soon as I saw Mr Coxon's file I knew they were perfect for each other. Fancy them walking into the office on the very same morning!'

Connie's face turned the colour of stale hummus. 'Miss Brodie?'

'Yes, I told you.'

'With Mr Coxon?'

'That's right. They're having a nice little chat in the waiting room. Why?'

'Because . . .' Connie's pallor acquired a nasty tinge of green. 'Oh God.'

'Connie?' Laurel was sure nobody's face should be that colour. 'Are you all right?'

But Connie just kept repeating the same mantra, over and over again. She ran inky fingers through her mousy curls, leaving black streaks. 'Oh God oh God oh God.'

This was just plain exasperating. 'Whatever is the matter?' demanded Laurel.

Connie looked up at Laurel with pleading eyes. 'Just tell me you haven't matched Gemma Brodie with—'

At that point, Connie was cut short as a masculine yelp resounded round the office, and Mr Adrian Coxon entered stage left, closely pursued by an extremely irate Gemma Brodie, a woman who looked as if she had something other than romance on her mind.

'Oh no,' groaned Connie. 'You have.'

Laurel paced up and down her office, with Connie trailing in her wake.

'You've prised them apart?' demanded Laurel.

Connie nodded.

'And they're both OK?'

'Yes, but—'

'And nobody's suing us?'

'No, but—'

'Thank God for that.'

'Everything's sorted out now,' said Connie, pausing by the fireplace to straighten the portrait of the first Mr Dovecote as Laurel caught it with her elbow.

'No thanks to me,' commented Laurel, flinging herself into the squeaky leather armchair. 'How could I be so stupid?'

'You weren't to know they used to live together, were you? It's my fault, I should've warned you about those two. I meant to add a note to Miss Brodie's file.' Connie hovered between the desk and the door. 'The thing is,' she began, then stopped and began fiddling with the Sellotape dispenser.

Laurel looked up and feared the worst. 'What? What's happened now?'

'Nothing's happened. It's just . . . well, you've not to get yourself all in a panic over this, that's all.'

'I've not?'

'Definitely not. Hey, we all make mistakes, don't we?'

Laurel caught sight of her reflection in the gilt-framed mirror by the door; she'd bitten most of her lipstick off, her nose was all shiny, and her hair was sticking up on one side like a honey-blonde cockade. 'Oh no, how long have I been walking around like this?'

9

'A while. I didn't like to say.'

Laurel did her best to flatten down the unruly tuft. 'Thanks a bunch Connie, I look like a one-eared koala!'

Their eyes met and after a brief moment's awkwardness they both burst out laughing.

'Have a biscuit,' urged Connie. 'Go on, there's a chocolate one under all those digestives.'

'I'm not sure I deserve a chocolate one,' said Laurel, biting into it ruefully.

'It's OK, it's medicinal.' Connie perched her pink polyester bottom on the windowsill, munching. 'Don't be so hard on yourself, everybody gets stuff wrong to start off with.' She chuckled. 'And you'd be amazed, some of the folk we get in here. Ask Bette about the time she had that Sir Marlon what's-his-face on the phone, and she thought he was a heavy breather!'

'No!' Laurel gasped.

Connie's cheeks coloured. 'Then there was the time I got locked in the loo with an Arab sheikh who was looking for wife number fifty-two.'

Laurel choked on a biscuit crumb. 'How on earth did you manage that?'

'It's a long story. If we hadn't found a twenty-four-hour locksmith it could've turned into a diplomatic incident! So you see, matching up the gruesome twosome isn't really in the same league, is it?'

'Well, since you put it like that.' Laurel decided she could forgive herself enough to the extent of a Bourbon cream and two fig rolls. As she nibbled, she mused. 'Looks like I'm going to need help,' she announced.

'No problem.' Connie didn't just look willing,

thought Laurel; she positively oozed eagerness. 'Whatever you need.'

'Thanks. I suppose Mr Case had some kind of routine for running this place?' Not that he bothered leaving me any notes or anything, Laurel added silently. That would be far too helpful.

'Well yes, as a matter of fact he did. I know you wouldn't think so from all the cardboard boxes and the equipment here's straight out of the Ark, but we've kind of built up a system over the years. You know, ways of doing stuff, places to put things so they don't get lost.'

'Ah, so that's why the spare safe key's with the custard creams.' Laurel swallowed the last mouthful of biscuit, wiped her hands on her skirt and came to the only sensible decision. 'OK then, no more jumping in at the deep end for me. I'd be really grateful if you could help me get into the same daily routine, so I can ease myself in gently, get a proper idea of how this place has been run in the past. And then . . .'

'Then?' enquired Connie.

Laurel winked. 'Then we start making changes.'

That afternoon, Connie was humming to herself as she sorted through her files, piecing together Mr Case's typical working week. Haphazard Dovecote & Marsh's systems might be, but Connie's own files were as ordered and professional-looking as pink cardboard would allow. Of course it hadn't helped that Mr Case had been in the habit of taking files home, only to leave them on the bus, have them chewed by his dogs or return them back to front and covered in jam. But

11

Connie was made of stern stuff: her desk drawers never lacked for Sellotape, a damp cloth or the telephone number of the bus company.

As she was hammering out a list on her antiquated typewriter, she spotted a flash of red lurex jumper out of the corner of her eye. Looking up, she was just in time to see Stacey's three-inch steel stilettos tottering past her door for the fifth time that afternoon.

'Stace?'

Stacey didn't seem to notice, so Connie raised her voice and bawled. 'Stacey Biggs!'

A startled ginger poodle perm appeared in her doorway, framing a heart-shaped face dominated by large doll-blue eyes. 'Did you say something?'

'Honestly Stace, you're in a world of your own half the time.'

The doll-blue eyes blinked. 'Sorry.'

'And don't think I haven't noticed you accidentally wandering past my door every five minutes.'

Stacey coloured up. 'I was just on my way to, er—'

Connie wagged a mock reproving finger. 'It's no good, you won't get a look at Miss Page now, she's gone off to buy a fireproof filing cabinet.' She smiled at Stacey's crestfallen expression. 'It's OK, she's fine.'

The bounce returned to Stacey's poodle curls, making her look more than ever like a twenty-five-year-old version of Shirley Temple. 'Really?'

'Breath of fresh air if you ask me. You'll like her.' She nodded towards the main office. 'Go on, tell the others, you know you're dying to.'

It wasn't until Stacey had skipped happily out of

12

earshot that Connie added under her breath: 'Oh yes. This one I can really make something of.'

By the time Laurel had bought a nice electric-orange filing cabinet, arranged for it to be delivered to D&M, had a coffee and chatted with her staff about paper clips, it was getting on for five and she decided to go home. After all, she was her own boss now: who was going to tell her off for stealing the odd five minutes here and there?

Besides, she was knackered. She stifled a contented yawn as she turned off the London Road into Oriel Gardens, and parked outside a square-cut, cream-coloured Georgian pile with several TV aerials bristling out of it like cocktail sticks from a lump of cheese. It rejoiced in the name of Rivendell, but the nearest it had ever got to an elf was the solitary garden gnome, dangling its fishing rod rather pointlessly over the rockery.

Grabbing her briefcase from the passenger seat, she walked up to the front door, unlocked it and stepped into a rainbow of softly coloured light, filtered through the stained-glass panel. There were several neat piles of post on the half-moon-shaped hall table, one for each of the six flats. Laurel's consisted of a TV licence reminder, a mailshot about cosmetic surgery, and a picture postcard depicting a cowboy roping a steer.

Laurel climbed up the stairs to her first-floor flat, made a beeline for the fridge and drank half a litre of orange juice straight from the carton. Then she flicked on the CD player, threw her itchy jacket and skirt over

13

the sofa bed and flopped into the chintzy depths of her favourite armchair to read the postcard.

Dear Laurel, it ran. *having a lovely time here in Montana with your Uncle Greg. Going to rodeo tomorrow, your dad's threatening to take part!!! Weather hot, noses peeling, you'd love it. Love Mum and Dad XXX. PS How's the love life?*

Laurel shook her head and smiled. *The love life?* God Mum, you never give up do you? Laurel had lost count of the number of times she'd told her mum she'd given up men for ever, end of story. One of these days it might finally sink in. Yeah, and the Isle of Man might win the World Cup.

Hauling herself out of the chair, she ambled over to the cork board she'd hung above the telly and pinned up her mum's postcard with all the others. So far she had Tipperary, Copenhagen, Reykjavik, Boston, Louisiana and Montana. Who'd have thought the Page family could have spread itself so widely, or that Laurel's parents might take it into their heads to visit every last one of their distant relatives? A tiny flicker of irritation disrupted Laurel's serenity; there was something annoying about being less well-travelled than your own mother, even if you'd never particularly felt the urge to go llama-trekking in the Andes.

She took a deep, calming breath and sprinkled a few flakes of fish food into the aquarium. 'Hi Neil. How's my favourite guy today?'

Neil mouthed back soundlessly, a little piece of the tropics that had come to her. Not a very interesting piece admittedly, but Laurel liked to think she saw through

14

those drab greyish-brown scales to the essential Neil beneath.

'Not bad for a first day,' she reflected out loud. 'OK, so I nearly witnessed a murder in my own office, but hey, things could definitely have gone worse.' She bent down and looked Neil in the eye. 'What do you reckon? Any words of fishy wisdom on offer?'

But Neil just scarpered and hid, quivering, behind a lump of plastic coral.

'OK, be like that.' She stuck out her tongue at him. 'I'm off down the pub.'

Chapter 2

Nice quiet drink: that's what I need, thought Laurel as her inner remote control guided her out of Rivendell, across the road, past the corner shop and into the saloon bar of her local. Ah yes, some quality time slumped in a corner with a half of lager, letting the day's adrenalin seep away into the sweat-stained moquette. Just the very thing.

Unfortunately the Ram was not the best place to find it, at least not tonight. Half the chairs and tables had been stacked up against the wall, and in the middle of an improvised stage a man in a sequinned stetson was directing colourful oaths at a tatty old amplifier. Bugger, thought Laurel; I forgot Monday was country and western night.

Heads swivelled at her arrival, clocked the newcomer as One Of Them From The Flats, then returned to the much more interesting spectacle of Burford Bill trying to thump some life into his amp.

'Plug it in,' somebody shouted helpfully. Everybody laughed. Burford Bill made an obscene gesture.

'Nah, give it a kick.'

He tried that, but all he got out of it was a dull thud and a sore toe. 'Buggerin' thing's busted.'

Thank you God, thought Laurel, getting herself a bottle of Beck's and squeezing into the remotest corner she could find. And please could you see your divine way to giving him laryngitis as well, just for tonight?

Kicking off her shoes, she slid down on the poorly disguised church pew that called itself a settle, took a swig from the bottle and pondered the day she'd just had.

Dovecote & Marsh. The very name had an inch-thick layer of dust on it. There was oak panelling in the one and only toilet, one of the desks looked like genuine Chippendale, and a stack of brochures she'd found in the stationery cupboard listed all the prices in guineas. If anybody had asked her a few weeks ago whether places like that still existed, she'd probably have laughed. If they'd told her she'd be managing one of them, she'd have told them to get their heads examined. Still, at least D&M was distinctive. And that was what she'd been looking for lately, wasn't it? An escape from dot com hysteria, a little time to stop and smell the flowers rather than flog them over the Internet.

She smiled, recalling the big Deco vase on her office windowsill. Freesias, a great big scented cloud of them. They smelt great.

And then there were the staff. Four of them, too many for such a small business if it hadn't been so resolutely old-fashioned. You could probably run the whole outfit with one iMac and a mobile, but that wasn't really the point. And the staff seemed normal enough, from the little she'd seen of them. At any rate nobody had more than one head, and the rumours of cloven hooves had been vastly exaggerated.

But first impressions were only that, and maybe she had them completely wrong. After all, she'd made mistakes in the past. There were some who might say she was no judge of people at all.

Her hand closed on a beer mat and scrunched the cardboard circle until it snapped in two. Not going to think about the past, she told herself firmly. The past can't hurt you any more. What matters is what you're doing now, and the people you're doing it with.

Fluffy Stacey, eager Connie, jokey Ravi, and Connie's no-nonsense sister, Bette. Laurel could already frame their faces in her mind's eye, make dumb, one-dimensional guesses about their lives; so what were the odds that at this very minute they were doing exactly the same about her?

It was quite an uncomfortable thought.

The minute Bette got home to the Connelly stables, she threw her work shoes into the back of the Land Rover and slipped on the pair of gumboots she always kept under the passenger seat. If you lived around horses you had to dress the part, and Bette couldn't recall a single happy episode in her life that hadn't had a horse in it.

'Where's Jack?' she asked a girl grooming a bay mare in the stable yard.

'Top field, Mrs C.'

'He's not with that damn donkey again?'

' 'Fraid so.'

The ground squelched comfortably underfoot as she thrust her hands deep in the pockets of her ubiquitous Puffa jacket and headed for the top field. As she took a brisk and muddy short cut, she wasn't thinking about her husband and his stupid donkey fetish, but weighing up the new manager of D&M like a piece of prime bloodstock.

Sixteen hands, presentable teeth, mane could do with a trim but coat in passable condition. No obvious problems with colic or staggers, nice athletic build and a good solid rump. Ah, but temperament, that was the key, ask any tipster. How would the filly shape up when the pressure was on and you were hanging on to the rail with two furlongs still to go?

As she reached the top field, where a tatty grey giant of a donkey was stuffing itself with carrots, a man in a checked cap and Barbour jacket waved to her and called: 'How'd she shape up?'

'Game filly. Haven't checked out her form yet though.'

Yes, Bette nodded to herself, that was the important question. Did Laurel Page have the stamina to go the full distance, or would wily old Edwin Case bring her down at the first fence?

The pink Fiesta lurched backwards into the residents' car park, only just missing the tub of marigolds it had clipped on its way out that morning. It wasn't easy to park while wearing three-inch heels, and Stacey was thrilled to bits whenever she got between the white lines first time.

20

More through habit than anything else, she checked out her reflection in the rear-view mirror before grabbing her shopping and heading for the seventies' block of flats where she lived. She liked to look nice; in fact, she thought everybody had a duty to make the most of what they'd been given, even if what they'd been given was a bit mousy and past its best. You could do an awful lot with a bottle of hair dye and an uplift bra, as she was always trying to reassure Connie, not that Connie ever stopped working long enough to listen. And Bette; well, Bette was just plain not interested.

All Stacey really wanted was to make the world a lovelier place, filled with kittens and big red hearts and people being nice to each other. It was a pity not everybody saw things that way.

As she tottered up the stairs to her flat, she wondered if Miss Page saw things that way. Of course she did, or why would she want to run a marriage bureau? Why would anybody, if they didn't think romance was the whizziest, spiffiest, gorgeousest thing in the whole wide world? Mind you, she reminded herself as she unlocked the door, Mr Case used to run D&M and all he cared about was patting people on the bottom, which certainly didn't count as romantic in Stacey's book.

'Home!' she called as she closed the front door behind her.

A distant voice called back, 'In the kitchen.'

Stacey followed the voice to the kitchen and found her niece there, up to her elbows in flour and concentration. 'Hi Alex. Homework?' she panted, dumping her bags on a chair.

21

'Done it.'

Stacey ruffled the mop of flour-streaked hair. 'Don't believe you.'

'Don't then. How's the new boss?'

Stacey pondered for a few moments. 'Relaxed. Nice I think. Tell you what though.'

The girl looked up. 'What?'

'I'd love to know who does her highlights. They're lush.'

The sign on the door read RAVI'S ROOM: PRIVATE!, but it might as well have said 'Piccadilly Circus' for all the notice anybody took of it.

'Push off, Ash,' said Ravi, one eye on the TV as he peeled off his tie and threw it onto the pile of other ones slung over the back of a chair. 'I'm knackered.'

His younger brother evidently took this as an invitation, since he came in and flopped down on the end of Ravi's bed. 'Well?'

'Well what?'

'You asked her out yet then?'

Ravi squirmed. It was bad enough having a younger brother at all, without him ferreting out every tiny detail of Ravi's so-called personal life. 'No,' he admitted.

'Taking your time, aren't you?'

'What's that supposed to mean?'

'Come on mate, when you were back at school you asked the Deputy Head out on a date! They're still talking about it now.'

'Yeah, and I got detention for it. Budge over.' Ravi

pulled a creased sports top from under his brother's backside.

'Oh I get it, you're chicken!' Ash dodged a swipe from a Juventus pillowcase. 'So what's she like?'

Ravi retrieved the pillow from the floor. 'Who?'

'Your new boss, stupid. What's her name ... Holly Bush or something?'

'Laurel Page.' Ravi pulled the sports top over his head and wriggled into his second-best black jeans. 'I dunno, thirtyish, maybe thirty-five tops. Sort of blonde, nice bum, not too thin.'

Ash grinned. 'Older woman eh? Sounds tasty.'

Ravi shrugged. 'If you like that sort of thing.'

Then, just as Ash was about to ask Ravi if he liked that sort of thing, a voice drifted up the stairwell in the nick of time. 'Food!'

In her father's dismal time warp of a kitchen, Connie gripped the washing-up sponge and counted to ten.

'Don't reckon much to this fish,' he droned through the open doorway from the dining room. 'We ate better in Korea.'

'So go back to bloody Korea,' growled Connie, *sotto voce*.

'What's that? Speak up, you're always mumbling.'

'I said, hurry up, Dad, your pudding's going cold.' Dad sniffed. Connie washed up the same plate for the fourth time, unable to relax, anticipating every petty whinge and hating herself for resenting it. 'Did you have a nice day?'

'No.'

'I thought you were going down the Legion.'

'I was. Then I didn't.'

'Oh.' Try again. 'I've got a new boss at work.' Pause. Nothing. 'She seems nice.' Still nothing. 'I think she's going to modernise things a bit.'

'There's bones in this fish.'

'I did say to be careful, Dad.' Connie took a deep breath and waited for the inevitable.

It came. 'Why can't you cook like your sister? Your sister can cook.'

'Because I'm not my sister,' she muttered between clenched teeth, then raised her voice to a peak of forced pleasantness. 'It's haddock, Dad, you know you love your haddock. I did it just the way Mum used to.'

There was a pause. Then: 'Your sister cooks a bit of haddock better than that Delia woman any day.'

Tears pricking the undersides of her eyelids, Connie swung round and marched to the door of the dining room. As if it wasn't bad enough working with Bette, she had to put up with her Dad eulogising her at every turn, as if being rich and having kids was the be-all and end-all of everything. 'Well my sainted sister doesn't want anything to do with you,' she flared, 'so you'll just have to put up with my haddock, won't you?'

Dad's small, red eyes contracted to malevolent pits in his withered potato of a face. 'Don't you talk about her like that! Bette's a good girl, made something of herself. Not like some. Now take this much away and bring me my pudding.'

It wasn't that you could have heard a pin drop; more

like you could have heard a snowflake falling on cotton wool. The Ram hadn't seen anything like it in twelve years of country and western nights. It was safe to say that Burford Bill and the Burfordettes were not going down all that well. As the silence turned to jeers and insults, one of the Burfordettes burst into tears and got hiccups; while the great man himself snatched up his guitar and stormed off into the Gents as the beermats came flying.

The landlord tapped the mike to get attention. 'Change of plan ladies and gents, Alan's going to fetch out his Big Green Karaoke Machine.' A cheer went up. 'So, what lovely lady's going to set the ball rolling?'

In two bounds, Laurel was out of the door. That was quite enough people for one day.

Chapter 3

First thing on Thursday morning, Connie was waiting by Laurel's desk with a small cardboard box. If she had been smiling any more broadly, the top half of her head would have toppled off backwards.

Intrigued, Laurel hung her jacket on one of the pegs behind the door. 'Morning Connie, what've you been up to? Nobody should look that cheerful this early in the morning!'

'I've brought you this.' Connie laid the box on the desk as gently as if it contained new-laid eggs – which, for all Laurel knew, it did.

'What is it? An office pet?' Laurel's imagination started running away with her. 'It's not a hamster, is it? I've always fancied a hamster.'

Connie laughed. 'Good grief no, nothing like that. I've just spent this week working on some ideas, that's all.'

Laurel frowned. 'Ideas? What ideas?'

'Mine. Ones I had. You did say you were thinking of maybe changing a few things round here?'

'Yes, I suppose I did. Once I've settled in, found my feet . . .'

'So I thought, why not jot down some of my ideas and show them to you?' Connie looked eagerly at the box, like a schoolgirl presenting her teacher with a gift-wrapped packet of Quality Street.

'Oh,' said Laurel, somewhat taken aback. Slipping a fingertip under one of the flaps, she peered cautiously inside. 'Connie – that's an encyclopaedia in there!'

Connie's face beamed like a tropical sun. 'Oh, not really. Just a few . . . you know . . . thoughts.'

Laurel flicked through the two-inch pile of paper. 'All week?'

'Uh-huh.' The tropical sun went supernova. 'But only in my own time, of course.'

'Wow.' Laurel felt distinctly punch-drunk. 'That's very, um, *pro-active* of you.'

Connie looked so proud she might explode. 'You can read it now if you like.'

Laurel let go of the cardboard flap and it pinged back onto the box. 'Not just this minute, Connie. The thing is, I'm ever so busy right now.'

'But you will read it later?'

'Oh yes. Definitely later. You couldn't be a saint and get me a coffee, could you? Only I've got someone coming to see me in ten minutes.'

Not until Connie was gone did Laurel allow herself a sigh of relief. With the door securely closed, she lifted the pile of papers out of the box, scanned the first page then replaced the whole lot hurriedly, her heart inexplicably thumping. Yes, Dovecote & Marsh certainly could

28

use some changes; in the fullness of time. But she'd been thinking of starting with new curtains, not a fully budgeted Five-Year Economic Plan! What had appealed most about the agency was the fact that it didn't seem to have changed its approach to business since it first opened its doors. After all that had happened to her, Laurel couldn't help but feel relieved at the sanctuary D&M offered from the twenty-first century. What she wanted now was a quiet life. But it seemed her new colleagues had other ideas.

'Bloody hell, Connie!' she whistled. 'You certainly don't hang about, do you?'

By Friday afternoon, Laurel was beginning to feel almost at home. She had her own mug on the rack in the office kitchenette, Bette had enrolled her in the Lottery syndicate, and Stacey was threatening to knit her some red leg warmers.

'So, d'you fancy Villa for the Cup then?' she enquired as she and Ravi sorted through some ancient files.

'Nah. Got to be United every time.' He shook half a dozen dead spiders out of the top file, and sneezed loudly.

'*Gesundheit*. What, even with five out injured?'

'It's all a big PR con, you mark my words. Oh yeuch, get a load of this.' He dropped half a twenty-year-old Twix into his waste bin. 'You a fan then?'

'On and off. I used to go to—'

She didn't get a chance to say 'Goodison Park', because for some reason Ravi's entire body was overtaken by a sudden spasm and he leapt out of his chair as though five thousand volts had just zapped through the seat of his trousers.

'Ravi?' She stared at him. 'Ravi, why are you standing to attention?' As she spoke the words she followed his eye-line and pivoted round, to find herself gazing right over the head of a short man with tall hair.

Five foot five with a seven-foot personality, that was Edwin Case. Not to mention the hundred-decibel voice.

'No need to stand on ceremony,' he boomed, and Laurel's eardrums recoiled from the onslaught. 'For God's sake relax, boy!'

'Yes Colonel, thank you Colonel,' said Ravi, and sat straight back down again, looking anything but relaxed.

'And get a haircut, it's halfway down your back.'

'Yes Colonel.'

Laurel looked quizzically at Edwin Case. 'Colonel?' Then she set off after him in exasperation as he walked straight past her and into her office. 'You didn't tell me you were a colonel.'

'What?' He looked her up and down as though he had just discovered her behind the toilet cistern and was working out what best to spray her with. 'Oh, that. I was in the Guards for a while, nothing to make a song and dance about, what?' Slipping off his gloves, he laid them on Laurel's desk. 'Just thought I'd drop by to see how you're getting on.'

His eyes lighted on Laurel's pride and joy: her lovely, brand-new, hundred-per-cent fireproof filing cabinet.

'Ye gods, woman, what on earth is that?'

'It's a filing cabinet.'

30

'I can see that. But ...' His voice dropped to an outraged whisper. 'But the bloody thing's *orange*!'

Laurel polished its gleaming top protectively with the sleeve of her blouse. 'What's the matter with that?'

'The matter? *The matter!*' Edwin's whispered rage rose to such a high-pitched squeak that dogs five miles away started howling. 'You listen to me, young lady.' His finger wagged at her chest. 'I didn't hire you just so you could go buying orange filing cabinets!'

'No,' agreed Laurel. 'You hired me to run this agency.'

'Bureau.'

'All right, to run this *bureau*. Which I'm doing.'

'Incorrect, Miss Page!' By now, Edwin was so puffed up with indignation that he looked like a bullfrog with wind. 'I hired you to uphold my mother's principles. To the very. Last. Letter. And that is what I expect you to do. There will be no radical changes. Is that quite clear?'

Laurel manoeuvred herself in front of the desk. Perhaps now would not be such a great moment for Colonel Case to clock an eyeful of Connie's in-depth report. 'Perfectly clear, thank you.'

'Because if you're not willing to do that,' Edwin's eyes narrowed, 'you can find yourself a new job.'

Chapter 4

'Oh dear.' Mr Graeme Lillee smiled a small, mortified smile. 'I really should have warned you about the smell.'

Laurel exchanged quizzical looks with Stacey, whose turn it was to sit in on Laurel's interviews. Stacey looked none the wiser. 'Smell?' Laurel sniffed the air. 'What smell?'

Dovecote & Marsh's newest client shifted uncomfortably in his chair. He was one of those men, Laurel mused, who would always look as though their suits were wearing them, rather than vice versa. And what with him being blond, that black two-piece made him look like a pint of Guinness.

'*My* smell. It doesn't matter how often I wash or change my clothes, it just won't go away.'

Laurel really was confused now. All she could smell was soap and aftershave. 'But you don't—'

'Please, there's no need to be polite.' He leaned forward and lowered his voice. 'I know my clients tend to, um, *linger* around me. And once people find out what I do for a living . . .'

Laurel consulted the open file on her desk and instantly understood his paranoia. 'Ah.'

'Exactly. And that's why I came to you.' Mr Lillee fiddled despondently with the end of his tie. 'I mean, I don't want you to waste your time on me if there's no chance, only I thought maybe *somewhere* there might be a . . . a . . .'

'A woman with no sense of smell?' quipped Laurel. Then she caught the look of disbelief on Stacey's face, realised what she'd just said and clapped a hand over her mouth. 'Oh gosh Mr Lillee, I'm so sorry, I can't believe I said that!'

There was a short but very uncomfortable silence, broken only by the gentle sound of Stacey's heel tapping on the polished parquet. Whoops. Laurel grimaced inwardly. Nice one, Loz, ever considered a career in the diplomatic corps? The poor man's only been here five minutes and already you've upset him.

Then, miraculously, Mr Lillee threw back his head and guffawed. 'No sense of smell, I like that! You've hit the nail on the head there.'

Phew, thought Laurel as the spectre of litigation receded. 'You know, Mr Lillee, you mustn't run yourself down.'

He sighed good-naturedly. 'That's easier said than done.'

'Not if you keep reminding yourself you're worth it. Try and, you know, think positive.'

It sounded so trite, but then she looked him up and down properly for the first time and thought perhaps it wasn't. Passably good-looking, under forty, vaguely blond, nice, polite, good-humoured ... Good grief, he even had his own hair, which set him apart from at least thirty per cent of Dovecote & Marsh's male clientele. So what if he was a wee bit neurotic? Who was she to talk? This was the kind of guy who really deserved to have somebody.

'You've seen our motto, haven't you?' She indicated the framed poster on the wall by the door. ' "There's someone for everyone at D&M"?'

'Sometimes I can't help thinking it means everyone but me.'

It was then that a moment of true epiphany descended from the heavens and thumped Laurel smack between the eyes. Mr Graeme Lillee, she declared silently, you *will* have someone. Someone really special. Yes I, Laurel Page, am going to take your life and completely rebuild it for you.

And if that works, her subconscious added, maybe I'll even think about rebuilding my own.

Laurel paused outside Connie's office. Through the door came the furious rattle of fingers bashing hell out of an elderly typewriter.

'Go on then.' Laurel looked soulfully at Stacey.

The large blue eyes blinked in innocent incomprehension. 'Go on what?'

'Tell me what a mess I made of it.' She squared her shoulders. 'It's OK, be honest, I can take it.'

Laurel held her breath and waited for Stacey to give her the full scathing rundown on the way she'd handled

Mr Lillee. Tactless, clumsy, promising more than D&M could deliver.

'Well, it is Monday,' said Stacey brightly.

'Uh?'

'People are never at their best on Mondays, are they? Leastways, that's what my magazine said. Your biorhythms are all up the creek, see. Tuesday mornings about eleven o'clock are best for social interaction. Monday mornings, you might as well not bother.'

'Oh,' said Laurel. 'I'll remember that.'

'And actually, I thought you did really well,' Stacey went on.

'For a Monday?'

Stacey smiled. 'Even for a Friday.'

'Even though I practically insulted him?'

'Well, he seemed quite happy when he went.'

'Either that or he was just too nice to complain.'

'And you'll get lots better at it with experience. Besides,' Stacey pointed out encouragingly, 'we're here to help you out when you're stuck. We're good at calming people down, we had loads of practice with Mr Case.'

As Laurel opened her mouth to demand the full SP on Edwin Case, the door to Connie's office opened and she appeared with a brick-sized pile of envelopes held together with blue elastic bands.

'There you go, boss,' she announced, thrusting the envelopes at Laurel's chest.

Laurel took them. 'What's this?'

'Your share of the letters from the *Courant* – you know, for the agony page?'

Laurel contemplated the solid chunk of paper. '*My* share?'

'That's right. We take a pile each and pick out the best ones.'

'You mean the ones we think we can help,' Stacey corrected her.

'And the ones that are printable!' Connie retorted.

'Then we think up the replies between us. Mr Case knows the editor, we've been doing it for years. The company gets paid a monthly fee and we get a discount on advertising.' Stacey read the return address scrawled across the top envelope in vivid green ink. 'Ooh look, there's one from Rampant of Rodborough, can I read it after you?'

'So what exactly am I supposed to do with these?' asked Laurel.

Connie winked. 'Same as we've always done. Read, inwardly digest and try not to be sick when you get to the one from Lovelorn of Leckhampton.'

'You mean you've already read them?'

'Oh no, Lovelorn's just one of our regulars.'

'Hmm.' Laurel twanged a rubber band. 'Be still my beating heart.'

'Well, you did say you wanted to learn the routine before you made any changes!'

Connie vanished back into her office and Laurel had just turned to leave when her secretary popped out again. 'Er, speaking of changes . . .'

Laurel, fresh from her run-in with Edwin Case, tensed. 'Yes?'

'I was sort of wondering. Don't suppose you've read my report yet?'

It was a perfectly innocent question, but Connie might just as well have taken an axe to a hornet's nest.

'No Connie, I haven't!' snapped Laurel, and left Connie wondering what on earth she'd done wrong.

Connie was the last one to depart that evening. As she closed the door of the office behind her, she saw Laurel on her hands and knees on the landing, doing something to her new orange filing cabinet.

Correction. Her half-orange filing cabinet. For the top half had already disappeared under a coat of gunmetal-grey paint.

She walked up behind Laurel. 'Hello.'

Silence.

'Why are you painting it grey?'

Laurel's brush paused momentarily, but she didn't turn round or answer.

'I thought you liked it orange.' The words hung in the paint-scented air for a few moments, then seemed to spiral like smoke down the stairwell and out through the door to St Thaddeus Place. 'About my report. I was just wondering –'

This time, Laurel looked up at Connie just long enough to say, 'I'm busy.' And then turned her attentions back to her short, impatient brush strokes.

'Oh,' said Connie. ' 'Night then.'

She paused halfway down the stairs for the answering ' 'Night', but Laurel didn't reply.

*

On Tuesday afternoon, Laurel was in a much sunnier mood, humming happily to herself as she arranged some stargazer lilies in her office. She'd decided on the arty green glass vase; it would really brighten up that bare windowsill. Even Case couldn't object to her adding a vase to her office space.

There was a knock at the door. Before she had time to decide between 'Come in' and 'Bog off', Connie walked right in.

'Is something wrong?' demanded Laurel, slightly put out.

'No, nothing,' replied Connie. 'I just wondered if you'd got round to . . .' Her gaze took in the entire room before lighting on the cardboard box perched on Laurel's topmost shelf. 'Oh, there it is!'

'Not yet.'

Connie fidgeted on the threshold. 'Oh. So when do you reckon you might have a look at it?'

'What do you think?' breezed Laurel, practically frogmarching Connie across to the window. 'Vase in the centre or to the left?'

By Wednesday lunchtime, nowhere in the entire building was sacred any more; not even the toilet. When Laurel opened the cubicle door, she found Connie lying in wait outside.

'I was just wondering,' began Connie.

'You asked me ten minutes ago!' protested Laurel.

'Yes I know, but I don't suppose you've managed to read my report yet?'

'No, I haven't!' Laurel stalked across to the washbasin, feeling more and more like a persecuted minority. 'And going on about it isn't going to make it happen any faster,' she added, her eyes meeting Connie's in the mirror. Oh please go away, she prayed silently. Can't you see I don't want to talk about this? What was the point in talking about Connie's extensive plans for the business when Case wouldn't let her change so much as the colour of their envelopes? But evidently the point hadn't got through, since Connie was still hopping up and down like a neurotic bedspring.

'Laurel . . .'

Hands dripping, the swung round and spattered Connie with soapsuds. 'What!' she barked.

'You've tucked your skirt in your knickers.'

The following morning, everyone knew something truly momentous was about to happen. It was written all over Laurel's face as she strode right past Ravi's desk and into Connie's office, without so much as a 'Hello, has the postman been?'

'Connie!' she closed the door behind her. 'Just the person I've been looking for.'

This came as such a surprise that Connie accidentally typed a whole line of Xs. 'I am?'

'Oh yes.' Laurel perched her bottom comfortably on Connie's window ledge and felt the sun warm her back through the glass. 'I've been thinking, Connie. About what we were discussing – you know, about making a few changes around here?'

'You *have*?' Sudden delight washed over Connie, so much so that she didn't even mind when Laurel

40

bounced off the windowsill and grabbed her by the shoulders.

'Oh yes. And you know what? You were right.'

There was a long, dramatic pause. A drum-roll sounded inside Connie's head. This was it: the moment she'd been waiting for, after all these years of Dickensian drudgery! At last, Dovecote & Marsh was about to take its first, faltering steps into the twentieth century (the twenty-first was still a bit too much to hope for).

Laurel continued, breathless with enthusiasm. 'So, bearing in mind what you said, I've done something I should have done the minute I took over at D&M.'

An i-Mac, fantasised Connie. Please God let mine be an i-Mac. I don't even care if it's a grey one. Hell, I don't even mind if it's not an i-Mac, as long as it's a computer and it works.

'Ready?'

Connie nodded fervently.

Reaching into her shopping basket, Laurel produced a clear plastic bag filled with water. 'See? I've bought us a fish!'

There was an atmosphere of hushed expectation as everyone gathered round the brand new fish tank. Everyone, that was, except Connie, who lurked in the background muttering darkly about some people not having a clue how to run a modern business, and deserving to be told where to stick their precious fish.

Bette gave her sister a hearty elbow in the ribs. 'Shut up, Connie, it's a nice fish. Granted it's not a racehorse, but you can't have everything.'

41

Connie scowled. 'A couple of lovely computers and a cute little fax machine would be a damn sight more use.' She lowered her voice to a mutinous whisper. 'All that talk about livening things up around here? That's all it was, talk! She's turning out even worse than old Case.'

Bette sighed and thrust her hands into the pockets of her quilted waistcoat. "Well *I* like her,' she said. 'And so do those two.'

Dead on cue, Ravi and Stacey cheered and clapped as a rather beautiful black and yellow angelfish plopped elegantly into its new home. Connie's scowl, on the other hand, deepened.

'Oh look!' enthused Stacey, 'it's wiggling its fins, I think it's saying hello.'

Ravi gave her a funny look. 'Have you been watching *Teletubbies* videos again?'

'Won't it be lonely in there?' enquired Bette, watching the new arrival gliding around the empty tank.

'Not in the least,' replied Laurel. 'And d'you know why? Because I've bought it a friend!' She produced a second polythene bag. 'See? Say hello to Fish Number Two, everyone.'

She held up the bag and everybody inspected the small creature inside.

'It's all brown,' commented Stacey disappointedly. 'And boring.'

'What sort is it?' asked Ravi.

'I think it's a colomesus,' replied Laurel, 'but the shopkeeper wasn't sure.'

42

'Well it's not a bloody Pentium 4,' muttered Connie, with an edge of bitterness.

Laurel ignored the jibe and handed Ravi the bag. 'Why don't you do the honours? Go on, introduce it to its little fishy friend.'

Ravi undid the bag carefully and emptied the contents into the tank. The newcomer flicked its tail, looped the loop, sized up its new surroundings – and then went straight for the angelfish, like a Rottweiler scenting a postman's leg.

'Aaaah!' squeaked Stacey, turning white and dropping her coffee cup. 'Do something, Ravi!'

'Oh shit,' said Ravi, covering his eyes.

'You vicious little horror.' Laurel grabbed a net and made frantic attempts at recapturing the fishy felon.

Connie sniffed and folded her arms. 'See?' she said, though no one was listening. 'I told you this was a bad idea.'

The mystery killer fish of Old Cheltenham Town was positively strutting around its tank in splendid isolation, a ragged shred of angelfish fin dangling from its jaws. It looked radiantly pleased with itself, but frankly it was the only happy thing in the whole office.

The tall, dark, Gallic-looking young man cast a dubious glance around all the glum faces as he opened the door of Dovecote & Marsh and stepped inside.

'Hello?'

There were three people in the office, but nobody said anything. Not even the girl with the huge ginger perm, who looked like the kind of person who'd seldom be lost for words. She was too busy sobbing into a box of pink Kleenex.

'Is this a bad time? Should I come back later?'

Since this still failed to elicit a response, he tried tapping the nearest shoulder, which just happened to belong to Ravi. The killer fish's unwitting accomplice looked up with guilt-etched eyes. 'Yeah?'

'Hi.' At this small sign of life, the newcomer's face relaxed a little. 'I was hoping maybe you could, you know, fix me up an appointment to . . . er . . .' He waved his hands around uncertainly, then gestured in the vague direction of his heart.

'To register, you mean?'

'Yeah. Register, that's it. I'm a bit new to this. Can I see the boss?' the stranger asked.

Ravi dragged himself listlessly to his fee. 'Yeah, sure, whatever. Follow me, I'll take you to see her.'

Ravi plodded off to Laurel's office, head down, hands in pockets. Reaching her open door, Ravi halted in his tracks and recoiled at the shouts coming from within. 'She's ah, on the phone,' he announced, indicating a chair just inside the door. 'Have a seat.' He nudged the stranger forward. 'I expect she'll be finished in a minute.'

And before the stranger had a chance to protest, the door had clicked shut behind him.

Laurel wiped the blood off the telephone receiver, and shouted into it. 'What the hell kind of fish *is* it?' she demanded. 'A Balinese Passionfish! You never said it was a piscicidal maniac!'

44

An indistinct voice on the other end of the line answered in hushed, apologetic tones.

'Oh really? Well that's not good enough,' retorted Laurel, her much-prized inner serenity severely ruffled. 'Bastard thing nearly had my fingers off!'

The same voice mumbled something fatuous about feeding.

'Special diet? Are you kidding? What am I supposed to do, throw in a cow and retire to a safe distance?'

Mumble, mumble, mumble.

In exasperation, Laurel crashed the receiver back down. Turning round to find another sticking plaster, she found herself confronted not by Ravi with the first-aid kit, but by a vision of knicker-dampening masculine perfection. A man so tall, dark and handsome he might have stepped straight out of her own subconscious. A man who looked uncannily like . . .

'Jason?' she gasped.

Chapter 5

By the time Laurel managed to pull herself together, the handsome stranger had already taken a few hesitant steps forward. He hovered uncertainly in the middle of her office, looking like someone who rather wished he had chosen this moment to be somewhere else.

Laurel made an effort to rescue what few wits she could scrape together. My God, she thought as she gazed at him; he's not that much like Jason really, but standing in profile with the light at that angle . . .

She dropkicked her two-timing bastard of an ex-boyfriend to the back of her mind. 'Hello.'

'Aye. Well.' The stranger's blue eyes seemed to glitter against his tanned skin. His voice was so deep Laurel could practically feel the vibrations running up and down her spine; the rough edge of his accent titillating like sugar crystals sprinkled on double cream. No, not like Jason at all. A thousand times sexier. She might have vowed to give up men but that didn't stop her looking or indeed appreciating a man who was so . . . well . . . aesthetically pleasing.

'So you'd be Ms Page then?'

'Call me Laurel.' She gazed up at him like an awestruck teenager. '*Please*. Would you ... I mean is there something I can do for you?'

He shuffled his feet in a gruff, manly sort of way and stared down at the parquet floor. A Byronic lock of very black hair slipped down over his forehead. 'I – that is, a friend of mine ...'

Laurel smiled understandingly. 'Ah, I see. So would this *friend* be thinking about meeting that special someone?'

The stranger looked puzzled. 'Friend? No. He just reckons I ought to – you know – get out and meet people. This was all his idea,' he added with just a hint of accusation.

Laurel gazed up into those sapphire eyes and had to make a concerted effort not to drool. 'Oh, well I'm sure we can help you. Absolutely!' She took a step forward and got her right foot wedged in the wastepaper basket. Blushing crimson, she shook the basket off, laddered her tights and sent her shoe skidding across the floor. 'Damn.'

Perfectly unruffled, Prince Charming bent down to retrieve the shoe. 'Are you all right?'

'Yes, yes, everything's fine,' she gabbled in embarrassment. 'I can manage, really, honestly I'm that clumsy it's a wonder I'm not covered in bruises. Why don't you ... I mean, where was I? Oh, yes. We've helped thousands of people over the years, would you like a coffee, milk and sugar?' Laurel tried to slide her shoe back on as discreetly as she could. 'Cup?

48

Saucer? Biscuit?' (Oh shit, now I sound demented.)

He stared at her open-mouthed and she could almost feel herself curling up at the edges.

'Sorry about that.' She flashed him a smile. Deep breath and start again. 'Do make yourself comfortable.' As she indicated the two lumpy old leather armchairs flanking the original Regency fireplace, she noticed the newcomer staring intently at the two portraits on either side of the chimneybreast. 'Don't let them put you off,' she laughed, 'that's just Mr Dovecote and Mr Marsh – they think they still own the business, don't you, guys?'

No doubt deeply shocked by such informality, Mr Dovecote and Mr Marsh glowered down from their frames. But Laurel was far too preoccupied with the handsome stranger to worry about the evil eye. She hovered by his chosen chair, torn between the desperate urge to escape and the even more desperate one not to. 'So,' she ventured.

'Well.'

'I, um—'

'Yes,' he agreed, probably wondering why Laurel's indecisive bottom was hovering a foot above the seat of the other chair.

It could have gone on like that until her thigh muscles gave out, neither of them actually managing to say anything sensible, if Laurel's nerve hadn't yielded first. 'I'll go and organise us that coffee, shall I?'

'I'd rather have tea if you've got it.'

'Yes, tea, right, sorry, should've asked. Would that be Earl Grey or Darjeeling – or herbal? Cranberry and

49

elderflower? I think we've got some of that somewhere if we haven't run out.' Oh no, she was gabbling
again. She was so out of practice at talking to men.
Especially good-looking men who had the power to
make her go weak at the knees with just a glance. In
fact she couldn't even remember the last time she'd
found herself as drawn to a man as she was to this
one. 'And how about a biscuit or two? Rich Tea?
Chocolate Fingers? Or I could send Ravi out to buy
some Hobnobs . . .'

Before her visitor had a chance to escape from this
biscuit-obsessed madwoman, she fled, leaving him to
make whatever polite conversation he could with Mr
Dovecote and Mr Marsh. At least they might make
some sense.

As Laurel approached her desk at the speed of sound,
Connie stopped swearing at her bottle of dried-up Tipp-
Ex and went back to just looking sullen.

'Connie, just the person,' panted Laurel. 'Can I ask
you a big, big favour?'

'I'm busy.' The look on her secretary's face said
'Naff off, I'm not speaking to you, you're not my
friend any more.' She lobbed the Tipp-Ex back into
her desk drawer as though it were a hand grenade.
'Typing out fifty identical letters, remember? Of
course, if I had a nice little computer with mail-merge
software . . .'

Oh please, willed Laurel. Don't do this to me, not
now. 'I'd be ever so grateful,' she wheedled.

Connie let out an exasperated sigh. 'What favour?'

'Just some tea.' Laurel hopped from one foot to the other. 'And maybe just a few biscuits?'

Connie looked her up and down. 'What's going on?'

'Going on?'

'You've gone bright red. And what happened to your tights?'

Laurel edged her skirt down self-consciously. 'Nothing's up, I'm fine. There's a . . . a new gentleman client in my office and he'd like some tea, that's all.'

'What new client? There's nothing in the diary about a new client, not till half-past ten on Monday. Shouldn't Stacey be sitting in with you?'

'No, I've been flying solo since Wednesday, didn't she tell you? Thought I'd go for the baptism of fire.'

Yes, added Laurel to herself, and it's really opened my eyes. There I was, half-expecting all D&M's clients to be crusty old colonels or complete inadequates, and it turns out they're not like that at all. They're just ordinary people. People who need to be loved. People like me.

Connie's finger jabbed at the virgin page. "Look, nothing! It's not that one Ravi dragged in off the street, is it? What's his name?'

With a start Laurel realised she hadn't even thought to ask. She covered up her own inadequacy by snapping, 'Just organise some tea, will you? Cups, not mugs. And maybe we should have those pretty flowery saucers, or are they a bit girly? Oh I don't know. Anyway, make sure they're clean. I'm just off to the loo.'

Connie's lip curled as she watched Laurel vanish

51

through the door marked Water Closet. 'Make sure they're clean?' Even the miniature teddy bear on top of her desk-tidy looked outraged. 'My cups are always clean! Laurel Page, I was wrong about you. You're turning out to be a total waste of space.'

She flounced off to the kitchenette, with its silver sugar tongs and its stupid old-fashioned whistling kettle. Reaching into the cupboard under the gas ring, she withdrew an aged toffee tin.

'My second-best biscuits,' she told herself firmly. 'That's all she's getting off me.' Her eyes narrowed to steely slits. 'And I won't even warm the pot.'

Laurel felt rather better by the time she got back to her own office. For one thing, she'd had a chance to give her hair and lippy some much-needed attention; and for another, the nameless hunk in her office looked much more at ease, stretched out in one of the armchairs and munching biscuits.

Ah, nice ordinary digestives. That, at least, was a relief. Connie normally had this fetish for those horrible fancy biscuits with bits that got stuck in your teeth – and dislodged bridgework was not exactly top of Laurel's wish list right now.

Pausing for a moment just outside the door, she wriggled the tension out of her shoulders, took a deep breath and launched herself into the office with a thousand-carat smile.

'Hello again, sorry about the wait.' She stuck out her hand and he engulfed it in a manly grip that simply oozed testosterone.

'Ms Page.'

'Laurel,' she reminded him. As she closed the door behind her, her entire body rippled with excitement, in a way it hadn't since she'd locked herself in the stationery cupboard with the Head Boy, way back in the Lower Sixth. I've changed so much since then, she thought with a pang of nostalgia. But then again, so have a lot of things. Even Milky Ways don't taste the same.

'I've been well looked-after, thanks.' His accent had a rugged, Pennine quality to it that made Laurel think of wild, windswept moors, Yorkshire pudding and ooh, Sean Bean.

'That's good. It's so much easier to work with people when they feel comfortable with us and what we do.' Laurel eased herself into the chair opposite, balancing a clipboard and pen on her lap. 'Incidentally, how much *do* you know about us?'

'Not a lot,' admitted Mr. Irresistible, swallowing a mouthful of tea. He leaned forward in a confiding sort of way, those blue eyes twinkling like rough-cut jewels. 'I'll be honest, it was all my mate Don's idea. He does your printing or something – leaflets and that?'

'Oh, that Don.' Laurel recalled a brief conversation with a pleasant Scottish man who'd spent most of his time looking at Connie.

'He reckons I should get out and,' he gave an embarrassed cough, 'meet girls.'

Laurel laughed, a little too conspicuously; and glancing down, realised that she was showing an awful lot of leg. You hussy! she thought, tugging the hem down' you're supposed to be interviewing this guy and you're flirting with him instead. Pull yourself together, you shameless tart. You're not like that any more, remember?

'Well, we are an introductions agency,' she smiled. 'That's our business, introducing people to other people.'

'It says "marriage bureau" on the door outside,' he commented, a flicker of unease crossing his face. 'I thought they went out with whalebone corsets. To be honest, I'm not sure I'm looking that far ahead.'

'Marriage, friendship, penfriends, casual dating: whatever you're looking for, we can supply it,' Laurel assured him in the kind of sing-song voice normally reserved for ten-seconds ads on local radio. And boy, could I supply it, she added with a silent growl. Just try me for size. 'But we do pride ourselves on giving clients an old-fashioned personal service.'

'So you're not just going to feed my details into a computer and see what comes out?'

'Absolutely not! Every client's personal introductions are carefully chosen by one of our highly skilled matchmakers. You're entitled to unlimited follow-up consultations with your matchmaker, who's there to help you every step of the way. And we have a *very* high customer satisfaction rating,' she added, then realised she was running the tip of her tongue over her lips, and closed her mouth abruptly.

'Hmm.' He listened, bit into a biscuit, and nodded. 'Sounds like it might be the kind of thing I'm looking for,' he conceded.

Something danced a jig in Laurel's pants. 'Well, that's marvellous.' She reached for her clipboard and pen. 'So, shall I take something off – I mean down?' A small muscle twitched in her cheek. 'Perhaps we could start with your full name?'

'Gabriel Jouet.'

She looked up. 'Sorry?'

'Jouet. J-O-U-E-T. It's French,' he explained, half-apologetically.

That would explain the dark hair and brooding expression, mused Laurel. Not to mention that hint of an oh-so-sexy Gallic pout. 'Gosh, how romantic.'

He laughed. 'Try telling that to a snotty kid whose mates are all called Sidebotham.'

She went on. 'Occupation?'

'Painter.'

'Wow!' Laurel recalled the way he had looked at the portraits over the fireplace – this explained why. 'What do you paint?'

There was a pause. 'Walls.'

'Walls?'

'Walls.' Seeing her crestfallen expression, he added, 'Some of them are quite big walls, though.'

It was no use; Laurel just couldn't resist following Gabriel down the stairs and out into St Thaddeus Place.

'Do drop in and see us,' she sparkled as they said

goodbye outside the One-Stop Copy Shop, her hand lingering just a little too long in his. 'Any time.'

'I might do that.'

'Oh yes, please do. I – we – can tell you how we're getting on with finding that special someone for you.'

'Well, I'll be seeing you soon then.'

'I do hope so.'

You bet I do, she said to herself as she watched him cross the road, turn the corner into Henrietta Street and disappear. She closed her eyes, leaned back against the wall and let out a huge, smiley sigh.

Uh-oh, steady girl, she cautioned herself. *You know you mustn't.*

Why not? her other self protested. Sandwich-eating business types drifted by on the opposite pavement, blissfully unaware of her inner turmoil. Lucky them. She bet they never had arguments with themselves about who they mustn't fancy and why fancying people was a totally bad idea in the first place, at least for her. She didn't do relationships any more. It was the code she lived by and it had kept her sane.

But what about a beautiful platonic friendship? Beautiful platonic friendships are OK, aren't they? I could do platonic, no problem.

Platonic? Who was she kidding? There was nothing platonic about the thoughts scurrying through Laurel's mind.

Aw, why can't I . . .?

You know why not.

But what if I want to? she reasoned, backing her Puritan other self into a corner. *What if I really, really, REALLY want to?*

Tough, you still can't. And that's all there is to it. So deal with it.

And that was that. But ten minutes later, when she was back at her desk, her heart was still thumping.

That afternoon, Laurel just couldn't seem to concentrate on work.

She stretched, spun round in her chair and looked out of her office window. The May sunshine had obviously got its dates mixed up, because down in the street below people were strolling past in shirtsleeves and T-shirts with not a goose bump in sight.

She glanced at the clock. Half-past three. On a Friday afternoon. Another glance out of the window and her mind was made up. It was much too nice an afternoon to spend indoors and besides, she was practically her own boss now. Who said she had to stay till five thirty?

Grabbing her jacket off the back of the chair, she flicked a little ball of Blu-Tack at the opposite wall and managed to get Mr Dovecote right on the nose. She was humming to herself as she stuck her head into Connie's office. 'I'm off.'

Connie looked at her over the top of her reading glasses. 'Off? Where to?'

'Home.'

Disbelief battled outrage for control of Connie's face, and lost. 'But it's only—'

'Half-past three, I know.'

Connie brandished a clutch of pink cardboard folders. 'What about these?'

'I'm sure they can wait till Monday. 'Bye then, have a good weekend, don't forget to lock up the office when you leave.'

She didn't give Connie a chance to protest any further. A few large bounds later and Laurel was out of the office, down the stairs and away, breathing the sweet air of freedom.

This was the life. Rummaging in her bag for loose change, she went to the newsagent's at the corner of the street, bought the biggest chocolate ice cream she could find, and skipped off down the road, swinging her brief-case back and forth.

If it was the quiet life you were after, there were few better places to find it than Rivendell on a Friday night. Anybody under ninety who had any sort of a social life was out having it, and the rest ... well, the rest just amounted to Laurel.

Nothing but the tranquil sound of bubbles broke the silence as she replaced the lid on the fish tank and knelt down to peer inside. Sure enough, a small dark shape was lurking in the shadows, almost entirely hidden by weed. Five weeks she'd had Neil now, five whole weeks she'd been coaxing him with choice titbits and relaxing music. Heck, she'd have tried reflexology on him if fish had had feet. But not once had she managed to entice him out of his foliage. She was starting to get quite concerned.

'Come on, Neil,' she urged, remembering to put a smile in her voice. She didn't actually know if he could tell the difference, of course, but it couldn't hurt to try. After all, she was forever telling her staff that it worked with customers on the telephone. 'Come and say hello.'

The fish remained immobile, for all the world like a small brown plastic submarine that had escaped from a cornflake packet. Laurel tried miming a fish taking in water, opening and closing her mouth until her jaw hurt; but Neil was resolute.

Eventually she got cramp in her buttock and had to move. Getting to her feet, she limped across to the CD player. Obviously fish didn't like Saint-Saëns; and to be frank he was starting to get on Laurel's nerves a bit, too. She scratched her nose, changed the CD, pressed 'play', and all round the room the plants seemed to flatten themselves against the walls.

'OK Neil,' she shouted, 'how about Sisters of Mercy?' Anything was worth a try.

The kitchen looked like a bomb had hit it.

Normally Laurel kept it quite tidy, unlike her bedroom; if only because she rarely did anything that might have messed the kitchen up. It was hard to create real chaos making beans on toast. But tonight there was stuff all over the place. She'd spent half an hour turning out the contents of every cupboard, unearthing everything from six-year-old Spam to Odor-Eaters, before finally tracking down the jar of cardamom pods she'd been looking for all along.

She set it down triumphantly amid the unruly crowd of ingredients on the kitchen counter. An onion, only slightly sprouted; three potatoes; half a pound of slightly stale Cheddar; two tins of chickpeas; some tomatoes; and a jar of Balti paste. She ought to be able to fashion something out of this lot, particularly if she could find that packet of polenta. If they could do it on daytime TV, how difficult could it be?

'And now on Four,' announced a bright voice from the living room, 'someone's in for a visit from the police in *Hollyoaks*.'

Laurel wavered, torn between her determination to cook a proper meal for once, and her inclination to veg out in front of the TV. 'Go on girl,' she told herself. 'You've got all the stuff out, you might as well cook it now. It'll be lovely and domestic. Besides, you can watch *Hollyoaks* any time.'

Then she went to the fridge, got out a half-bottle of red and a bagel, and sloped off to watch TV.

Later that evening, Laurel lounged half-dressed on her bed, watching the evening sun making shifting patterns on the ceiling. Outside the open window, birds were twittering prettily and flower-scents mingled with a distant, comforting aroma of stale lager. She closed her eyes with a contented sigh, let her thoughts drift on the warm evening air, and tuned in to a blackbird singing his heart out in the hedgerow.

Bliss.

After a few moments' calming meditation, she said to no one in particular: 'I do not and will not fancy him.

Men are childish, selfish idiots.'

Reassured by her own resolve, she wriggled her head into a more comfortable position on the pillow.

'He is cute, though.'

Chapter 6

It was a fabulously warm day, and Cheltenham's café society had ventured out to the pavement cafés along the Promenade, sipping Pernod under gaudy parasols and pretending not to be Eurosceptic.

But not everyone was happy. Take Anton, for example. No question about it, his attention was definitely somewhere else, and if there was one thing Steph Mihailovic hated it was not being the centre of attention. After all, she was the great-great-niece of a Serbian count, even if she had grown up on a council estate. She gave her wavy, flame-red locks a petulant toss. If you were charitable enough to let a man take you out to lunch, the least he could do was be pathetically grateful.

'Anton,' she tried for the umpteenth time.

He just went on staring into space. 'Mmm?'

Her fingers walked up his arm. 'Anton, *darling*.'

She hitched her skirt a little more conspicuously up her thigh. But Anton was serenely unmoved. 'Anton!' This time she positively snapped his name, and he turned and gave her a sort of vague smile.

'Sorry?'

Steph was about to inform him that he soon would be when the waitress turned up, with two starters and an overcrowded bosom. 'Melon Supreme, sir?' she enquired bending over him in her tiny scoop-necked T-shirt.

In the blink of an eye, Anton was transformed from a lifeless sack of potatoes into Cary Grant. 'Now there's an offer I can't refuse!' he grinned. To Steph's absolute disgust, not only did the little tart burst into a giggle that made her breasts quiver like strawberry blancmange, Anton actually *winked* at her!

Well, frankly, that was the final straw. A girl could only take just so much, after all. Hauling her own assets into their optimum configuration, Steph stood up, leaned over and thrust them right in Anton's face. To his credit, he responded pretty much instantaneously. A silly smile spread over his face, and he murmured a gruff 'Oh *darling*!' Bless the poor helpless creature, his tongue was practically hanging out.

Steph smiled with satisfaction. When you've got it, you've got it, she told herself; and then she tipped a bowl of red-hot consommé into Anton's lap and flounced off down the Prom.

It wasn't until she was half way to the High Street that she took stock of just how angry she was: with herself for getting so angry over such a useless waste of Armani. As she passed a high-class jeweller's and glanced at the window display, she had to admit that the search for Husband Number Three was not going well.

64

Stepping up closer, she examined her reflection in the window for clues. Nose too big? No, it was absolutely perfect. Skin showing signs of premature wear and tear? No, there wasn't a single laughter line. Thanks to that nice doctor and his Botox injections, she'd never looked more alluring in her life. And as for her body ... well, her body was so good she'd fancy herself if she wasn't a girl. So what on earth was going wrong?

Maybe it was time to swallow her pride and get some help.

Stacey cursed her three-inch heels as she tottered up the steep staircase to Dovecote & Marsh with her lunchtime shopping: three chocolate bars, two sherry trifles, some calves' liver and a pot of double cream for that new Jamie Oliver recipe, and a diet yoghurt. Not that she would have dreamed of swapping her stilettos for something more sensible. A girl had to think of appearances, especially when she was only five foot one in thick socks.

Gingerly negotiating the final stretch, she was surprised to find the top step occupied – not by an unscheduled delivery of self-seal envelopes, but by a very small, suntanned boy with angelic blond curls.

Stacey melted like a Mars Bar in the sun. 'Well! Hello there!' she cooed, flashing the child a brilliant smile. 'Aren't you a little sweetie!'

The child glanced up at her dubiously, then went on swinging his sandalled heels against the treads, and said nothing.

With immense difficulty, Stacey squatted down to the child's level, hoping her hobble skirt wasn't going to split up the back. 'What's your name then?' she ventured. 'Mine's Stacey.' She pointed to her gold identity necklace. 'See? Stay-cee. What's yours?'

Silence.

'Where's your mummy? Are you waiting for her?'

As this produced no response, she tried a different tack. 'That's a lovely blue jumper, I wish I had one like that. With pretty orange frogs on.'

The small, nut-brown boy simply went on gazing glumly at his feet, as though not even a blue and orange jumper could make up for the basic ickiness of life. Stacey tried pulling faces, but that didn't work either. 'Oh dear.' She scratched her head. 'Well we can't leave you here like an unclaimed parcel, can we?'

Time to summon reinforcements.

'Ravi!' she called out. 'Ravi, are you there?'

The door to the office opened and a head appeared. 'What's up now? If it's a big box, I've got my new shirt on.'

'Nothing's up. Look Ravi!' she trilled, her voice ascending a squeaky octave. 'We've got a special visitor. Isn't that lovely?'

'Hmm.' Ravi eyed the child up and down. 'Does it bite?'

'Don't be silly. Any idea who he belongs to? He won't tell me his name.'

'Nope, never seen him before.' He patted the small boy on the shoulder. 'If you're after a date, kid, come back in about twenty years' time.'

Stacey smiled encouragingly at the child. He was a cute little mite, even by Stacey's undemanding standards, though there was something vaguely unusual about him, something she couldn't quite put her finger on. And he looked so lost, sitting there all on his own.

She nodded down the stairs towards the crèche that occupied the bottom half of the building. 'Maybe he's come from the Happy Nappy?'

Ravi was doubtful. 'Bit old isn't he? What is he – five, six?'

'Dunno, he won't say anything.' Stacey fluttered her blond eyelashes appealingly. Ravi sighed.

'Oh all right, I'll phone down and check. Get 'em to send somebody up with a big butterfly net.' He disappeared into the office, closing the door on Stacey's disapproving pout.

'Don't you take any notice of Uncle Ravi,' she advised the small boy. 'He's just a silly man. Don't you worry, we'll soon find your mummy.'

Stacey sat down on the top step and put a protective arm round the child. Following his gaze, she saw it linger expectantly on her shopping.

'Ah!' she exclaimed. 'You're hungry, aren't you! I bet I know what *you'd* like.' And she slid her hand into one of the plastic carrier bags.

Kathy from the Happy Nappy might only be young, but she was good in a crisis. At any rate, having a small boy snivelling into her skirt didn't seem to faze her in the least.

'It's all right, Edward,' she reassured him in her soft Gloucestershire brogue, gently stroking his quivering curls. 'Everything's all right, the scary thing's gone now.'

Frankly, Laurel wasn't sure who needed comforting more – the little boy or Stacey. At any rate, when Kathy returned from taking Edward back to the crèche, poor Stacey's voice was more than halfway to a sob. 'What d-did I do? I was only fetching out a b-bar of chocolate!'

Beneath her Tweenies tabard, Kathy's bosom heaved an understanding sigh. 'I know, but the thing is . . . well, you weren't to know, but Edward's had one or two problems lately. It weren't the chocolate that did it, see, it were the sight of all that raw liver.'

'What's liver got to do with anything?' asked Laurel, sitting herself down on the top step next to Stacey and handing her a tissue.

Stacey blew her nose loudly. 'Is he vegetarian?'

'No, it's Jocasta,' explained Kathy. 'His stepsister. You'd think she'd know better, what with her being so much older than him, but one day she takes him into the kitchen, opens up the freezer and shows him . . . his placenta.'

Stacey's blue eyes expanded to twice their normal roundness. 'His *what*?'

'Exactly. Only turns out his mum's been keeping it there ever since he was born, sitting in there with all the frozen peas and that. And now the poor kid thinks he was made by Bird's Eye. Honestly,' she shook her head sorrowfully, 'some parents.'

'You're not wrong there,' empathised Laurel, subconsciously wiping the hand that had brushed the bag of liver on the seat of her work trousers. 'Still,' she mused, 'at least his mum didn't fry it up for tea with chicken nuggets.'

Stacey looked as if she was going to be sick. Kathy hesitated for a moment, then threw back her pink-streaked head and laughed. 'Chicken nuggets, I like it. She's nothing like Mr Case, is she?' she prompted Stacey.

'Chalk and cheese,' agreed Stacey.

'Is that bad or good?' enquired Laurel.

Kathy pulled a silly face. 'Do you have to ask?' Then she turned round and skipped back down the stairs. 'Better get back,' she threw back over her shoulder. 'If I don't find Tommy the Tiger there'll be hell to pay.'

Laurel and Stacey were still sitting side by side on the narrow staircase.

'It's such a shame,' commented Stacey, mopping blue mascara from her cheek.

'A shame?' Laurel took a fresh tissue from her pocket. 'here, let me do that, you're making it look worse. What – about Edward you mean?'

'No.' Stacey's eyes almost crossed as the tissue scrubbed away at her face. 'Well yes, it is, but I meant about Kathy.'

'Kathy? Why's it a shame about her? She seems really nice.'

'Exactly!' nodded Stacey. 'She *is* nice, a really lovely person, so she ought to have someone, oughtn't she?'

Laurel was taken aback. 'You mean she hasn't?'

Stacey shook her head. 'Nobody. Nobody at all.'

'But she's nice, she's young, even with the Bagpuss hairdo she's attractive, and she's obviously great with kids. How come?'

Stacey shrugged. 'Dunno. I guess life's like that sometimes.'

Well it's not right, Laurel declared silently. Not right at all.

In a corner of the saloon bar at the Merry Hind, the atmosphere was filled with suspense.

'You did it then?' Don held his breath. 'You really did it?'

Gabriel answered with an expressive shrug of his broad shoulders. The strong and silent type, that was Gabriel: big as a barn door and hardly the world's biggest talker, but good-looking as heck. Don wished he could be even half as cool, but that wasn't easy with a face as memorable as tapioca pudding.

'Aw thanks Gabe, you're a real mate.' Don took a swig from his beer glass and wiped his mouth nervously with the back of his hand. 'I can't tell you how much this means to me,' he blathered on in his faint Highland brogue. 'I mean, I'm crazy about Connie and we've known each other for God knows how long, but I've never quite managed to pluck up the courage to come right out and tell her I want to ... you know ...' Suddenly bashful, he buried his face in his glass. '*Thing.*'

Gabriel prodded his empty beer glass round the table like an ice-hockey puck. 'For God's sake Don, why can't you just go over there yourself? Better still, just ask her straight out if she's got a boyfriend?'

Don squirmed. 'I've tried, man, I really have. But Connie just has this look, you know?' He tried mimicking it, and all his freckles tried to stand on top of each other. 'There's only so many times I can take a catalogue over there and try and make conversation. And at least with you joining you have an excuse to visit. Maybe you'll find out more about Connie for me. Put in a good word like?'

Gabriel let out a kind of expiring groan. 'But it's not going to work. You do realise I didn't speak to her at all? I just saw the woman who runs the place, Laurel something.' There was a deafening pause, accentuated by the loud crash of somebody dropping a try of glasses. 'It was all very embarrassing.'

This produced the kind of crestfallen look normally associated with a spurned marriage proposal on live TV. 'So you'll not go back, then?'

Gabriel didn't answer, but instead fidgeted with his empty glass, held it up to the light and peered meaningfully into the dregs. For once, Don was swift on the uptake.

'Ah, yes, empty glass.' He picked it up. 'Can't have that, I'll get them in. Same again is it?' As he was standing up, Gabriel shifted uneasily on his stool and Don hesitated.

'I didn't say I wouldn't go back,' said Gabriel slowly.

Don's face lit up like the Blackpool Illuminations. 'Aw Gabe, you're a mate.'

'Just don't expect me to interrogate your Connie, OK?'

'Whatever you say, mate.' Happy again, Don headed off to the bar for another two pints of heavy.

Gabriel watched him, smiled to himself and shook

his head. Believe me, your Connie would be the last thing on my mind.

'Connie,' hissed Laurel, 'why the *hell* is that woman in my office?'

Connie peeked through the door of her own office into Laurel's where a tall, chic woman in a grey suit was gazing out of the window, visibly trying to ignore the whispered argument going on outside the room.

'Her name's Janice Foster,' said Connie. 'Dr Janice Foster – she's a computer consultant.'

'I'm well aware of that, Connie, and I didn't ask *who* I asked *why*!' Laurel could feel the blood zooming up to the top of her head, and threatening to erupt like a miniature crimson geyser. 'What on earth gave you the idea that—'

Connie snapped back, 'You did.'

'I did!' Laurel's finger wagged reprovingly in Connie's face. 'I most certainly did not.'

'Changes. You definitely mentioned changes.'

Laurel seized Connie by the elbow and steered her to the other side of Connie's office, a few feet further out of Dr Foster's earshot. 'I said there *might* be some changes. In the fullness of time.'

'What! You implied there were going to be big changes. And computers, there were definitely going to be computers. A network, even. So naturally when I got the brochure from Dr Foster's consultancy . . .'

Laurel scowled. 'You decided to fix up a meeting behind my back, with not one word to me, because you knew if you asked me I'd say no!'

'That's rubbish!'

The two of them were locked in such a heated debate that neither of them noticed Dr Janice Foster slipping out of Laurel's office. Having concluded that Dovecote & Marsh were a bunch of lunatics, she had not unreasonably decided to make good her escape, head straight for the nearest pub and down several long, calming drinks.

Everyone in the main office was trying ludicrously hard not to notice that Laurel and Connie were whispering nose to nose and eyeball to eyeball in Connie's office, like two pitbull terriers with laryngitis. And most probably nobody had even realised that there was a naturally tanned, very soignée redhead standing by the door, gazing open-mouthed at it all.

As Janice darted past on her way to freedom, she gave the redhead's arm a brief squeeze. 'I wouldn't bother staying if I were you,' were her parting words. 'If you ask me they're all nutters.'

A few moments later, Laurel came storming out of Connie's office and walked slap-bang into the soignée redhead.

Laurel took a step back; blinked; looked the redhead up and down, and then backed away another two steps.

And then the redhead beamed and spread her arms wide. 'Lozzie! It *is* you! God, how long's it been?' Still grinning broadly, she enveloped Laurel like a Gucci octopus, and kissed her on both cheeks.

'Lord,' squeaked Laurel, almost inaudibly. So much for vowing to put her past behind her: her past, it seemed, had other ideas.

*

73

'Well, well, well!' Steph sat in Laurel's office chair, sipped her cup of Earl Grey (lemon, no sugar) and eyed Laurel with obvious pleasure and surprise. 'My God Loz, it's been years. How many?'

Not enough, thought Laurel as she stared at the woman she'd once regarded as her best friend. Before, that is, her best friend and her fiancé had got too damned close for comfort. 'I'm not sure. A few.'

'So what've you been up to? How on earth did you get to be here?' She surveyed the Pickwickian surroundings.

'Well. You know,' hedged Laurel.

'But – a place like this!'

Laurel felt instinctively defensive. 'Like what?'

Steph's perfect nose wrinkled. 'Like ... *this*! Old-fashioned, quaint, behind the times.'

Laurel shrugged. 'It's a business, it needed a manager. I manage things.'

Steph's crimson mouth pursed in disappointment. 'Oh Lozzie, don't say you haven't forgiven me yet? After all this time? After all, I've forgiven you,' she pointed out charitably.

But Steph's pointed look didn't prod the hoped-for answer out of Laurel. In fact Laurel didn't react at all.

'Oh Lozzie,' sighed Steph, setting her cup down on Laurel's desk. 'I know we parted on bad terms, but—'

'Not on there,' interrupted Laurel, whisking Steph's teacup off a pile of client photographs and shoving a copy of *Gloucestershire Today* underneath it.

'But we were mates for years and years before that, weren't we? Doesn't that count for anything? Well,

74

doesn't it?' Steph took in Laurel's less-than-radiant expression and was forced to consider the possibility that perhaps it didn't. 'You've changed, Lozzie,' she said quietly.

This at least provoked a small smile. If only Steph knew how much. 'At least you haven't,' retorted Laurel.

Taking this as a promising sign, Steph winked. 'Yeah, you know me! Same old Steph.'

Laurel cut to the chase. 'So why are you here?'

'Why do you think?' giggled Steph. 'I want a man.'

'A man!' snorted Laurel. That really was preposterous, like a jam-pot advertising for flies. 'Steph, if you want a man, all you've got to do is take a five-minute walk down the High Street!' It was easy enough when you wanted *my* man, she added silently.

'Yes, I know,' conceded Steph without a trace of modesty or pride or even embarrassment, given what had happened with Jason. 'But I don't want the hassle of having to filter them all out until I find the right one.'

Laurel sat down heavily on the squeaky leather sofa. 'One? As in settling down?' She nearly added 'again', but she wasn't that much of a bitch. Besides, who was she to criticise Steph's current love life? *Anybody's* love life.

'As in settling down. I've decided I'm at that . . . age. You know, *our* age.'

'Good God.' Laurel poured herself a cup of tea from Steph's pot, and knocked it back in one like a shot of vodka. 'OK, I was wrong, you *have* changed.'

'Maybe on the surface. I'm still the same person underneath though,' insisted Steph. 'Remember when we gatecrashed the sixth-form disco and you—'

'I did not! That was you, you fitted me up.'

'All right then, who was it who got pissed on Pernod at Mr Fletcher's leaving do and danced on the table with no knickers on?'

Laurel blushed faintly at the blurred memory and swiftly changed the subject. 'I suppose you've come here to register then?'

'Of course I have,' smiled Steph. 'I heard about you taking over the agency through the old school gang. I thought, if it's Lozzie's gig it'll be like keeping it in the family, sort of thing. But I thought first we could maybe go out for a drink, have a little chat about old times?' Steph's sublimely sexy mouth crinkled as another recollection came dancing back. 'Hey, do you remember the time we—?'

Oh I remember, thought Laurel soberly as Steph rattled on about childhood escapades. I remember everything. Your mum was in the next bed to mine in the maternity ward: how could you not have been my first, best friend? We did everything together right through school; told each other everything, trusted each other better than we trusted our own sisters. And then you betrayed me, and things could never be the same again.

'I really am sorry,' lied Laurel, getting to her feet, 'but I'm running behind schedule. I mean, I'd love to chat only I've got to be at the bank by four – you know how it is when you're running a business.' She stuffed a bundle of paper into Steph's hand and towed her towards the door. 'Registration forms. If you'd just like to fill these in.'

Steph's face fell. 'Oh. All right.'

The door open, Laurel ejected her visitor so swiftly and smoothly that it looked like sleight of hand. 'Don't worry, we'll find you the right guy,' she promised.

Steph turned, smiled sweetly and delivered her parting shot. 'Of course you will, Lozzie. I've got complete faith in you. I always did have.'

Chapter 7

The tail on the cat-shaped clock above the mantlepiece swished back and forth, counting off the seconds.

It was Saturday morning, the June sun had chased every cloud from the sky, and Seuss & Goldman were having a Blue Cross Event; Laurel could almost hear her mother's voice, urging her to get off her backside and have some fun. Instead of which she was sitting in her pyjamas by the fish tank, a yellowed Boots' photo album open on her knees.

As she ran her fingers over the pages they seemed to crackle like static; like the electric charge of anger and resentment that had sparked between her and Steph. She closed her eyes but she could still feel it crawling up her back, unbidden; forcing the memories back into her head.

The way Jason had tasted of white chocolate. The ghost of his hand holding hers. The cold, cruel way Steph had invited her for lunch and announced that she and Jason had been screwing behind her back.

I won't remember this, Laurel willed herself. I won't. Her fingers clenched, the nails raking across a bare rectangle of paper where a photo had once been. But she couldn't escape from the memories. Oh, all her photos of Jason had long since been burned and forgotten; every little thing he'd ever given her mislaid in the homes of a thousand strangers, thanks to Cheltenham's myriad of charity shops. But still her pictures of Steph remained, almost reverentially untouched.

Pictures of two gawky girls in school uniform and far too much lipstick; pictures of two young women arm in arm and laughing on some cut-price Mediterranean beach; pictures of Steph holding the silly trophy they'd won at Butlin's. A reminder of the time when it was her and Steph against the rest of the world. Of when things were right.

One large, fat teardrop rolled down the side of Laurel's nose and plopped onto Steph's photo. 'Oh Steph,' she whispered, 'it wasn't that Jason cheated on me, though that hurt; it was you . . . He was just a man. But you, Steph. How could *you* cheat on me?'

Laurel opened her eyes to wipe the wetness from her cheek, and saw that Neil had emerged from his plastic castle. He didn't even swim away when she stroked the glass of his tank.

'You understand, don't you?' Neil mouthed silently back. 'She was my best mate in the whole world. When she cheated on me, how was I ever going to trust anyone ever again?'

Despite the billing and cooing doves on the letterhead, all was not sweetness and harmony at Dovecote & Marsh.

80

For a start, something very odd seemed to have happened to Laurel. On Friday she'd been her usual self – laid-back, friendly and always first to the chocolate Hobnobs. But the minute she walked through the door on the Monday of her fourth week, you couldn't help but notice the difference. For laid-back, read flat. For friendly, read distracted.

'Is Laurel ill?' asked Stacey on Monday afternoon. 'Look.' She held out a teacup and a plate as evidence. 'She hasn't touched her biscuits!'

'And she's hardly been out of her office all day,' added Ravi. 'What do you reckon's going on?'

'Don't ask me,' sniffed Connie, stalking up to Ravi's desk with a huge pile of pink folders. 'I'm not here to think, remember? Madam made that *quite* clear. Here.' She dumped the folders on the desk, completely burying Ravi's in-tray. 'She says these are for you. M to Q, R to V to follow.'

'Oh bloody hell,' groaned Ravi. 'Not more! I haven't finished the last lot yet. I thought she said she was going to match this lot up herself.'

Connie shrugged ill-temperedly. 'Tough. Now she says you're doing them.'

'But—'

'Don't take it out on me, I'm just passing on the message from on high.' She jerked her head towards the closed door of Laurel's office. 'If you want to complain, complain to her.'

'All right, I will then.' Ravi was half out of his seat when Connie interrupted him.

'You can't, she says she doesn't want to be disturbed.'

Grudgingly, Ravi lowered himself back into his chair and flipped open the first folder. 'Who was it said things were going to get better once Mr Case got somebody else in to run the agency?' He snapped his fingers. 'Oh yes, I remember. It was you.'

Connie coloured up. 'Yes, well, that was before she arrived.'

'Complete revamp, that's what you said. Space-age technology. Soft toilet paper.' He contemplated his leaky biro. 'Huh.'

'B-but how was I to know?' stammered Connie.

Stacey poured oil on troubled waters, the only way she knew how. 'Prune, anybody?' she trilled, waving an enormous cardboard drum under Ravi's nose. 'They're virtually fat-free,' she added enticingly when he failed to respond.

'Ugh,' said Ravi. 'How can you?'

Connie recoiled from the proferred blue squishy thing, but at least the interruption gave her an opportunity to withdraw with some dignity intact. 'Haven't you got work to be getting on with?' she demanded. 'Some of us have been hard at it since half-past eight you know. And it was supposed to be my half-day.'

Do Not Disturb notice or not, Connie was going in.

Giving the door a swift knock, she pushed it open without waiting for an answer and stepped into Laurel's office. The new manager of Dovecote & Marsh was still slumped over her desk, her crossed arms propping up her chin. In front of her lay a whole gallery of client photos, propped up against several books and a vase of tastefully arranged carnations. Mutinous thoughts seethed inside Connie's head. Typical. The woman couldn't run a business to save her life, but give her a vase of flowers to arrange and she was in heaven.

'Excuse me,' began Connie.

Laurel didn't answer. Connie's irritation was mounting by the moment.

'I've given Ravi the files, like you said.'

Still no answer.

'He isn't very happy about it.'

Silence. This was getting really, really irritating.

'You're not still annoyed about Dr Foster, are you?'

At last Laurel's head lifted. She looked puzzled. 'What?'

'Dr Foster. The computer consultant.'

'Oh, her. Yes. As a matter of fact I am. After all, you did overstep the mark so far you practically emigrated.'

'Oh come on, I only—'

'Who's supposed to be the boss around here, you or me?'

'But we need computers!' protested Connie.

She knew she'd said absolutely the wrong thing, yet again, because Laurel directed a cold, hard look at her. 'That will be all.'

Connie wavered. 'Couldn't we talk about it?'

'All.'

With the worst of bad graces, Connie left. Once the door had closed behind her, Laurel straightened up in her chair, let out a long sigh of relief and surveyed the three piles of photographs in front of her.

'Hmm,' she murmured, turning to the pile on the right. 'This is tougher than I thought. If I fix you up with anyone from this lot, you'll know I'm taking the piss.' She pushed the rejects aside and turned her attentions to the left-hand pile, trying not to notice that Steph's photo was in there. 'You lot, on the other hand, are too bloody glamorous by half.' She pushed those aside too, which left her with just the middle pile.

Picking up the top photo, she propped it up against a long-forgotten mug of coffee, promptly changed her mind and went for the second photo instead. Aha! This one would do. Nice smile. Modestly pretty and presentable but hardly a contender for the front cover of *Vogue*. Yes, this one would do just fine.

Seconds later, remorse kicked in; and Laurel pushed Miss Impressive Overbite regretfully to one side. Selecting a photo from the glamorous pile, she sighed.

'Oh all right, Gabriel and Ms Phelps it is, then.' She looked at the photo and Briony Phelps smiled back sweetly, all bright eyes, glossy lips and platinum power bob. 'Shit. Why do I have to be cursed with a conscience?'

The Merry Hind was quiet tonight. Don positioned his pint exactly in the centre of the beer mat and sat down. 'Haven't seen you in a while,' he commented.

'I've been busy,' replied Gabriel.

Don waited but Gabriel didn't elaborate. At the best of times Gabriel was a man of few words. 'You're not avoiding Dovecote & Marsh, are you?'

'No. Matter of fact, they've fixed me up with a date tomorrow. I'm dropping into the office later to pick up the details.'

'Hey! That's great.' Don raised his glass in salute. 'Looking forward to it?'

'Not really,' admitted Gabriel, 'but I'll make the best of it.'

'Good man.'

Dropping his voice, Gabriel added, 'Between you and me, if I had a choice I'd rather go out with Laurel Page.'

It took Don several sips of beer to evaluate this startling revelation. 'Laurel Page? You're having me on. Don't you think she's a bit . . . odd?'

'Not so as I've noticed.'

'Hmm, well, takes all sorts I s'pose. Any rate she's single, so Connie says, so why don't you go for it?' Another thought struck him and he brightened. 'Hey, if you went out with her, you'd have loads of chances to put in a word for me with Connie.'

Gabriel was looking more doubtful by the minute. 'Look, mate. About this Connie. I don't want to hurt your feelings or anything but . . .'

'But what?'

'I can't help thinking you could do better for yourself.' He crunched on a pork scratching. 'I mean, she's attractive enough I guess, but you could find someone who actually notices you're alive, for a start-off.'

Don's face fell. 'Yeah, I know.'

Gabriel stopped chewing. 'So why do you do it, then?'

'I dunno,' Don confessed. 'Why does anybody do anything? All I know is, I want Connie and I'm not beaten yet.'

The Wishing Fish clock in the shopping mall was about to strike one as Gabriel sauntered up, hands in pockets that were almost as deep as his thoughts.

It was funny about Laurel Page. Very funny. He'd had the distinct impression that she couldn't make eye contact with him, that day in her office. And then there was all the blushing, which was surely a good sign. But maybe he'd been mistaken, or maybe there were things about her that Don didn't know.

Maybe he just wasn't her type.

Pity. Still, Briony Phelps seemed like a very decent second prize. He recognised her from her photo the moment he saw her waiting there – blonde hair, nice smile, cute little turned-up nose – and extended a hand in greeting.

'Hi. I'm Gabriel.'

She took his hand and smiled. 'Briony.' There was a pleasantly dreamy, faraway look in her eyes. 'Pleased to meet you.'

He waved a hand in the vague direction of several restaurants. 'Shall we?'

'Yes, let's.'

They hadn't walked more than five yards down the shopping arcade when the clock struck one behind them and started playing 'The Sun Has Got His Hat On'.

'Oh look,' Briony giggled delightedly as they turned to watch it. 'I forgot it blows bubbles and—'

That was as far as she got; because half a second later she fell in a dead faint at Gabriel's feet.

Connie felt as if the whole world was weighing down on her shoulders as she trudged up the short, ugly street to her overdue OU assignment and her house. No, not her house – her father's. She just lived there.

And cleaned it, cooked in it, gardened, sewed and once – in a howling gale – had clung to its roof, trying to re-secure the slates. Ah yes. How she loved going home. It had been a horrible week, and the prospect of a weekend with her father didn't make it any better.

Still, the way things were with her life right now, she doubted it could actually get much worse. On the other hand, just when you thought things couldn't get any more depressing they generally did.

Despite Connie's resolve to wallow in self-pity, her mood started to lift as she neared home, and without realising it she began to quicken her step. Today was the day Dad went down the Legion to play dominoes, so for once the house would be empty. By the time she reached the front door, she was almost running.

In the front hallway, she shed her handbag, jacket and uncomfortable shoes like some speeded-up stripper, then dashed up the stairs two at a time, to the only place she wanted to be.

It was the spare bedroom, but it was more than that: it was a temple to lurve. Its striped wallpaper was almost invisible beneath a mosaic of picture postcards and photographs of men; and at its centre stood a cheap little trolley with a computer on it. She switched on the machine and paced up and down impatiently as it booted up. Finally the desktop appeared, complete with photo of a semi-naked fireman, and she dived for the Internet button.

Only once she had accessed her own little private chat room did she surrender to the thrill of the moment. 'C'mon God,' she pleaded to the ether. 'One person, just one. I really need someone to be there today.'

She waited, hardly daring to hope. Then, just when she was on the point of despair, her prayer was answered.

Hi said the on-screen message. *I'm Joe*.

With a gasp of pure relief, Connie began to type.

Chapter 8

Laurel sat down next to Gabriel on the little two-seater sofa in D&M's waiting room; taking care to position herself as far away from him as possible, without actually moving herself to one of the armchairs arranged around the table.

This was not going to be easy. In fact it was downright embarrassing. Putting her coffee cup on the low table in front of her, Laurel tugged down the hem of her skirt and tidied away an escaped wisp of hair. She didn't know quite what to say, and she hated admitting it to herself, but she was really rather pleased that Mr Jouet's date with Briony Phelps had been a complete disaster. No, not rather pleased. Excessively pleased.

'About Ms Phelps,' she began awkwardly.

'Aye. Well.'

There was a kind of deep, velvety warmth in Gabriel Jouet's eyes. She'd noticed that the first time they met. That, and the way those eyes crinkled at the corners when he smiled. She tried not to meet his gaze, but it was like trying not to eat the last spoonful in a tub of

Häagen-Dazs. She gave herself a mental slap on the wrist. Mooning over clients: unethical. Having impure thoughts about them: completely *verboten*.

Finally she managed to break the spell and force a few words out. 'I'm really, really sorry Mr Jouet, I had no idea . . . I mean, narcolepsy!' She laughed nervously. 'Who'd have thought it?'

'Aye.'

Fuelled by several strong cups of coffee, the few gathered speed and turned into a torrent. 'That is, I realise I should have done my research properly, but the thing is what with the power cut on Wednesday and then my secretary having to go to the chiropodist or was it the optician – yes that's right, it was the optician, and well, I mean, narcolepsy, wow, would you like another pot of Earl Grey, or a biscuit, I could send Connie out for some?'

Gabriel drew back his manly chin and gave her a funny look. 'What?'

'Oh. Sorry.' Laurel felt herself flush crimson. 'I'm not making any sense, am I?'

'Not so's you'd notice.'

She knew she was going to start gabbling again, but every time she came within ten feet of Gabriel Jouet he had the same embarrassing effect on her, turning her into a deliquescing mess of gooey girlie.

Laurel cleared her throat and tried not to drool. 'I haven't been here very long, you see. I suppose I should have looked at the file more closely, or maybe interviewed her myself, but you know how it is with hindsight, and people don't always disclose these things, and like I said . . .'

Her voice tailed off as Gabriel started to shift position on the sofa, and moved slowly round to face her. 'Go on.'

'I—' The words suddenly stuck. Not really aware that she was doing it, Laurel began to turn her face towards his. 'I – I mean. About Ms Phelps's . . . disorder. She – that is, I . . .'

Something had jumbled up all the words inside her head like tickets in a tombola machine, and they weren't coming out right at all. It didn't help that she wasn't the least bit sorry things had gone awry with Briony Phelps. It didn't help one bit. And her face was ever so close to Gabriel's now; it was sooo distracting . . .

Involuntarily, her lips parted and her tongue flicked across, moistening them to a glistening pout. But no sound came out. And Gabriel wasn't saying much either. In fact, it seemed as if he was caught in the same trap.

'Actually, I were wondering,' he began, after an endless silence.

'Wondering?'

'If you'd . . .' His voice tailed off.

'If I'd what?'

He cleared his throat and gulped down half a cup of tea. 'Oh, you know. Nothing important.'

There was something almost pleading in those big grey eyes.

'As a matter of fact,' Laurel heard herself say, 'I was wondering if you'd . . . um . . .'

'Yes?'

In the nick of time, Laurel realised what she was doing, gave a silent yelp of panic and slammed on the brakes. Go on! screamed her moistening body. Ask him out for a drink, you know you want to. Don't you bloody dare! her brain screamed back. It's a trap, do you hear, a trap! Your stupid hormones are trying to make you do the very thing you've absolutely, definitely, decided not to do. Never again. No way!

Unless . . .

No! Springing to her feet, Laurel delivered Gabriel a hearty slap on the back, making him cough into the Bourbon creams. (Oooh, such a broad, strong back; muscles like tempered steel rippling under that crisp white shirt . . .)

'Ow!' He started as though rudely awakened from a trance. 'What was that for?'

'You mustn't let this one little setback with Ms Phelps get you down,' Laurel said, fixing a slightly manic smile to her face. 'Don't you worry, Mr Jouet, we'll soon find you Miss Right.'

It was a beautiful June evening, with the gentlest of breezes swaying the sycamores that lined the road; but the public bar at the Ram could still rustle up a good crowd for a darts match, even on a Monday.

Laurel's heart was thumping as she waited for her turn to throw, but it had nothing to do with the grudge match against the Feathers she'd somehow been talked into taking part in on account of the first, second and third reserves all flying off to Turin for Wednesday's big match. Even after two halves of Frimley's Old Irregular, she was still racked with doubt. Should she, or shouldn't she? Should she have asked Gabriel Jouet out for a drink, or had she done the right thing in keeping her mouth shut? Should she have listened to fifty million screaming hormones?

A cheer went up from the regulars as the landlord's dart flew straight to double top.

No! she told herself again and again, stabbing the point of a dart into the table top. Never get involved, ever again. Remember? It doesn't matter how gorgeous, hunky, brooding, thoughtful, downright sexy this – she seized on the most disparaging word in her vocabulary – this *man* is, he's not for you, OK? Besides, what is he, this cross between frog's legs and Yorkshire pudding? A painter and decorator, that's what! He paints walls for a living, his conversation's limited to about three words a minute.

Ah yes, cut in the devil on her shoulder, but you don't want him for his conversation, do you?

Somebody elbowed her in the ribs. 'Oi, sleeping beauty, you're up next. Ninety-six to win.'

'Not that there's any pressure, like,' grinned the captain of the Feathers team, replacing his mono-grammed arrows in their box.

Oh great, thought Laurel; that's all I need, the entire match resting on me just when I'm not in the mood.

She did try though really she did. And she almost hit double fourteen, only the bloody dart hit the wire instead, bounced out and speared Luke from the Feathers right in the arm.

Well, after that things just went from bad to worse. Or they would've done if Laurel hadn't pleaded a raging

93

headache and the Feathers hadn't let the landlord throw her last two darts for her.

After the match, when the Ram had sneaked through to the next round of the Challenge Trophy by the skin of their teeth, Laurel found herself sitting in not-so-splendid isolation at the bar.

Still, at least the landlord's wife had a kind word to say for her. 'Time of the month is it, dearie?'

'Er, yes.' It was easier than being honest.

'Not to worry, I 'spect you've got something on your mind, haven't you? Brings the pains on terrible, does stress. Tot of whisky and a hot water bottle, that's what you need.'

Laurel nodded mutely. Something? she thought to herself. No, not something; someone.

Connie hesitated in the hallway, one hand on the banisters and the other clutching her empty cereal bowl. She glanced thoughtfully at the clock above the telephone table. It was Tuesday morning, so there was Dad's leg ulcer to dress and the rubbish still to put out, not to mention a load of circulars that wanted mailing at the office; but even so, maybe she did have time.

A voice boomed out of the kitchen. 'There's lumps in this porridge.'

'Oh for God's sake,' she muttered under her breath, then raised her voice to a yell because Dad was bound not to have switched his hearing aid on. He never bloody did, except when it suited him. 'All right Dad, I'll sort it out in a minute.'

Dashing upstairs, she scooped Darcy off her chair, plugged in the computer and switched it on. The blue Persian stalked off with a disgusted 'Waaah' and very nearly tripped her up as she made a dash for the bathroom, scrubbing her teeth clean in double-quick time as the machine booted up.

By the time she'd spat out the last mouthful of minty foam, the computer was ready and waiting, and she hastily rattled off a message to Joe. 'Be there, please be there!' she begged the flashing cursor.

And he was! *Been up all night*, he typed back. *Big building design project to finish. What's your excuse?*

She replied swiftly; fifteen years of touch-typing came in very handy when you were in a hurry. *Only logged on for quick chat, getting ready 4 work.*

Oh, came back the response. *What U wearing then?*

Grey suit, white blouse, black shoes.

Oooh, boring, he teased.

Not boring, smart!

Bet U look like Miss Marple.

Oddly, though it was just a joke, it stung. Her fingers hovered over the keys as the cursor flashed expectantly. She thought for a few seconds, muttered a quick request for divine forgiveness, then plunged right in. *Have 2 look like this 4 work, but bet U can't guess what I'm wearing underneath.*

The reply came back lightning-fast. *So tell me.*

The letters chased each other playfully across the screen, the flashing cursor inviting her to play. A frisson of excitement ran like a soft-legged spider up her spine. And she forgot all about work, and began to type.

Wednesday evening found Laurel sitting alone in her front room, working through the address book on her organiser.

Lots of people, she told herself; I know lots and lots of people. OK, so maybe I can't actually remember who any of them are just now, but I'm definitely very nearly almost sure I know lots of them.

She toyed with the idea of e-mailing her sister in New Zealand for a chat, but it was the middle of the night in Auckland, and anyway she was a bit tired of Jools going on about potty training and her latest pregnancy. Mum and Dad were somewhere in the Amazon rainforest, and even if they did answer their mobile Mum would be sure to interrogate Laurel about her non-existent love life. And Laurel was running out of boyfriends to invent.

Flicking a Malteser into the air with her thumbnail, she caught it on her tongue, crunched it in two and started looking for likely numbers to dial. Around her, a semi-circle of Maltesers glistened on the carpet like a minefield.

As soon as Connie got home the following evening, she dashed upstairs and sent a message to Joe. Then she waited.

And kept on waiting – so long that she let her cup of tea go cold. She waited all through teatime as Dad went

96

on about his new pills. She waited right through the downpour that soaked all her nice clean washing on the line outside. Even waited while Darcy stretched out on her best work jacket and went to sleep. Connie waited and waited and waited.

And then she waited some more.

Laurel bolted out of the cinema at top speed, and into the warm night. Leaning on the railing by the zebra crossing, she watched cars disappearing into the darkness while a laughing group of teenagers jostled past her, swigging Bacardi Breezers.

It wasn't that it was a bad film; in fact it was quite funny. It wasn't that her seat was uncomfortable; far from it. And the popcorn was just right.

It was just that, when the house lights went up, she had realised something that made her feel deeply uncomfortable. It was Friday night, and she was the only person there on their own.

And that stank.

For once, Connie took her time over her Saturday chores.

It was remarkable just how many things you could find that needed doing when you bothered to look. Really important things, like arranging all your cookery books in alphabetical order; or rationalising your make-up bag so that all the lipsticks were pointing the same way.

When she'd finished tidying the shed and polishing the lawn mower, she put a really nice casserole in the oven and sat down to groom Darcy for the first time in weeks. The poor beast was developing a six-inch Afro. She even tried to watch *The Bill* with her dad, despite the fact that he had the volume turned up loud enough to deafen polar bears in Alaska.

But all the time her thoughts kept drifting upstairs to the computer. Several times she thought about going up and turning it on, and each time she told herself off. What was the point? There wouldn't be anything. Not from *him*. Besides, she was busy.

The cat protested and jumped off her lap as she tugged absent-mindedly at a matted tuft of fur. Dad fell asleep in his chair. Deprived of something to do, Connie fought the urge – but not for long.

'Oh well, maybe just one last try.'

She covered the distance to the computer in record time, switched on and drummed her fingers impatiently as the modem warbled into life. 'Come on, come on!'

To her joy, there was one new message in her inbox. A message from Joe. Her heart jumped as she opened it.

It was short and to the point: *What colour knickers did you wear today then? ;-) J.*

On Sunday afternoon, Laurel's answering machine finally registered a call. She felt like doing a lap of honour as she walked into the living room and saw the little green light flashing invitingly at her. Wha-hey, a message!

Grabbing a pen and paper, she settled herself beside the machine with great ceremony and pressed the 'play' button.

Two seconds later, as the message chirped into life, her heart sank into her slingbacks.

'Hi Laurel!'

Oh shit. It was Steph.

'I'm at a loose end right now, but you're obviously not!' There was a girlish giggle. 'So don't keep the men all to yourself, give me a call and we'll go out together. You can show me all the hot spots. Speak to you soon, bye-ee!'

The message ended with an anticlimactic beep. Laurel watched the machine in silence for a moment. 'Nope,' she decided, flinging down the pen. 'I may be desperate, but I'm not *that* desperate.'

Chapter 9

Despite Laurel's resolve, Steph's call was still preying on her mind on Monday morning.

As she glared into Killer's tank, trying to stare the little git out, she found herself contemplating the stark, solitary reality of her life – and Killer's for that matter, not that solitary confinement seemed to bother him. But there was no avoiding the facts: virtually everyone Laurel had ever known or liked or had anything much to do with at all, she'd left behind. And not by accident, either. It had seemed like such a good idea at the time, after all that bad stuff with Jason. Make a fresh start, break with the past, build a completely new life . . .

Fair enough, retorted her reflection, *but what life? If you were a D&M client, you'd have yourself marked down as a saddo within fifteen seconds.*

She was sure Killer was smirking at her from behind his wall of toughened glass.

'Ooh Rav, you've got a new haircut!' trilled Stacey as he walked into the office. 'Good weekend?'

Ravi ran a hand gingerly over his freshly shaven head. 'Bit too good, know what I mean? Woke up bald as a coot yesterday morning, can't remember a thing about it. Auntie Geeta went ape when she saw it – don't let me touch alcohol ever again, you got that?'

'I might hold you to that!' giggled Stacey. 'Anyway, you tell your auntie it suits you. Good weekend, Bette?'

Connie's big sister Bette slapped a copy of the *Racing Post* down on her desk and wriggled out of her ubiquitous Puffa jacket. Officially she only worked two half-days a week at D&M, doing the books; but she always seemed to be thereabouts, dispensing pithy advice and working her way through another jar of Kenco. Almost as if she didn't really want to go home.

'Fabulous actually. Cakes on me today. Three winners in a row at Kempton Park.'

The sounds of merry banter bounced back and forth across the office, making Laurel feel more isolated than ever, not that that was anybody's fault but her own. Even Connie sounded as if she'd had a decent time: she was humming as she filled up the paper-towel dispenser, for goodness sake! And Laurel was certain she'd never worn that bright red shade of lipstick before.

Nobody bothered to ask Laurel what, if anything, she'd done – least of all Connie, who was pointedly being nice to everyone except her. She suspected the others imagined her climbing inside her coffin at half-past five on a Friday, and not emerging until dawn broke on Monday morning, like some kind of bizarre reverse vampire.

She and Killer exchanged unblinking stares. Maybe I really ought to start over, thought Laurel, drumming her fingers on the glass. Only do it right this time. And maybe Gabriel Jouet's a good place to start. I'm sure he fancies me. At least I *think* he does. Or am I imagining it? Maybe he'd have been horrified if I'd asked him out for that drink.

She turned to the piscine assassin. 'You're a fish of the world. What do you reckon?'

But Killer's only response was a disdainful flick of his tail. Then he turned his back on Laurel, and swam off to rip a mealworm to shreds.

Laurel stayed distracted all through the rest of Monday and most of Tuesday, and by teatime she'd gathered so much wool she could have knitted her thoughts into a gross of Fair Isle ponchos.

Cake: the universal panacea. That was the one great truth Laurel had learned as a teenager, and it had stayed with her ever since. Zen and the art of cake-making? She could write a book about it: when in doubt, trouble, debt, prison, limbo, Middlesbrough, need of comfort, inspiration or just plain hungry, look no further than Mrs Beeton and something family-sized and sticky.

Which was why she was standing in the kitchen of her flat with a big treacly bowl of fruit-cake batter, so thick and heavy it made the wooden spoon bend every time she tried to stir it.

Really she ought to be running through that batch of applications she'd brought home with her, but right now the thought of other people's problems kept reminding

103

her of her own. She remembered the most recent client she'd interviewed, a lovely lady, a widow who still seemed a little bit lost after the death of her husband of thirty-two years. She'd confided, after a couple of rounds of Earl Grey, that she'd even gone so far as to place an advertisement in a Lonely Hearts column in an effort to find friends. But 'Lonely widow seeks companionship' hadn't elicited the type of company she'd been looking for. In hushed tones she'd confided to Laurel that all she wanted was some company, someone to go on outings with – perhaps lunch and a movie – rather than S-E-X. While the professional Laurel was pleased that they'd be able to help Mrs Perkins find a suitable male friend, on a personal level she'd been tempted to ask her if she'd kept their contact details.

Or maybe she ought to place her own ad.

'Aphrodite seeks Love God with Big Thunderbolt,' she murmured, absent-mindedly licking cake-mix off her finger. 'Ball of String seeks Minotaur.' She giggled to herself at the thought of how the ad might look on the Lonely Hearts page of the *Courant*. Or how about: 'Young Free and Single seeks . . .'? Nah, who was she kidding? She decided to get real: 'F, Used, Abused and Slightly Shop-soiled, seeks M, Not Too Fussy, Preferably Continent and With Own Teeth.'

Lost in the silly game, she heaved the spoon through the mixture, completely failing to notice as half of it slopped over the edge of the bowl and formed a glutinous slag heap on the work surface.

Come on, she scolded herself. Stop running yourself down and do this thing properly. Use the jargon, make it sound the business. 'F 32, blonde—' No, better not say blonde, they'll stink you're stupid which maybe you are but you don't want to advertise it for God's sake and anyway it's out of a bottle. 'F professional 32, single, into music, books, cake, windy hillsides, seeks M pref tall, dark, artistic, brooding . . .'

No, Scrub that.

'Cathy Seeks Heathcliff.'

A pleasurable shiver ran down Laurel's spine and she glanced down at the worktop. Almost without realising, she had drawn a big heart in a patch of spilt flour. Smiling to herself, she added the initials L and G, and finished it off with an arrow.

'But I ca-an't!' protested Ravi, sounding more and more like Orville the Duck as his last few, precious inches of empty desk vanished under another stack of paperwork. 'I can't possibly take any more files!'

'Tough,' replied Connie, dumping another armload on the desk and stalking back to the filing cabinet. 'She says you have to, so you have to.'

'She's already got me working through my lunch hour! Who does she think she is?'

'Your boss,' said Bette, ever the practical one. Feet comfortably resting on the desk, chair balanced on its two back legs, she glanced up from the latest form guide. 'She's in charge, remember?'

'God knows why,' sniffed Connie, elbowing her way past her sister and almost tipping her off her chair. 'Expecting people to run a modern office without a computer – we'll never get things straight. It's no wonder all this paperwork's been piling up for months. All Case ever did was shove things into boxes and forget about them, and Madam's not exactly going to set the world on fire, is she?'

'Shh,' urged Stacey, round-eyed. 'Laurel'll hear you!'

'Good! Fine!' Bright-eyed and reckless, Connie practically hurled the next consignment at Ravi, sending him tottering backwards into the fish tank.

'Hey, why do I get all this bad karma?' he moaned. 'What have I done? How come I get landed with all the extra work? Why's it always me?'

'Buggered if I know,' replied Connie, making Stacey choke on a carrot baton and cough till she turned purple at the thought that Connie actually knew how to swear. 'Just get on with it and stop whingeing.'

Being accused of whingeing only added insult to Ravi's injury. 'This is because I'm the only bloke round here, isn't it? If you ask me—'

'I didn't and I'm not going to.'

'Somebody's got it in for me.'

But Ravi's complaints just bounced off Connie's thick skull. She wrenched open the bottom drawer of the filing cabinet. 'And another thing.' She swung round with a fresh armful of files, narrowly missing Stacey's head. 'How much money is she throwing away on flowers and stupid fish? Tell me that!'

Nobody dared tell Connie anything, least of all Ravi, who was trying to head off a landslide.

'Hundreds, I bet you!'

'She brought us all fruit cake today though,' pointed out Stacey, as always keen to see the good in everyone.

'Home-made fruit cake,' she added as if that made all the difference. 'With nuts and everything.'

'Huh!' Connie just turned round and jabbed a finger at Bette's chest. Bette looked at it and moved it firmly to one side, but Connie seemed not to notice. '*And* she spends all bloody day arranging the damn things. But can I have a computer so I can do my job properly? Can I hell.'

'Oh nooo!' wailed Ravi, as a stack of files tottered, slipped sideways and cascaded onto the floor like slates off a roof. He flung himself after them, but only succeeded in banging his knee on the leg of the desk. 'Well thank you Connie,' he muttered between clenched teeth. 'Thank you very bloody much.'

'Don't thank me, thank our blessed leader,' replied Connie, flouncing off back to her office.

'Connie's been in a funny mood all day,' said Ravi gloomily. 'Up, down, manic, scary. Even the humming was better than this.'

'It's OK,' said Stacey, joining Ravi on the floor. 'Don't worry, I'll help.' Then she lowered her voice, squeezed his hand and whispered in his ear. 'I'll help you with *everything*.'

The seaweed sushi roll with extra wasabi sauce was wrenched from the silver sugar tongs in a flurry of small, sharp teeth.

Hastily replacing the lid on Killer's tank, Laurel eased her hands out of the double-strength leather gardening gloves. She prayed that the local zoo would get a move on with sorting out its special reinforced isolation tank, so it could take the blasted Balinese Passionfish off her hands before it ate not only the sushi, but the tank, the office and everybody in it.

'Right. Now, where were we?' She turned back towards the office and dropped the gloves on Ravi's desk. At least now Killer had been fed he'd stopped head-butting the glass of his tank. Maybe now she could get on with her meeting and the even more daunting task of motivating her troops.

Nobody said anything. Ravi fiddled with the stubble on his scalp. Stacey beamed in her infuriatingly perky way. Connie and Bette stood shoulder to rigid shoulder, as silently antagonistic as two prizefighters preparing to sort out some private grievance round the back of the gasworks.

Laurel sighed. Took a sip of lukewarm tea. Smiled and clapped her hands, as much to encourage herself as anybody else. 'All right then, matchmaking. That's what we do, right?'

This produced a sort of general mutter of agreement from everybody, and deepened the scowl on Connie's face.

'Only sometimes there are people who don't get matched up, and what does that mean?'

There was a short silence. Ravi shuffled his feet. 'Refunds?' he hazarded.

'Well yes, refunds,' agreed Laurel. 'Sometimes. And what else? Well?'

Silence.

Laurel gave in and answered her own question. 'Unhappy people, that's what. And we don't want them,

108

do we? Because unhappy people tell other people and that means bad publicity. So what do we do?'

This one was a gift for Stacey. 'Make people happy?'

'Exactly! We make people happy. By matching them up.' Laurel perched on the end of Ravi's desk, at the risk of starting another landslide. 'The question is, how do we do that? How do we improve our matching rates?'

This at least produced a reaction.

'We don't,' declared Bette. 'Some people are unmatchable.' Laurel had begun to wonder if working in a marriage bureau was quite the job for someone as naturally cynical as Bette. But just as she was about to interject, Connie rounded on her sister.

'What would you know about people? All you know about are horses!'

'Well pardon me I'm sure, Professor Freud.'

'I don't think anybody's unmatchable,' said Stacey. 'They just haven't met that special person to walk hand in hand with along the exciting adventure that is life's uncharted pathway.'

Stacey's word-perfect grasp of D&M's excruciating advertising material was as impressive as it was faintly disturbing, mused Laurel. Einstein she might not be, but steeped in the D&M ethos she most assuredly was.

'Couldn't have put it better myself,' lied Laurel. 'OK, so if they're not meeting the right people, how can we make sure that they do?'

'Buggered if I know,' said Bette. 'If you ask me, culling's probably the kindest answer. Captive bolt, clean and quick. It's what we do with the unwanted foals.'

109

'A get-together,' declared Stacey, wriggling her bottom excitedly. 'We could hold one of our special Getting To Know You evenings!'

This produced several groans and a muted jeer.

'What's wrong with a get-together?' demanded Laurel. 'Sounds like a good idea to me.' And clients like that nice Mrs Perkins would really like it too – an opportunity to widen her social circle.

Ravi sighed. 'What's wrong is that nobody ever turns up.'

'Oh,' said Laurel. 'Why not?'

'Put it this way,' said Connie. 'Would you turn up for an evening of Mr Case's antiquated mates playing jazz standards in a draughty church hall?'

'Possibly not,' admitted Laurel. 'But what if we replaced them with a black-tie dinner and a really cool band in a nice hotel somewhere? Or a really posh disco?'

'They still wouldn't turn up,' insisted Ravi. 'There's the babysitting for a start.'

Seeing the mystified look on Laurel's face, Stacey chimed in. 'Haven't you noticed how many of our clients are single parents?'

'Yeah,' nodded Ravi. 'Try getting forty babysitters sorted out for forty people in the same town on the same night!'

To everybody's surprise, Laurel burst out laughing. 'Well if that's the only problem,' she said recklessly, 'consider it sorted.'

As Laurel walked through the doors of the Happy Nappy, she couldn't help wondering if she'd been a mite over-confident. After all, she hadn't even mentioned the idea to Kathy yet, and she had a feeling that Connie would be absolutely delighted if she came back to D&M with egg all over her face.

Not just egg either, but soup, chocolate, orange juice, baby rice and a thousand different flavours of beige stuff out of little jars. Yes, it was bang on lunchtime at the crèche, and as Laurel picked her way across a mine-field of discarded teddy bears she wondered if it might not be wiser to turn right round and come back later.

But it was too late: Kathy had already spotted her.

'Hello, haven't seen much of you lately.' She aero-planed a spoonful of something slushy into one of her tiny clients' gaping mouth, ducked and deftly avoided the blow-back as he burped all down his front.

'It's been a bit crazy upstairs. Mind if I sit down?'

'Be my guest – but not there!' Kathy dexterously whisked the red plastic chair from under Laurel's bottom. 'Tarquin had an accident.'

Laurel inspected a giant plastic toadstool for bio-logical contamination, then lowered herself gingerly onto the top of it like an oversized pixie. 'We were thinking of having a get-together – you know, D&M?'

'That's nice. Cindy, watch Leanne, she's trying to bite Jack's ear again.' Another spoonful of sludge flew unerringly to its target. 'Good boy. So what's this get-together got to do with me?'

'Weeell, it's like this . . .' Laurel had rehearsed her sales pitch thoroughly, but it wasn't easy to sparkle convincingly when you were trying not to slide off a big plastic toadstool. She explained about Stacey's idea, and how it wasn't going to work unless somebody – somebody really skilled and experienced and professional, like Kathy – could organise childcare for the evening. 'I'd be really, really grateful,' she added, in the hope that the sympathy vote might prevail. 'You'd be getting me out of a hole.'

Kathy wiped orange mush from a dribbling mouth. 'Fine,' she said with a shrug.

'Pardon?'

'Fine. We can handle that, no problem. Couple of extra people from the Swindon branch, maybe get an entertainer in – just let me know when and how many.'

'You mean it's that easy?'

Kathy looked at Laurel and laughed. 'What did you expect? You want babysitting, babysitting's what we do, right?'

'Hey, great!' Laurel began to relax and almost enjoy having her eardrums assailed by Tarquin's impression of a fire engine. 'Hey, tell you what – why don't you find somebody else to run it and come along to the get-together?'

Kathy's laughing mouth sagged slightly at the corners. 'I don't know.'

'You'd enjoy it, there'll be lots of blokes there!'

'No thanks.'

'Oh go on, I'm sure they could manage without you.'

The corners tightened, and a slight edge came into the voice. 'I said no, OK?'

Laurel looked at her, taken aback. 'I'm sorry.'

Kathy's eyes met hers, and for a split second Laurel thought she almost glimpsed fear. 'No, I'm sorry, I shouldn't have snapped. Maybe I'll drop in for ten minutes, but my first responsibility's to the kids. Now, make yourself useful and pass me that juice.'

All things considered, the week hadn't turned out as badly as Ravi had feared it would. For a start-off, there was Stacey. Not only had she given up loads of her time to help him with his work, she'd even spent an entire half-hour on the phone to Briony Phelps, listening to her complain about the new depths her self-esteem had plummeted to since her secret got out. What's more, despite the fact that Connie had spent most of the week whining for a computer, when Laurel wasn't around she seemed unaccountably cheerful ... *And* he'd made the first XI for Sunday's match. So all in all, he couldn't really complain.

At five o'clock on the average Friday, Ravi was usually the first one out of the office. But when teatime came on that particular day, Ravi was feeling so well disposed towards the world that he decided to stay on late. Maybe in the quiet of the early evening he could actually get some work done.

Clearing a space on the floor, he spread out all the photos from his new caseload. When he'd finished, he got up and walked round them like a battle-hardened general inspecting his troops. OK, there were some faces in there that only a mother could love, but he liked a challenge. And one or two of them were positively presentable.

Like that one, for example. The evening sunlight glanced off his bald scalp as he bent to pick it up and read the name on the back: 'Stephanie Mihailovic'. 'Nice,' he murmured to himself, flipping open her file to find out more about her. Redhead, sexy, not too old, interesting past.

He tapped his chin thoughtfully with the photo, letting all the facts settle in his head, waiting for inspiration to strike. 'Now, if I were going out with you . . .' The thought trailed off wistfully. He should be so lucky. '*If* I were going out with you, I'd want to look like . . .' He scanned the array on the floor. 'Ah.'

Stooping, he picked out another photo. 'Like you.'

Chapter 10

Line dancing, Terry Wogan at the Town Hall, an amateur production of *Carousel* and a demonstration of decorative knot-tying. Laurel crumpled up the *Cheltenham Courant*, and hurled it halfway across her living room with a snort of disgust. Not a thing worth going to in the local listings; not a single bloody thing – not unless you were dead, senile or landed with your granny for the weekend.

She crawled to the sofa, extracted the TV remote from down the side of a cushion and zapped the screen into life. A man on a moving conveyor belt was juggling melons while people in chicken suits threw eggs at him. Clearly BBC2 had gone downhill since she last watched telly on a Friday night. Channel-hopping, she found AIDS on Channel 4, earthquakes on Channel 5, incest on ITV, tidal waves on BBC1 and nude Bolivian house-wives on Channel 6.

'And you can forget that for a start-off,' she scolded herself as her free hand reached instinctively for the open packet of Jaffa Cakes. 'Your bum's quite big enough already. And anyway, what excuse have you got for being bored?'

All that did was remind her of her late grandma, sternly assuring her that the starving children in Africa would be glad of lumpy semolina pudding. On one memorable occasion Laurel had even put some in an envelope and tried to mail it second-class to Ouagadougou. It had come back three weeks later, covered in green mould and marked 'gone away'.

Laurel didn't respond well to advice, particularly her own. 'Who asked you, anyway?' she snapped back.

But her smug subconscious wasn't letting her off the hook. 'Hey, why don't you go for a walk? Or do your t'ai chi? It's no wonder you're out of condition, slobbing around the house all day and feeling sorry for yourself. Then after that you could ... er,' the inner voice dwindled to a lame halt, 'clean the bathroom.'

Clean the bathroom? Laurel almost laughed out loud. 'All right, suppose I do clean the bathroom,' she sneered. 'What am I supposed to do with the other forty-seven hours of my weekend?'

No answer came. Short of running up and down the road naked in the hope of getting arrested, it looked like Laurel was doomed to another weekend spent listening to the sounds of frenzied shagging through the wall from next door.

She got up, paced up and down, picked up a favourite CD and promptly put it down again. Nothing appealed. Maybe she'd read a book, improve her mind. Flopping down on the lovely chesterfield hardly anybody ever sat on any more, she surveyed the pile of unread books on her genuine Moroccan coffee table. A history of pre-dynastic Egypt (even more boring than it sounded), *Cooking for Friends* (great if you had any), *Fun with Fish* (yeah, right), something on Japanese flower-arranging that she knew off by heart anyway, two half-read crime novels and *The Big Book of Erotic Fiction* (a none-too-subtle hint from her ever-optimistic mum).

It was no use, she couldn't just sit here. She had to do something. If only there was a shop where you could buy yourself an instant social life. 'I'd like four close friends, a couple of imaginative lovers and two dozen assorted acquaintances, please.' 'Of course, madam, can I interest you in our Frequent Shagger discount?'

Finally her gaze wandered back to the phone. There was one other possibility. What if she called Steph?

An electric shock of horror made all the hairs on the back of her neck stand on end. No, bad idea, terrible idea, worst idea she'd ever had. But what if I'm cutting off my nose to spite my face? she demanded. What if . . .?

She looked at the phone. It looked back at her, challenging her willpower. Uneasiness invaded every cell in her body. So maybe it's a bad idea, and maybe it isn't, she mused. If she was ever going to put the past behind her then part of the process was forgiving Steph. And once upon a time they had been mates, however unlikely that might seem now. She'd never been bored or lonely on a Friday night when Steph was around. Mind you, neither had Jason.

Without making any positive decision, she found her hand curling around the receiver, tightening, lifting it off the hook, pressing it to her ear. As her index finger punched out the numbers she felt like some medieval sailor, travelling to the ends of the earth and fully expecting to fall off at any moment.

The ring tone chirped into life, each rhythmic pulse testing her nerve a little further.

'Hello?'

Steph's voice made Laurel jump. The breath caught in her throat, and an endless moment passed in silence.

'Hel-lo-o? Is there anybody there?'

Laurel's voice returned from a far-off place. 'Steph? Yeah, it's me. Listen, you free tomorrow night?'

Despite second, third and fourth thoughts, Laurel didn't dodge out of the deal. The following evening, she left Neil minding the house and headed downtown to meet Steph.

Laurel had never been inside Bar Pravda before, though she'd occasionally tripped over one of its patrons in the gutter outside. Somehow the idea of a bar that sold nothing but forty different kinds of vodka struck her as a bit lacking in imagination. But as she took a deep breath and stepped inside she could see that it was the perfect setting for Steph: smart, expensive, designed to buggery and full of sad thirty-somethings still raving about Ayia Napa.

She'd half expected Steph to be half an hour late, the way she always used to be. In fact she'd been counting on it, to give herself time to find a dark corner, gulp down a drink and get her head together. But as she turned towards the bar she froze.

Steph had beaten her to it.

More than that, she appeared to have made herself thoroughly at home. Perched on a bar stool with a shot of something ice-blue, she looked like Bond-girl-meets-Jewish-princess, her dyed red hair curling sexily down over her pushed-up breasts. Certainly the guy whose leg she was stroking seemed to appreciate the way she was slavering all over him.

Was that how she'd behaved with Jason?

The bitter taste of bile filled Laurel's mouth, and she felt her stomach clench into a fist of pain. This had been a totally big mistake.

Just as she was about to walk right out again, Steph spotted her. 'Coo-ee, Lozzie! Over here!'

Some force she couldn't fight took hold of Laurel's body and drew her over to the bar.

'Hi Lozzie, this is—?' Steph prompted him with a quizzical eyebrow.

Two rows of perfect teeth flashed in an expanse of permatan: 'Martin.'

'Martin, of course, silly me. Sit down Lozzie, that T-shirt is so cute, what can I get you?' Laurel didn't answer. Steph stopped gushing and peered down at her from the dizzy heights of her bar stool. 'Is something wrong?'

'Wrong?' A dry laugh caught in the back of Laurel's throat. 'Why should anything be wrong? I mean, you're obviously having a great time, does anything else matter?' She flung a look of disgust at Martin. 'I'll see you around.'

Her face was burning as she pushed her way back out

through the door and into Regent Street. Theatregoers streamed past on their way to the Saturday night show at the Everyman, leaving Laurel standing alone and very still, like a pebble in a swollen river.

She closed her eyes and breathed deeply. Things would be OK again in a minute.

A voice sounded behind her. 'Lozzie, what the hell's the matter?'

She sullenly kept her back turned. 'Hadn't you better get back before lover boy goes off the boil?' A hand touched Laurel's arm, but she snatched it away. 'Don't touch me.'

'Lozzie!' Steph refused to be detached, and, when Laurel tried to avoid looking at her, she planted herself right in her line of sight. 'What's up with you?'

'With me?' sniped Laurel, as three years and more of pent-up anger and frustration released themselves. 'That's a good one. I'm not the one who'll shag anything with less than four legs.'

Steph blinked. 'What?'

'How long have you known him – must be five minutes at least. And you've not even got his pants off yet. Oh dear, you're not losing your touch, are you?'

'You cheeky cow!'

'Do you want to know something?' Laurel spat the words out with spiteful pain. 'I used to wish you were dead. Now I just feel really sorry for you.'

'You? Feel sorry for me?' Steph's perfect mouth turned into a thin red sneer of disbelief. 'Laurel no-mates, hermit of this parish? I can't believe I'm hearing this.'

'Believe it.'

'Bloody hell but you've changed.'

'Like I said, you haven't.'

They glared at each other.

'Well if that's how you feel.'

'It is.'

'You might as well sod off.'

'Don't worry, I wouldn't waste another minute on you if your arse was on fire.'

Laurel stalked off across the road, only daring to breathe once she was safely cocooned by the Saturday evening crowds. When she turned round to sneak a backward look, Steph was nowhere to be seen.

It was dark by the time Laurel's wanderings took her to Montpellier Gardens, but the bandstand stood out clearly against the amber glow of the nearby street lamps. Besides, she'd been here so many times that she could have found the way blindfold.

She could only see Steph's back, but she knew it was her. She was perched on the wrought-iron hand rail, shoulders hunched and her Prada-shod feet dangling limply like two lengths of designer string.

'Hello,' said Laurel, suddenly six years old again.

'Hello,' said Steph without turning round.

'I knew you'd be here.' Laurel climbed the steps and hitched herself up onto the rail next to Steph.

'That's my line.' Steph stopped gazing down at her feet, straightened up and turned to look at Laurel. 'I was thinking about the time we shaved Liam Anderson's eyebrows off when he was asleep. Boy, did we get into trouble.'

121

The corners of Laurel's mouth twitched. 'We were always getting into trouble.'

'And we always ended up here.'

'It was our special place.' She ran a hand along the age-smoothed handrail, reabsorbing a lifetime of memories. 'I guess it still is.' She took a deep breath. 'Look, about earlier, I just wanted to say I'm—'

'So am I.'

'I didn't say what.'

'You didn't have to.' Steph swung her feet back and forth, the pink sequinned mules hanging from her manicured toes. 'We've got some sorting out to do, yeah?'

'Yeah.'

'I am sorry about Jason, you know.'

'Oh really.'

'Yes, really. I was angry and I . . .' For once Steph ran out of words.

Laurel didn't know what to say either.

They sat in silence for a few moments.

'It wasn't *all* my fault,' said Steph.

Laurel looked up sharply. 'Says who?'

'I mean, you sacked my Carlos, didn't you?'

Laurel's anger flamed. 'And that's supposed to make it all right for you to sleep with Jason?'

'Well if you hadn't neglected him like you did . . .'

'What!' Laurel leapt to her feet, ready to do battle.

'You were always at work,' Steph said simply. 'Never had any time for any fun. Never had any time for him.'

'Which of course you did!'

Steph had the decency to lower her eyes. Feeling suddenly weary, Laurel sat down again.

'I didn't mean to—'

'Oh put a sock in it, Steph.'

Laurel's heart ached, like a muscle that had been abruptly reawakened after years of inactivity. It ached with the old anger and hurt. But most of all it ached with the horrible suspicion that Steph might be a little bit right.

After a long and uncomfortable pause Steph chuckled to herself, as if she'd just remembered the punchline to a dirty joke.

'What are you laughing at?' demanded Laurel.

'Remember how we always used to sort things out when we had a fight? Tell the truth or down a bottle of my gran's Cinzano?'

Laurel shuddered. 'Don't remind me. The times I've thrown up on this bandstand.'

'It always used to work.'

'Things have happened since then.'

Their eyes met in the amber-tinted darkness. 'For old times' sake,' urged Steph.

And Laurel couldn't think of a good reason why not.

'And the slice of orange,' insisted Steph.

Laurel groaned and ate it, peel and all. 'You know I hate cocktails.'

Steph was implacable. 'Now the cherry.'

Laurel eyed the bright shiny thing on the end of her swizzle stick. 'All right, all right. But it's your fault if I spew.'

'That's all part of the fun.'

Drinking games at McSquiffy's. Answer the question or drink the drink – no matter how gruesome it might be. What on earth had possessed Laurel to agree? They weren't rampant fifteen-year-olds any more, even if Steph persisted in behaving like one. There were things that couldn't be settled just by getting hideously drunk.

The cherry slid down Laurel's well-oiled throat and plopped into the alcoholic maelstrom in her stomach. Already feeling light-headed, she shook herself to jolt Steph back into focus and fixed her with a defiant stare. Steph stared back – in fact both Stephs did. And then, just as Laurel was on the point of falling backwards off her bar stool, Steph blinked.

Thank God for that, thought Laurel, rubbing her bleary eyes. 'Ha! My turn. Name … oh God, I don't know. The most romantic city you've ever been to?'

'Romantic? I think your job's getting to you. Once upon a time you'd have asked me which was the most exotic city I'd ever had sex in.' She chuckled. 'Or something a bit more risqué. It's Antananarivo by the way. To both.' Steph yawned. 'I flew there once. The time that African prince asked me to be his thirteenth wife. I met him on one of my flights.'

'I forgot you used to be an air hostess.'

'Flight attendant!'

'Trolley dolly.'

'Whatever. Anyway, I win.'

'Shit.' Laurel's stomach lurched. 'What are you going to inflict on me next?'

Steph scanned the cocktail menu. 'A nice big celery and mango daiquiri. With extra crème de menthe.'

Laurel put her hands up. 'OK, truth, I surrender. No one could drink that and live.'

124

Steph threw a cashew nut into their air and caught it in her teeth. 'Does that mean I get to ask you anything I like?'

'Only if I get to ask you first. Tell me what you've been up to since I saw you last. Or should I say who?'

By half-past nine, they were drinking peach schnapps at the Cap and Whistle.

'. . . so anyway, when I saw the books I started thinking there ought to be more money in my savings account,' explained Steph. She shrugged ruefully and raised her glass. 'Cheers, Mr Cheating Git.'

Laurel gazed at her in frank amazement. 'But at school you were totally crap at maths!' she protested.

'I was crap at everything that didn't involve sex or blowing things up,' Steph reminded her. 'Anyhow, it turns out that revenue accounts aren't that hard to follow once you get the hang of them – and besides, Richard hadn't covered his tracks very well.'

'Bastard!' whistled Laurel.

Steph drained her glass. 'Thick bastard,' she corrected her. 'I could almost have forgiven him if he'd had half a brain. And if I hadn't been married to him,' she added with a grimace. 'Still, he went to jail and I got both houses, so it worked out OK in the end.'

'Maybe I should get you to do my books.'

This produced a look of disgust. 'God no Lozzie, I couldn't! It'd be like sorting through your used knickers!'

'As opposed to my used boyfriends,' Laurel muttered but this time she managed to laugh and Steph joined in.

As Laurel reached for the bottle, she happened to glance across the bar. Steph's eyes followed, and three blokes immediately waved to her from the other side of the room.

'I've. Been. Think-ing,' said Laurel, trying not to slur her words. It was getting hard to keep her brain from slipping out of focus.

'Naughty, naughty.' A finger wagged in her face.

'Shush, listen. I've been wondering. About why you came to see me.'

Steph's hand was so unsteady as she refilled her glass that it sounded like somebody playing the marimba. 'I told you why,' she objected.

Laurel shook her head. 'Not true. You said it was 'cause you wanted a man, but you've got loads of men.' She swept an arm across the bar, knocking over a dish of crisps. 'Everywhere! Look at them!'

'Loads,' agreed Steph. 'Too many. And they're all crap.' She sighed. 'I just seem to keep picking the bad ones.'

The black humour of it all made Laurel snort into her schnapps.

'What's so funny?'

She looked up into Steph's puzzled face, and a sudden wave of sorrow washed over her. 'We all pick the bad ones, Steph. Why should you be any different?'

Steph looked away. 'Yeah well, maybe it's what I deserve.'

By the time they hit the Jolly Hercules, they were so wasted that they couldn't have cared less about the beer-stained beer mats, the sticky upholstery or the Daniel O'Donnell album on the jukebox. Even the watery ale was just a means to an end. Besides, the floodgates were wide open now and there was no way to stem the tide of confessions until oblivion kicked in.

'Lozzie?' repeated Steph. She sounded like she was calling from a long way away. 'Lozzie, I know it was a crap thing I did, but he was just a bloke. You used to eat blokes for breakfast. What happened to make you change so much?'

It was a stupid question, yet it was the key to everything.

At last a tiny voice came out. 'That would have been the breakdown,' Laurel said, sounding suddenly sober.

Steph's face turned white. 'The what?'

'Breakdown. The mental . . . breakdown.' She tried so hard to sound matter-of-fact and hard-faced, as if it were something of no more consequence than a cold sore, but her lower lip was starting to tremble. 'You know, that thing where you feel like you're losing your mind.'

'You were?'

'After Jason I . . .' Her fingers gripped the bartop. 'You have to realise, I'd lost the man I thought I was going to spend the rest of my life with, I'd lost my best friend. I couldn't concentrate at work. Then I lost my job because I couldn't cope and I couldn't talk about why. Then I got ill for a while.' The last dregs of Laurel's bitterness evaporated and her head drooped onto her chest.

'How ill? You mean hospital ill?'

Laurel nodded. 'Three weeks with this scary woman in the next room trying to carve swastikas in her arms. I couldn't sleep nights, listening to the poor cow screaming through the wall.'

Steph was shaking now. 'You mean they put you in a—?'

'Psychiatric ward? Yeah. But I signed myself in. I knew I needed help. Unfortunately, it's not as easy to sign yourself out. Once you're there it's up to them to decide.'

Steph's many gold rings clattered against the neck of the bottle as she tried to pour herself another drink. 'Oh Jesus.'

'And then when they finally worked out I wasn't a danger to myself or anybody else, they let me out. I saw a counsellor for a while. That helped a lot, it's good to talk . . . and all that.' Laurel smiled humourlessly.

'Why didn't you tell me? Why didn't you say something?'

'We weren't on speaking terms at the time and you were kind of part of the problem.'

'Touché,' said Steph.

'And when you showed up again, out of the blue . . . well, it's a bit of a conversation-stopper. Anyhow,' she went on, 'after a while I came out of counselling and that's when I decided: no more men, no more love, no more getting close.'

'Is that what they said you should do?'

'Not exactly,' admitted Laurel. The fact was, her counsellor had been less than impressed by Laurel's radical approach to her problems. 'But I knew it was what I needed to do.' And – grateful though she was to the counsellor for helping put her life back together – the other thing she'd needed to do was call a halt to their sessions. She'd grown tired of talking about what had happened, she just wanted to forget everything. All the same, Laurel still kept his number on a battered slip of paper in her wallet, like a lucky charm, just in case.

'Oh Lozzie.' Steph's head sank slowly towards the table in front of her, but not before Laurel had seen the tear fall wetly onto the mahogany veneer. 'Oh my God, I never thought, I . . . I didn't . . . I'm so sorry, I never meant to . . .'

'Never meant to what? Make me crazy? Turn me into Mrs Mad Woman? Don't flatter yourself, you didn't.' Laurel paused, reconsidered. 'Well, it wasn't just . . .'

The look in Steph's eyes spoke guilty volumes. 'Oh Lozzie, I never knew, I never even dreamed. What can I say? What can I do?'

'Nothing. This isn't about you Steph, this is about me, OK?'

For a moment Laurel contemplated Steph's face with curious detachment, as though it belonged in some entirely different dimension. Then the scars of three years ripped asunder and emotion broke through like bright, arterial blood.

She laid a hand across Steph's trembling shoulders. 'Look Steph, it wasn't just you and Jason. It was lots of things. Everything got on top of me and I guess it was just all too much. It's one of those things that people never talk about but it happens more often than people realise.'

129

'But not to you, Loz, not to you!'

"People are like elastic, OK? And sometimes something stretches it too far. Hey, c'mon, I got over it,' she lied softly, knowing in her heart that she'd only begun to get over it about five seconds before. 'I'm fine now, I really am.'

'Really?'

'Well, as much as anyone can say that.'

Steph gave her a wry smile. 'I'm glad.' She laid a hand on Laurel's. 'I really am sorry, you know.'

'I know.'

'I never wanted you to go through all that, especially by yourself. And I wish I'd not done what I did. If there's anyway I can make it up to you . . .'

'You're here now,' replied Laurel. And surprisingly it did feel good to have Steph back in her life. Especially as she put her arms round Laurel and hugged her like it was the last hug left in the universe.

In the early hours of Sunday morning, two figures wove an unsteady path down the Strand, arm in arm to avoid falling over.

'I'd go for it,' advised Steph. 'Definitely.'

'You really think I ought?'

'Yeah, go on, you try it on with what's-his-name.' She leaned closer. 'What is his name?'

'Ah-ah,' admonished Laurel. 'Not telling.'

'Huh. Be like that.'

'I intend to.' Laurel pulled away and swung round the nearest lamp-post until she felt so dizzy that she had to cling on to it for support.

A smile crept across Steph's lips. 'Say, has this back-water town of yours got a fountain these days?'

Puzzled and breathless, Laurel nodded. 'Yes, why?'

Opening her handbag, Steph produced a couple of coins and shook them under Laurel's nose. 'For luck. Shall we?'

Laurel beamed. 'Oh yeah! C'mon.'

And they walked. And then they ran. And wished for all they were worth.

Chapter 11

Laurel hardly moved all day Sunday, just flopped around the house in a T-shirt and pyjama bottoms, eating chocolate spread straight from the jar. It was her tried and tested way of dealing with a hangover: if the sugar didn't knock out the headache, the endorphins made her so blissed-out she could have trepanned herself and not cared.

Around half-past three on Monday morning, just as the July sun was winking one sleepy eye over the brow of the hill, a massive energy burst kicked in. Maybe it was the chocolate spread, or the caffeine in the three litres of Lucozade she'd knocked back, or confessing her deepest, darkest secret to Steph and discovering the world hadn't ended, but whatever it was, Laurel felt bursting with energy. She knew she had to get out right now and do something. Climb a telegraph pole and shout 'knickers'; do backflips all along London Road; find a field full of sheep and paint them all red. Anything really, as long as it wasn't lolling around scratching her armpits.

In the end she settled for something constructive: doing the week's shopping at the all-night superstore. She was quite proud of the idea until she got there and remembered that it closed on Sunday nights. Giggling like a tipsy fourth-former, she bounced back into the car, wound down all the windows and turned the radio on as loud as she dared. Singing along with Radio Chelt FM, she didn't stop for breath until she reached the leafy summit of Cleeve Hill. Even then she was still so hyperactive she had to jump up and down on the spot for five minutes, freaking out the dawn chorus.

Half an hour later and feeling less manic, she was back in her own living room, freshly showered and towelling herself dry as she shared risqué confidences with Neil.

'He is just so . . . unbelievably . . . well he just is,' she gushed, leaning over the fish tank and dripping into the water. 'Tall, strong, silent, completely irresistible – you know the type, come on, you must do.'

Although a fish of few words, Neil advanced his head a couple of millimetres beyond the gateway to his plastic castle and seemed to nod, as if he understood.

'One look from that man and I just can't help myself.' Laurel closed her eyes and slithered the bath towel sensuously down her flanks. 'I go all goose-bumpy.'

Neil's only comment was a trail of air bubbles.

'And I'm sure – well, almost sure – he feels the same way about me. He even makes excuses to come into the office when he could easily have just phoned. That's a really good sign, isn't it? Don't you think?'

Neil looked quizzical.

'Yes, I know I said never again,' admitted Laurel, 'but a girl can change her mind, can't she?'

Suitably chastened, the fish withdrew into his castle keep. Laurel sat down on the arm of the sofa, squashing her nose up against the glass of the aquarium. 'I feel I'm ready to try relationships again and I'm telling you, Neil, if he walked through that door right now and offered to take me away from all this ...' She sighed luxuriously. 'What I wouldn't give to be locked in a bed showroom with Gabriel Jouet.'

Ga-bri-el. Jou-et. She rolled the words on her tongue like a mouthful of fresh crème brûlée. Oh yes. The very sound of his name moistened bits of her she'd almost forgotten existed.

Closing her eyes, she swished the towel around her shoulders like a cape. 'I can just feel his big strong arms lifting me up onto his big black stallion, slinging me across the saddle and riding away with me to his castle. I'd struggle a bit, of course, just for form's sake, but he'd kiss me ruthlessly, and start unlacing my bodice and slipping his hand inside my ...'

Whoa, girl. She swallowed hard, took a deep breath and confronted her flushed reflection in the mirror above the fireplace. 'All these years of pent-up lust? Steph's right. You've got to give it a go, before you blow a gasket.'

After all, what was there to lose? Apart, that was, from every remaining ounce of self-esteem when Gabriel laughed in her face. But he wasn't going to, that was defeatist talk. Besides, the air crackled with sexual tension whenever they were in a room together. The only question was, how to go about making this thing happen. Which would he prefer: the subtle approach or the in-your-face? Drumming her fingers on her chin, she pondered for several long minutes.

Then it came to her: Don! Don was Gabriel's mate. Maybe it was a rather juvenile approach for a woman in her thirties, but Laurel was painfully aware just how out of practice she was with the opposite sex. In the circumstances, Don seemed an ideal place to start.

Connie ran with all the laden panic of a convent schoolgirl, hardly daring to look at the display of accusing clocks in the front window of Samuel's. She yelped. Quarter to ten, and she was supposed to be on mornings this week! She could hardly believe she was this late – and neither would Laurel. This was bad, really bad; definitely a hanging offence given the mood she had been in these last few weeks. And Connie was fresh out of plausible excuses. She might as well jump under a bus right now.

Threading her way breathlessly between bus queues, she vaulted a stray binbag and almost skidded on a discarded pizza box. Her shoes flopped noisily against the paving stones, and she cursed her own stupid vanity in wearing silly high-heeled courts – not to mention the even sillier hobble skirt which right now was living up to its name. In desperation, she hitched it up a couple of inches, took off her shoes and ran like hell.

Oh, the trials of love, she told herself. The fact was she'd lost all track of time while she was chatting online with Joe. If it hadn't been for the fuss Darcy'd made about his empty biscuit bowl, she'd probably still be gazing longingly at the computer screen.

Maybe all wasn't lost just yet. Maybe Laurel had come in late and gone straight into her office, without even noticing that Connie wasn't there. Yeah, and maybe Chris Tarrant's face was naturally that colour. Laurel had made it quite clear to Ravi just last week that she wasn't going to put up with lateness, which she no doubt classified as disgraceful along with flexible working hours (except when they applied to herself), and everything else that was modern and sensible and cost-effective. They might as well have stuck with Edwin Case and put a dress on him. It's no good Connie, she told herself bitterly. Face it, you're gonna die.

Hurtling into St Thaddeus Place, she executed a ninety-degree turn any slalom skier would have sold his granny for, and raced up the stairs two at a time. Punching the door open, she burst into the office . . . to surprised looks all round.

'Good God,' said Bette, eyeing the purple-faced figure with the sagging tights, dishevelled hair and the skirt up round its bum. 'Is punk back in fashion?'

Connie didn't reply. In fact she didn't even hear Bette; she was staring haplessly at Ravi's desk, where Laurel – yes, Laurel – was sitting, arms folded and looking straight back at her.

Oh shit, oh shit, oh shit, she thought to herself. And then, to her complete amazement, Laurel smiled.

'Calm down, Connie!' she exclaimed. 'You'll do yourself a mischief. You know Kathy, don't you?'

The young woman from downstairs looked round Laurel and gave Connie a friendly wave.

'Er . . .' panted Connie.

'Now, get your diary out and have a chat with her about this get-together we're organising,' breezed Laurel. She cocked her head on one side and gave Connie a thorough appraisal. 'You know, you're awfully flushed. I think I'd better make you a cup of camomile tea.'

As Laurel strode off to the kitchenette, humming to herself, Connie couldn't decide whether to faint from shock or relief.

Mr Coxon was holding onto his teacup with both hands, but it still rattled on its saucer as he brought it to rest on Laurel's desk.

'This is all very embarrassing,' he blurted out. 'The thing is, I and Ms Brodie . . . that is my former . . .'

'Significant other?' suggested Laurel.

'Quite. I mean, we were never married or anything, but ten years is a long time.'

Laurel nodded with a sympathy that was largely genuine. The large purple lump on Mr Coxon's forehead bore ample testimony to the fact that life for him was hardly a bed of roses. Rules, however, were rules.

'I do appreciate that things have been awkward for both of you,' she replied. 'But you must understand that Dovecote & Marsh has to be given any information that might affect a client's suitability for a match.'

Mr Coxon shrank miserably into his armchair. 'I've asked her to leave me alone, but she won't have it,' he lamented. 'It's a power thing. Says if I get myself a new girlfriend she'll make my life a misery.'

'It's not for me to say, of course,' commented Laurel, 'but from where I'm sitting you're the one with the bruises.'

He seemed to deflate a little more inside his shiny suit. 'Nobody believes me. They never do.'

'Why shouldn't they?'

But Mr Coxon just shuffled his feet and looked uncomfortable. 'Anyhow, I thought you ought to know I've had stern words with her.'

'Then maybe she'll keep her distance now.'

He didn't look too optimistic. 'I suppose you're giving me the push then?'

'Well, strictly speaking I ought to cancel your membership here and now. We do have rules about members with existing attachments, you know. Even if those attachments are ones they don't actually want.' Laurel met his spaniel gaze and her iron resolve wilted at the edges. She sighed. 'But I suppose as long as everything's above board, and any prospective matches are aware of the situation with Ms Brodie . . .'

She thought he would look relieved, but if anything he was twitching more than ever, and staring fixedly at something behind her left shoulder. 'Is something the matter?'

'Sorry, I couldn't help but notice that animal over there. It's a bit . . .'

She swung round and looked straight into a gaping maw that boasted far more gums than teeth. 'Oh that,' she laughed. The four-foot-high stuffed black thing reared up at them on moth-eaten legs. 'That's just Mr Case's old stuffed bear. Hideous, isn't it?' It was just one more thing that she would love to do something about at D&M if only she had the chance.

'You sure you're feeling all right?' asked Laurel anxiously.

Don held out his cup for the waitress to refill. 'Aye, fine. Good coffee this, I might have another.'

Laurel couldn't help being impressed as Don started on his third double-strength grande Americano. By all the laws of biochemistry he ought to have turned into a caffeine-fuelled axe maniac by now, but frankly if he'd been any calmer she'd have had to check him for a pulse. God, but he was one freaky guy.

She glanced around the coffee bar with its square-cut retro sofas and baristas in baseball caps. Thankfully the Mean Bean was pretty quiet on weekday mornings, which was just as well because she didn't fancy half of Cheltenham listening in on what she was going to say. Assuming she ever got the balls to say it. It was all most embarrassing.

'Er . . .' she began, which wasn't a terribly good start. Come on, she willed Don. What's wrong with you – why don't you flaming well ask me? Anybody half normal would have ages ago. But Don just dipped into his jacket pocket and offered her a little paper bag.

'Chocolate-covered coffee bean? They're quite tasty if you eat them four at a time.'

She fended them off with her amaretto biscuit. 'No thanks, I'm jumpy enough already.'

He looked at her with the air of someone who had not got the joke. 'What?'

'Oh, nothing, take no notice.' She wriggled uncomfortably on her plastic stool, wishing she had worn tights, then her legs wouldn't make this awful sucking sound whenever she shifted position. 'Aren't you wondering why I asked you out for coffee?'

'Not really. You're a client, after all.'

He munched in painfully slow motion. It was like watching a Galapagos tortoise lapsing into hibernation. 'The thing is, Don, I wanted to sort of – you know – ask you about something.'

'Oh. Right.'

'Something I thought you might be able to help with.'

'Me?' He shrugged in unconcerned surprise. 'Well, if you're wanting publicity leaflets printed, you'd be best waiting a few weeks till the new machines arrive.'

'No Don, it's nothing to do with leaflets.' Laurel breathed deep and dived in. 'Let's just say – for argument's sake – there are these two people.' Grabbing the sugar bowl and the chocolate-sprinkler, she plonked them down in front of Don.

'People.' Don eyed the visual aids, considered the concept and decided he could handle it. 'Ri-ight.'

'For argument's sake, we'll call them Mr A and Miss B.'

'A and B, OK. I'm cool with that. Which one's which?'

'Oh God, I don't know, does it matter?' She could see from Don's face that it did. 'All right then, Miss B's the chocolate-sprinkler, OK?'

141

'You don't think the sugar bowl's more, you know, woman-shaped?'

Spot the designer, thought Laurel, growing increasingly agitated behind her calm veneer. 'Fine, sure, the sugar bowl. Whatever.'

'All right. So what about these two . . . people?'

'Well, say Miss B's got a bit of a problem.' Laurel nudged the chocolate-sprinkler forward, caught Don's eye and swapped it for the sugar bowl. 'She wants to know how Mr A feels about her.'

'Ri-i-ight.'

Laurel could see she was on the point of losing him already, but pressed on regardless. 'Only she can't tell just by looking if he feels the same way about her as she does about him, and she's afraid to come right out and ask him.' She paused for breath. 'With me so far?'

Don looked blank. God, seethed Laurel, I can't make this much more bleeding obvious.

Just as she thought she was going to have to draw Don a picture, a glimmer of enlightenment illuminated his craggy face. 'Oh – right, I get you. That sort of problem.' Glancing swiftly to right and left, he leaned across the table and whispered dramatically in Laurel's ear. 'This Miss B . . .' He picked up the sugar bowl and waggled it meaningfully. 'She wouldn't happen to be a "friend" of yours, would she?'

'We-ell, now you come to mention it.' Laurel took an inordinate interest in the brown-sugar sludge at the bottom of her coffee cup. 'I mean, we don't have to, do we? Not if we don't want to. Get specific I mean.'

Don patted the back of her hand. 'Now now, you shouldn't go fretting yourself over this.'

She looked up at him, slightly relieved. 'I shouldn't?'

'Not at all. I mean, it's hardly surprising Connie doesn't know how I feel about her, is it? I've never found a way of telling her.'

Completely thrown, Laurel's brain stalled in neutral and crunched to a half. 'Uh?'

'I've tried to let her know, mind, but well, I've never been your heart-on-sleeve type of man if you get my meaning.'

Don? Don and Connie? Oh my godfathers, thought Laurel, suddenly realising where the conversation was heading and selfishly desperate to divert it back to its original course. 'Don, I think you've got the wrong end of the stick.'

Another handful of coffee beans vanished into Don's meditative mouth. 'This problem,' he mused, gazing up at a framed black and white photograph of two loved-up teenagers buying pretzels from a New York street stand. 'D'you reckon it'd help if I tried to be a bit more ... romantic? I mean, I've tried often enough, but Connie's got this way of stopping me in my tracks. She's a fine woman you know, and when I see her, well, I just seem to trip over my tongue and then—'

'Don!'

'It all goes wrong.' His jaw stopped chewing, hung slackly for a moment, then started again at double speed. 'Hey, maybe I ought to do something dramatic!' His eyes snapped back to Laurel, glinting with a new-found evangelism. 'How d'you think Connie'd take it if I proposed to her?'

'What!' coughed Laurel, inhaling a mouthful of coffee.

'Proposed. You know, marriage.'

In the split second between having the thought and voicing it, Laurel made a determined attempt to beat it senseless. But like an unruly jack-in-the-box, it sprang out regardless. 'I don't know, Don. I think she has a boyfriend.'

Oh shit! She closed her eyes in a grimace, waiting for the inevitable outburst; but when nothing had happened after a couple of seconds, she opened first one and then the other.

Don was sitting there, chocolate coffee bean halfway to his lips, his mouth forming a perfect O.

'Boyfriend?' he enquired faintly.

'I'm sorry, Don. I think he's called Joe,' revealed Laurel. After all, she'd let the cat out of the bag now, there was no point in trying to backtrack. 'She's on about him the whole time at work.' For no sensible reason, she added again: 'Sorry.'

There was a small, intricately crafted pause. Then Don's mouth sagged into a resigned smile. 'Nothing's ever straightforward, is it?'

Bette fought her way through the beaded curtain into the Small World café, spotted the person she was looking for and made straight for the table brushing off the annoying laminated menu that some boy tried to shove under her nose.

Reaching her objective, she dragged over the nearest empty chair and sat down.

'Go away,' said Connie firmly.

Bette did not go away. In fact, she took off her waistcoat and slung it over the back of her chair. 'What the hell do you think you're doing in here, Connie? Have you seen the time?'

'What about it?'

'You should have been back at work an hour ago, that's what!' Bette swung round to confront the spotty hovering youth in the pink apron. 'Bring me a pot of tea, bloody strong, and then bugger off.' Her finger wagged in Connie's face. 'You can't go on neglecting your job like this, it's not good enough and you know it.'

Connie's chin jutted. 'Since when does your job include telling me how to do mine?'

'Since you stopped behaving like an adult and started damaging the business.'

Her younger sister glowered. 'Don't give me that crap, Laurel's got it coming to her.'

Bette laughed humourlessly. 'How do you work that one out?'

'Because if she bought computers for the office, I wouldn't need to come to this shitty cyber-café in my lunch hour to use the Internet, would I?' At the word 'shitty', the boy in the pink apron dumped the teapot next to Bette's elbow and fled. Connie's fingers jabbed irritably at the ketchup-smeared keys on the machine in front of her. 'You know something? I heard she used to work for a dot com company! Talk about hypocritical.'

Bette let out something between a groan, a growl and a sigh. 'Anyway, what's so damned important about the Internet that it can't wait until after work?'

Connie tossed back her head with righteous pride. 'My Joe, that's what.'

'Your Joe!' Bette snorted in derision. 'If you ask me, your Joe's about as real as Peter Pan's bus pass.'

'How dare you!' seethed Connie. 'Of course he's real!'

Bette folded her arms and called Connie's bluff. 'All right then, if he's so bloody real why hasn't anybody seen him? Hmm?' She threw five sugar lumps into her tea mug and stirred it with a clatter. 'Go on – I want to meet this Joe of yours. In fact, I insist!'

Connie's eyes narrowed. 'What right have you got to insist on anything?'

'Right?' Bette's face loomed half an inch from hers. 'I don't need a right, Connie. I'm your big sister. I get to vet all your boyfriends, have done ever since Ma passed on.' She flung a mouthful of scalding tea down her throat. 'But of course there's nothing to vet, is there?'

'You bitch!'

'No, Connie, not a bitch. A realist. All I want is for you to face up to your responsibilities.'

'Oh?' Connie smiled with venomous sweetness. 'You mean like you face up to your responsibilities with Dad?'

Bette drew in breath. She might have coloured slightly too, but with her weather-beaten complexion it was hard to tell. Pushing back her chair, she got to her feet and snatched up her waistcoat. 'Don't be long, you're needed back at the office.'

146

'When the going gets tough . . .' spat Connie as the beaded curtain swished back into place. 'I'll show you,' she muttered under her breath as her fingers rattled over the keys. 'I'll damn well show you all.'

Getting launched on this dating lark was even harder than Laurel remembered. And it didn't help that her conversation with Don had gone so emphatically pear-shaped. After inadvertently dropping the bombshell about Joe, she hadn't felt comfortable asking questions about Gabriel. So that little scheme had taken her precisely back to square one.

Twice she'd almost raided Gabriel's personal file for clues; and twice she'd mentally slapped herself on the wrist, glad that the file was safely locked away in Ravi's filing cabinet.

Then she'd spent a good half-hour sitting in her office, staring at the telephone on her desk. Ought she to phone Gabriel out of the blue? Could she do that? 'Course she could, why the hell not, she was no wimp. Besides, Steph was expecting great things. But she still couldn't quite bring herself to dial the number. What if he thought she was too forward? What if the one thing he couldn't stand was pushy women?

Relieved to have found an excuse not to be brave, she took an early lunch and sloped off to the High Street, to loiter outside all the places she thought Gabriel might frequent. But he didn't go to the Merry Hind for a pie and a pint, or to Noodle Doodle for sushi and a pot of jasmine tea – not that she'd really thought he would. That would have been far too

147

convenient. She'd just sort of vaguely hoped he might.

Laurel had squashed her face up against the front windows of countless takeaways, leaving her nose-print on every sandwich shop in town; but when an hour had elapsed and she suspected she was only five minutes away from being arrested for soliciting, she gave up and went back to Dovecote & Marsh.

'Buy anything nice?' enquired Stacey as Laurel headed for her office, peeling off her jacket.

She stopped and looked round. 'Sorry?'

Stacey pointed at Laurel's mini-backpack. 'Shopping. You were gone ages, couldn't you find what you were looking for?'

'Er . . . no. No, I didn't.' And you don't know the half of it, thought Laurel.

'They've got some lovely turquoise plunge tops in Seuss & Goldman, all velvet and sequins – did you see them? Go smashing with your colouring.' Stacey warmed to her subject. 'Ooh, and when I was in that new French boutique the other day—'

'Sorry, I'd love to stop and chat,' lied Laurel, 'but I've got loads of work to do. No calls unless they're urgent, OK?'

She felt restless and light-headed as she closed the office door behind her, leaned her back against it and let out a long, deflating sigh. Typical. Now she'd finally made up her mind to do something about the man, he was nowhere to be seen. Oh Gabriel, she moaned silently; why couldn't you just accidentally happen to be at the same place where I accidentally was?

148

The telephone beckoned her from across the room. Go on, it seemed to say; you know you want to.

And Laurel might even have picked up the receiver if there hadn't been a knock on the door.

'I'm busy.' She nipped swiftly behind her desk, sat down and opened a ledger at random.

The door opened a fraction and Stacey's cheery face appeared in the gap. 'Sorry, I know you said not to disturb you, only this just arrived Special Delivery and I thought it might be important.'

When Stacey had gone, closing the door very quietly behind her, Laurel contemplated the parcel warily. It was small, square, weighed virtually nothing and seemed to consist of something in a box, inside a padded envelope. She prodded it but it didn't squeak or explode. Picked it up, shook it and listened to its faint rattle. Belatedly she read the return label, and saw that it was from Steph.

Well, well, well. Intrigued, Laurel popped apart the staples and prised the lid from the box. Inside lay a diamanté tiara – a creation so magnificently tacky it was gorgeous; and so very like the one she'd sobbed over when she was nine and had accidentally sat down on it at Irish dancing. The note read:

Just a little prezzie to say I'm thinking of you. See you Saturday, love Steph XXX.

Tiptoeing over to the door, Laurel turned the key; then balanced the tiara on top of her head and whipped out her handbag mirror. She giggled delightedly at her

149

reflection. Lush. That was the only word for it. Now all she needed was a pink feather boa and a sequinned halter-top to be the Barbie princess of her childhood dreams.

Then it struck her. All this time she'd been wandering round Cheltenham, ineptly trying to bump into Gabriel, she could have been taking lessons from the mistress of power-seduction herself. It was the obvious thing to do: ask Steph for advice. If anybody knew the right way to pick up a bloke it was her.

Chapter 12

Another Saturday night, another gallon of Pimm's.

In the short time since Steph had tap-danced her way into Cheltenham, Laurel had been to more pubs, wine bars and dens of iniquity than she'd visited in the last twelve months put together. About a thousand per cent more, if she was honest. And now here she was in the Toucan, a bar she hadn't even known existed, half-pissed by half-past nine on a Saturday night. This was getting to be a habit. Not that that was necessarily a bad thing. Having Steph back in her life was just like old times – the good old times before Laurel's life had gone pear-shaped. And at least she was getting out and about even if her liver might be feeling the strain.

Steph winked at her over the top of an immense margarita. 'So, this mystery bloke of yours.'

'He's not my bloke,' she protested. 'Well – not yet.'

'That's my girl.' Steph chuckled dirtily. 'Get out there and do your stuff – he won't know what's hit him.' She ran her finger round the salt-encrusted rim of her glass. 'You going to tell me who he is then?'

'Nope.'

'Go on, he's a toyboy, isn't he?' fished Steph. 'You met him outside the sixth-form college and offered to help him with his homework.'

Laurel nearly choked on a mouthful of bar snack. 'What!'

'All right then, he's a ninety-four-year-old billionaire and he's going to leave you everything in his will.'

'You don't half talk bollocks sometimes.'

'Come on, you might as well tell me now – you'll have to eventually.'

'Well, you can wait until I've actually got round to asking him out.' However many centuries it takes me to pluck up the courage, thought Laurel. Aiming her drink at its coaster, her elbow missed the edge of the bar and she jabbed herself in the eye with a Twiglet. 'Ow!'

'Steady on,' giggled Steph. 'We've hardly started drinking yet!' With an expert hand she retrieved Laurel's diamanté tiara from round her neck and stuck it back on top of her head. 'There you go – perfect again. Just like my Gabriel!'

Laurel's brain took a couple of seconds to register. 'Who?'

'Gabriel.' Steph ran a lascivious tongue over her lips. 'Gabriel Jouet, my hunky new squeeze! Don't look all innocent, I know you engineered the whole thing.'

Laurel's jaw fell open. Suddenly she felt very, very sick.

If Steph had noticed the sudden change in Laurel's expression, she didn't give any sign. She just kept rattling on about Gabriel. Her Gabriel.

'I mean all right, I admit it, when that Indian boy at your office called me I did have my doubts. After all on paper a painter and decorator is hardly my type but maybe that's where I've been going wrong. Always dating wealthy men when what I needed all along was someone more ... down to earth. And our introductory date was perfect and it's so clever of you, it really is!'

Something had drained all the blood from Laurel's body and replaced it with ice-water. 'It. Is?'

'Of course it is, Lozzie! It was a stroke of genius matching me up with Gabriel and it's all going brilliantly and I know the whole thing's down to you and—' Belatedly, Steph clocked the look of total shock on Laurel's face. 'Oh dear, you really did hurt yourself with that Twiglet, didn't you? Your eye's watering.'

'No. No, it's OK, everything's fine,' gabbled Laurel, her mind a nauseous whirl, all her fluffy pink fantasies suddenly turned inside-out like a disembowelled pyjama case. She couldn't believe it Steph had done it again. Taken the one man that she really, really wanted.

'But I'm sure it's—'

Laurel warded off Steph's concerned hands. 'Stop fussing me, OK?'

Steph drew back. 'I'm sorry, I was just trying to help.'

Laurel brought down her fist on the counter, so hard that everything rattled. 'What I need is a drink. A bloody enormous one.'

A radiant smile blossomed on Steph's face. 'That's my Lozzie! Let's celebrate.'

Laurel swallowed and tried not to be sick. 'Yeah. Let's.'

I don't believe it. I do not bloody believe it!' Laurel fought the urge to punch her fist through the mirror in the Ladies' loo. 'You get over someone, you think never again, then you see someone else, and no sooner have you set eyes on him than Steph walks in and steals him from under your nose!'

Angry and upset, she applied a quivering slash of red gloss to her blanched lips. No way was Steph going to see her fall to bits again, not the way she'd done over Jason.

'Face it, Laurel,' she told her red-eyed reflection, 'as long as Steph's within five thousand miles of your life you might as well forget about men.'

Not that she cared, of course. Why should she? After all, hadn't she made up her mind never to get involved ever again?

'Lozzie?' A hand waved in front of her face. 'Anybody in there?'

Suddenly there was no fizz left in the Kir royal.

Something nasty had happened to Laurel. Just when she was certain things were really on the up, a great big cosmic piano had dropped on her from a great height, reducing her to a thin smear on the bar-room floor. Not that Steph had a clue what was going on, and why should she? How could Laurel tell her why she'd suddenly changed from party animal to tetchy drunk, all in the space of five minutes?

154

Steph tried again. 'Are you all right?'

'Fine!'

'Was it something I said?'

Silence.

'What did I say?'

'Nothing.'

'Then what are you upset about?'

'I told you, nothing's wrong,' snapped Laurel, avoiding Steph's gaze. And then, out of pure malice and because it made her feel better, she muttered, 'As if you give a shit.'

Steph drew back in surprise. 'Hey, that's a bit unfair, all I said was—'

'All you said, all you bloody said.' Laurel's eyes flashed, almost pleading with Steph to take the bait and fight; but all Steph looked was puzzled. 'As if everything always has to be about you, like you're the centre of the universe or something. Maybe if you kept your big mouth shut a bit more often . . .'

'Oh,' said Steph, caught between baffled and alarmed. 'Are you sure you're feeling all right, I mean there aren't any pills you ought to be taking or anything?'

'Stop pussyfooting and say it! Am I about to foam at the mouth and go doolally on you? No Steph; I don't think I'll bother going mad tonight, if that's OK. I think I'll just go home and watch *Newsnight* if it's all the same to you.'

Laurel scrambled off the bar stool and threw down the ludicrous tiara she'd been naive enough to think was fun; about as much fun as this whole disastrous

155

evening. 'This was a stupid idea,' she announced, stamping it cleanly into two pieces.

'What – the tiara? I'm sorry, I thought you liked it.'

'Not the stupid fucking tiara. All of it.'

Snatching up her handbag, Laurel pushed past Steph and headed for the exit. She had to get out of here, had to escape before the ludicrous truth came spilling out and she did something she'd really regret.

'Hang on, where are you going?' Steph asked her retreating back. Laurel didn't turn round.

'I don't know.'

'Can I come too?'

'No.'

'But—'

She threw her one last, pain-filled look. 'I said no, Steph. What are you – deaf or something? Just fucking leave me alone.'

Saturday night had ended badly and Sunday didn't start much better. Of course, brooding sulkily in your own front room was hardly the grown-up way to deal with a problem, especially when the problem was a bloke. Just one stupid, ordinary bloke. It wasn't even as if it was anything worth getting herself into a state about. Laurel had told herself that over and over, but she took some convincing; and dawn found her sitting in exactly the same position, still staring sightlessly at the blank television screen. And there she stayed in the same sullen heap for most of that day, barely moving a muscle as a bloodshot sun clambered wearily into the sky, staggered across it and finally collapsed in a grateful heap behind the western hills.

'It doesn't matter,' she said out loud, her grip tightening on a chocolate-stained scatter cushion. 'You know it doesn't.'

Neil peeked out warily from beneath his plastic portcullis.

'You can't be in love with the guy – you don't even know him. You're only upset 'cause Steph's got him.'

A knot twisted in her stomach, and she knew she was telling herself lies again. Sure, Steph was part of it: after all, Steph could have anyone she wanted and most of the ones she didn't want as well. It seemed so unfair that she should take the one small thing Laurel had been coveting for herself. Especially after Jason. But there was more to it than that, much more. It was like the first time she'd dared to even stick her head above the parapet after hiding behind it for so long, some bastard had decided to shoot it off. Maybe Neil had the right idea after all. Plants and plastic castles were a lot less threatening than the real world.

'Oh for God's sake get over it, you daft cow,' she said aloud. 'Stop feeling sorry for yourself.'

The exhortation hung in the air like the smoke from a charred Sunday roast.

'You know what your sister would say if you rang her now,' she lectured herself, picturing Jools' well-meaning smile at the other end of the line. 'I've told you a thousand times, come to new Zealand. I'll fix you up with a dozen hunky sheep farmers inside ten minutes.

157

Remember what Mum always says, plenty more fish in the sea.'

Plenty. More. Fish.

And that, she mused, was exactly why she wasn't phoning her sister. There might well be plenty more fish, bigger and better and shinier fish, but Gabriel was the fish she'd wanted and if she'd not farted about playing hard to get, he might even now have been swimming in her bowl instead of Steph's.

She flung the cushion at the floor, and Neil ducked behind a frond of weed. 'What if I don't want to know about the other fish?' she demanded, adding silently 'and what if the other fish don't want to know about me?'

A tiny sob of self-pity shuddered through her. Look, Laurel, she admonished herself sternly: you're supposed to be over this, remember? All grown-up? Self-sufficient? Sorted? We agreed. You were going to get real, give up chasing all this love crap. Face facts, girl: even if Steph hadn't got to him first, who says you'd ever have got up the courage to ask the bloke out? And even if you had got it together, well, there was never any guarantee, was there? Look how Jason had turned out. Like just wasn't fair. And every time you let your hopes build up, it's gonna hurt a bit more when the big foot of doom comes and kicks them all in your face.

Doomed, that's what I am, she concluded with a pang of masochistic relish. Doomed to be a loser in love.

Some time on Monday morning, between an OU programme about the history of sash windows and the start of the early morning news, Laurel downed two pints of cranberry juice, ate half a packet of Jaffa Cakes, and scraped herself upright. There was nothing else for it: she had to seek out the company of other people like her, Cheltenham's raggle-taggle army of the hopeful and hopeless in love.

Yes, she was going to work. Insane though it might seem at this time of the morning, that was where she wanted to be.

As nine o'clock chimed on the ormolu clock, the outer office began filling up with people and their voices. Annoyingly bright and happy voices.

'Anyway, after we've watched the video Alex says, "Let's make popcorn," which seemed like a great idea at the time, only she overdid it a bit.' Stacey's voice was punctuated by a winsome giggle. 'And we're still hoovering it out from behind the washing machine!'

And then Ravi's voice, bursting with irritating enthusiasm. '... fourteen different kinds of burger relish! You just wouldn't believe ...'

'Like I said,' boomed Bette, 'it was only the Maiden Fillies' Handicap Chase, but our Spearmint Fondue ran a damn fine race. Next weekend we're taking her down to Newmarket for the ...'

Laurel clenched her fists and fought the urge to jump ship. Coming to work had seemed like the right thing to do, but now she was here and the world had woken up, it was all proving too much to bear. It seemed like everybody, everywhere, had had a fantastic weekend. Well, almost everybody.

She stuck it out for as long as she could, making a real effort to bury herself in last month's profit and loss account; but her eyes kept wandering to the brass-framed 1940s' advertising poster hanging on the wall opposite her desk: Ladies! Let Dovecote & Marsh find you the Perfect Match.

The lump in her throat was turning into a tennis ball. She had to get out while she still had some self-control left. Retrieving her handbag from under the desk, she stood up straight and fixed a smile to her sagging face. Then she opened the door and stepped into the main office, setting a course straight for the Ladies' loo.

Damn. Stacey was heading right into her path, waving a sheet of D&M headed notepaper, complete with embossed pink doves. 'Oh Laurel, could you just have a look at this?'

But Laurel just kept coming straight at her like a Chieftain tank, forcing her to jump aside at the last moment for fear of being run over. 'Not now.' The elastic holding Lauren's taut smile in place was starting to fray at the ends.

Stacey's ginger curls wilted. 'But it'll only take a second.'

'Later.'

And then she was gone.

Laurel stood in the churchyard behind the High Street, half a large bag of currant buns dangling from her hand. Unfortunately there was only so much bread you could throw to the pigeons before even they lost interest and staggered bloatedly away.

160

Pulling herself together: that was what she was supposed to be doing here. It was a great idea, too – in theory. So was Einstein's Theory of Relativity, and she couldn't get her head round that one, either. Well, despite appearances Laurel wasn't entirely stupid. She knew she had to get back and shoulder all the responsibilities she'd hammered into herself, but every cold, lonely step that took her nearer to the D&M office increased the crushing gravity in her heart.

By the time she had climbed the stairs, she barely had the strength to push open the door. If she could just somehow get across the office without anybody saying anything to her, she'd be all right, she was sure she would.

And perhaps she would have been, but it didn't work out like that, because Ravi was one happy bunny and he wanted the whole world to know about it.

'Hey Laurel, come and look!' He bounded over, grabbed her by the arm and dragged her to his desk, where an enormous thank-you card had sprouted on top of his desk. 'Have you seen? Do I get "Employee of the Month", like in Mcdonald's?' He saw the look on her face and faltered.

Ravi's enormous grin trickled down his chin and plopped wetly onto the floor as his eyes locked with Laurel's. Something dark and scary grabbed him by the vitals, tied them into a reef-knot and left him with the unpleasant feeling that he was gazing into The Abyss.

He swallowed nervously. 'I got a thank-you card.' Snatching it from his desk, he hid it behind him. 'From your friend Miss Mihailovic.' The dark, scary thing was looming up like an iceberg now, and Ravi was the *Titanic*, garrulously steaming ahead. 'I matched her with Mr Jouet and she's really pleased.'

Laurel contemplated him in silence for a squirmingly long time. 'Fine.' She turned away.

'Fine?' Ravi thought of all the work he'd put in, all the time he'd spent shifting Laurel's backlog when he could have been having a social life, all the sheer dedication. And for what? All of a sudden he stopped feeling daunted and reverted to hard done-by. 'Fine?' he protested. 'Is that the best you can do?'

'Steady, boy,' urged Bette, placing a restraining hand on his shoulder as though he were a restive colt. But Ravi couldn't be pacified with a handful of pony nuts. He shook her off.

'Fine?' he squeaked. 'Is that all you can say?' His nose was uncomfortably close to Laurel's face and she turned away from him. 'I work my arse off for you, I carry this place, I carry you for chrissakes, and what do I get? I get "fine"! Well, d'you know something? It's not fine. It's not fine at all!'

Slowly, Laurel turned her face back towards him, and he saw that her eyes were bright and wet. 'What d'you want, Ravi?' she demanded softly. Then suddenly, abruptly, her voice rose to a shout. 'A bloody badge?'

Ravi flinched. 'I don't have to take this.'

Laurel's poor, sick heart pounded in the empty hollow of her chest. With all the poise she could summon up, she turned and walked away to her own office. The only sound in the shocked silence was the definitive click of her door, shutting out the world.

162

'She was crying,' whispered Stacey.

A sea of accusing faces turned on Ravi. 'Well, it's true!' he insisted. 'I don't have to take any of this. I'm not staying just so's madam can keep picking on me.' Plucking his leather jacket from the back of his chair, he slung it round his shoulders and stuck his favourite silver gel pen in his top pocket. 'See how you lot like it without me.'

And with that, he walked out.

Chapter 13

Just as Laurel was stepping out of the shower on Tuesday morning, the phone rang for the twenty-seventh time.

She hovered in the bedroom doorway, her wet hair dripping water on the carpet. She told herself she should probably ignore it, as she had done on the previous twenty-six occasions. It might be her mum, of course; but that was as good a reason as any not to answer. Laurel's mum could have hired herself out to the CIA as a lie-detector. And just now Laurel had no desire to be prodded out of the little trouble-free cocoon she'd spent all weekend constructing for herself.

A couple more rings, and it would stop. Just a couple more.

Only it didn't. It just kept on shrieking, as impossible to ignore as a crying baby in a library. With a sigh of impatience, Laurel snatched up the receiver.

'What?'

'I don't believe it – you're finally in!' Steph's triumphant shout was so loud that Laurel had to hold the phone away from her ear.

Shit, thought Laurel. 'Oh, it's you.'

'Yes, me! Your bosom chum, remember? How are you? In a better mood I hope.' Laurel didn't answer. 'What on earth have you been up to since God knows when? I was getting really worried.'

And if you believe that you'll believe anything, thought Laurel bitterly. 'Up to? Nothing.' Paranoia nibbled at the edges of Laurel's consciousness. 'Who told you I was up to anything?'

'Nobody did. Nobody ever tells me anything.' Steph was busy putting two and two together and adding five hundred. 'You *have* been up to something, haven't you? You dark horse. Is it a man?' Laurel's silence egged her on to a delighted conclusion. 'It is, isn't it? Go on, you can tell me.'

Laurel sat down heavily on the arm of the settee. 'There's nothing to tell,' she insisted, which was almost true since there was nothing she *wanted* to tell and even if there had been, Steph was the last person she'd have told it to. 'I've given up men, remember?'

'Don't give me that!' snorted Steph. 'Only last week you were talking about asking Mr Sexy-Pants out for a drink.'

A pang of hurt made Laurel's fingers clench on the arm of the chair. 'Yes, well, that was last week.'

'You mean – he knocked you back?'

'No, I just . . . changed my mind. Anyway, how are you?'

She should have known that Steph wasn't that easily diverted. 'So if it's not a man where have you been hiding yourself? And don't you dare say "nowhere".'

166

She steamed right on without leaving a pause for Laurel to reply, which was a relief really. If Steph knew Laurel had been moping around the house playing Radiohead, she'd probably turn up armed with two litres of Häagen-Dazs and even more questions. And that would lead inevitably to the awkward subject of her 'mystery man' – Gabriel Jouet.

'Go on,' insisted Steph. 'I want chapter and verse.'

'I know it's a disappointment to you and all that, but there's really nothing to tell,' replied Laurel. 'Look – I'm fine, I've not been doing anything, just slobbing around and being really boring.' She made a supreme effort to put on her breeziest voice. 'Never mind me, what've you been up to? How many fit blokes have you seduced since Saturday?'

That was the ace up Laurel's sleeve. If there was one thing Steph had never been able to resist talking about, it was sex. If there were two, the other one was herself. Laurel could visualise her twirling the telephone flex about her index finger, a Prada mule dangling from her perfectly varnished toes. 'Oh, maybe one or two,' she teased.

'Dozen you mean?'

'Hundred! And who says *I* was doing the seducing?'

All the muscles at the back of Laurel's neck ached with the effort of trying not to imagine Steph with Gabriel – and failing. She'd never have cast herself in the role of bunny-boiler, but the mental picture of the two of them grappling naked on black satin sheets tapped a vein of childish jealousy that made her want to sneak round to Steph's place and sew

167

well-rotted prawns into the hem of her bedroom curtains.

'Steph,' she retorted, 'you're *always* the one doing the seducing, you can't help yourself. One pout from you and they're putty in your hands.'

At her end of the phone line, Steph grinned broadly, recalling that Gabriel had not been at all like putty – in her hands or anywhere else. No, there was nothing soft about Gabriel Jouet, though she suspected a secret fondness for babies and fluffy kittens might lurk beneath that rugged, enigmatic exterior. Well, everybody had their faults.

She sprawled across her gilded chaise longue and dangled her bare feet over the end. 'Can I help it if I'm irresistible?' Laurel didn't reply. 'Well, can I?'

'So your second date with . . . er . . .?'

'Gabriel.'

'Gabriel. Right. It went . . . OK then?'

Laurel's voice didn't sound quite like Laurel, which puzzled Steph, but she let it pass. Maybe it was a bad time.

'Darling, it was won-der-ful.' Steph wriggled delightedly inside her silk brocade robe. 'He's so big and rugged and gorgeous. And a gentleman with it – I practically had to drag him inside for coffee.'

'You did?'

'Isn't that cute? I mean, how many men do you know like that?'

'You're forgetting,' replied Laurel, an edge of bitterness creeping into her voice. 'I don't know any men.'

168

'Of course you do – or you damn well ought to. All those men on your books to choose from, it's a sin not to sample the merchandise. Oh, did I tell you he bought me roses?'

'That's. Nice.' The words sounded clipped, almost disinterested, but Steph was in full flow now.

'And then he wanted to pay for dinner! He's so . . . so different!' Steph ran a hand through her still-damp hair. 'I'll have to take him shopping, mind, get him out of those boring clothes. Can't you just picture him all in black leather, or one of those Edwardian suits with the long jacket . . .'

'Steph—' began Laurel.

'I was going to play hard to get, Lozzie, I really was! But then I thought hey Steph, what's the point? Life's too short.'

'It's been great talking to you,' cut in Laurel, 'only I've got loads to do today, and I've only just started.'

Steph frowned. 'I thought you said you were just bumming around.'

'I was. All weekend and yesterday as well. That's why I've got so much to catch up on. Speak to you soon,' gabbled Laurel, 'have fun, 'bye.'

'Hang on a minute, I haven't finished!'

But Laurel had already clicked away into the ether, leaving Steph staring at the receiver. She'd never been the in-touch-with-your-emotions type, in fact an ex-squeeze had once accused her of being as sensitive as a triple-strength condom, but she wasn't stupid and even she could tell that something was wrong with Laurel. She cast her mind back and tried to play pop psychologist. All that crying, picking arguments in pubs, avoiding people – yes, something was definitely up. The question was, what?

She'd decided to attribute Laurel's behaviour in the bar to a bad case of PMT, which was preferable to admitting that it might be due to something more serious. Despite what she now knew about Laurel's past, Steph preferred not to think about it too much, if at all, and had filed away that particular piece of information in a far-flung corner of her brain 'Don't Go Here'. No, if there was something wrong with Laurel, Steph was determined it would be something that she could solve by taking her shopping or introducing Laurel to her plastic surgeon or . . .

'I wonder,' she mused, reaching out for her handbag and dipping a hand inside.

Ravi's departure had left several large holes at Dovecote & Marsh. Like chalk outlines at a murder scene, conspicuous gaps marked the places that had become his own. The row of plastic Thunderbirds figures had gone from the top of his filing cabinet, along with the Mills & Boon promotional coffee mug and a box of zebra-striped paper clips. No longer would people trip over the micro-scooter parked permanently in the kitchen, or moan about the fish and chip wrappers in his waste-paper basket. Even the wind-up false teeth that had annoyed the hell out of everybody seemed in retrospect to have possessed a certain vulgar charm.

It was Wednesday morning when his official letter of resignation arrived, but it could have been the eve of Armageddon for all the jollity there was in the office.

'Laurel,' ventured Stacey, shifting from one foot to the other.

'I told you, I'm busy.'

'But I was just wondering . . .'

Red faced and sweating, Laurel emerged from the giant stack of folders she was sorting through. 'You're just not listening, are you?' she snapped, dumping a pile into Stacey's outstretched arms. Even as she said it she knew she was being mean, but she couldn't stop herself. 'Here, renewals and reminders M–Q. Get a move on, you're getting R–Z tomorrow.'

Although sagging under the sheer bulk of pink cardboard, Stacey stood her ground. 'I only wanted to ask when you're going to advertise for Ravi's replacement.'

'Advertise? How the hell do I know? With him walking out on us like that I've hardly got time to breathe. For God's sake, Stacey, just go away and get on with your work.'

Stacey beat an honourable retreat, exchanging despairing looks with Bette, who was trying to have a delicate telephone conversation with one of their more elderly clients while ploughing her way through Ravi's A–Gs. Backing out with an armful of files, Laurel banged her head on the underside of some very solid oak shelving. 'Damn and bloody blast!'

'Are you all right, dear?' enquired Bette, putting her hand over the receiver.

'What do you fucking think?'

A moment's shocked silence descended on the office.

171

'No, Mrs Foyle,' said Bette, 'the line's rather crackly, you must have misheard.'

The usual low hubbub resumed. Laurel scrambled to her feet, beating the dust from her best black trousers. 'We've got the whole of the Cotswolds to cover, not to mention the international pen-friend service *and* the problem page for the *Courant*. And since that agency closed down in Tewkesbury, everyone and their mother's second cousin's stick insect are coming to D&M. How the hell are we going to get through all this work without Ravi?'

Connie scowled. 'You tell me. As if I care,' she muttered under her breath.

'Well, there's only one thing for it.' There was an alarmingly manic glint in Laurel's eyes. 'We're all going to have to work harder and faster.'

Connie's scowl became a sneer. 'Fine. Great. I'll ring the papyrus factory right away.'

Bette raised an eyebrow. 'Shush, Connie.'

'And while I'm at it, why don't I order us some of that newfangled stuff – what's it called? Oh yes, paper.'

In the midst of all the tantrums and traumas, Don walked in. At first he thought he had accidentally wandered into a sub-department of Dante's Inferno, but all things considered the place was a bit too untidy for Hell.

He stepped over a disembowelled box of ancient advertising brochures. 'What's going on?'

Stacey darted him a brief smile but hurried straight past him, so restricted by her tight skirt that she had to hitch it up to her bottom to step over a stack of folders somebody had left on the floor.

He turned to address Laurel, but had barely opened his mouth when she seized him by the shoulders and moved him firmly to one side, like an inconvenient hatstand. 'Not now, Don, I'm rushed off my feet.'

He barely dared move from his allocated square of polished parquet as he surveyed the scene. Ah, Connie. There she was, an erotic vision in sexy black T-shirt and skirt, and sheer nylons that he fervently hoped ended in a lacy black suspender belt. He cleared his throat and waved. 'Connie, what's happening?'

'For God's sake!' she hissed. 'One person short and the whole office turns to crap.' If looks could kill, Connie would have cornered the market in pest control. 'Working my arse off, and all *she* can do' – this was accompanied by a laser-beam glare in Laurel's direction – 'is fuck about and get on people's nerves.' She pushed him aside, so suddenly that he slipped on a glossy brochure and nearly fell over. 'Don't just stand there you stupid Scottish lump, you're in my light.'

He mumbled an apology, but by then Connie was already halfway across the office, brandishing the window pole like a javelin.

'It's Ravi,' explained Bette, who was sitting with her elbows on her desk and her chin in her hands. 'He's gone.'

Grateful for an oasis of calm, Don went over to talk to someone sane. 'Gone?'

'Resigned.' Bette lowered her voice to a confidential whisper. 'Reckoned Laurel was working him too hard.

Trouble is, we're a body short now and of course the business is busier than it's ever been. Murphy's Law. So we're *all* knee-deep in the mire.'

Don contemplated the mess that the office had turned into; to all appearances, a disorganised mess at that. If business was booming at Dovecote & Marsh, he couldn't imagine why. 'How come there's so much work coming in?'

Bette's gaze lighted on Connie, swearing as she kicked hell out of a helpless waste-paper basket. 'Dunno. Must be all that cheerful, friendly, personal service we lavish on our valued clientele.' She looked at Don and snorted. 'God help 'em.'

'So you're not coping then? With all the extra?'

'Not at the moment, but we *could* cope.' She was glaring at Connie, but Connie seemed immune to anything less than TNT. Bette raised her voice several dozen decibels. 'If everybody got on with what they were supposed to be doing, instead of acting like Godzilla with PMT.'

'Ah. Right,' nodded Don. But Bette had the distinct feeling his mind was somewhere else.

If anybody's got PMT, thought Laurel gloomily, it's me.

These last few days, everything seemed to irritate her. People, places, songs on the radio, hammocks, custard, even Neil – who had enough psychological problems already, without being the target for irrational annoyance. She was turning into the sort of person she really couldn't stand. Small wonder everybody at D&M was giving her a wide berth – apart from poor Stacey, bless

174

her, who was too nice to avoid anybody and had consequently become Laurel's right-hand flunkey.

Well, rather than snap at people and take it all out on Stacey, Laurel had decided that the only fair thing to do was to make herself scarce for a couple of hours. That was why she was sitting hunched over her third latte in the Mean Bean, wearing the kind of expression that could clear entire tables within seconds.

Much to her relief, nobody had ventured to sit anywhere near her. Well, nobody except one persistent German student who had tried to pick her up, and he wouldn't be trying *that* again anytime soon.

People came and went. Coffee got drunk and muffins munched. A light drizzle flecked the café's windows with moisture. Laurel's thoughts drifted. Try as she might to be hard and practical, the uneasy atmosphere in the office hurt her; all the more so since it was justified. After all, Ravi had only been doing his job, and he'd done it well. how was he to know that he'd twisted the invisible knife in her heart? How was he supposed to guess that his boss was an emotional basket case?

She stirred her coffee slowly, watching the hot milk and the dark espresso swirl together and blend. If only people could be that easily reconciled. If only Ravi would make the first move. She wanted him back in his job, but if she had to ask, she hadn't a clue where to start, and maybe it wouldn't work anyway.

'Penny for 'em,' said a quiet voice at her side.

Laurel looked up, preparing a scathing retort, but the words stuck in her throat. The man was familiar ... youngish, blondish, faintly attractive. Attractive?

175

Laurel felt a flush of colour rise to her cheeks as she smiled back, startled by her own reaction. It felt mildly adulterous.

'Hi. Hope you don't mind if I join you.' He sniffed his hand before he extended it, and recognition clicked inside Laurel's head.

'Mr Lillee, isn't it?'

'Please. Call me Graeme.' He sat down with his small cappuccino and emptied three sticks of sugar into it. 'Everybody needs a vice,' he laughed as he saw her watching him.

'Oh. Yes, I suppose so.' Laurel nibbled the corner off a flapjack because it seemed the thing to do. 'It's not much of a vice,' she added.

He tapped the side of his nose. 'Who said I've only got one?'

'Ah.' In spite of herself, she warmed to his smile, to the gentle light that danced behind his grey-blue eyes. 'So the truth is out.'

Graeme Lillee took another sip of coffee, watching her over the rim of his cup. 'Tell me to mind my own business if I'm being nosy,' he said, 'but I can't help noticing you look troubled.'

'Troubled?' She experimented with a carefree laugh, but it caught in her throat and turned into a cough. 'No, I'm fine. Really.'

In Laurel's head, a voice wanted to say, Ever feel that wherever you are, whatever you're doing, however well you're doing it, that you're in the wrong place, doing the wrong thing and all the time you've just been kidding yourself? But something stopped her mouth from

176

shaping the words. Instead, she found herself answering with a question: 'So, what brings you into town?'

Graeme's eyebrows formed an inverted V of surprise. 'You did.'

'*I* did? How?'

'You hired me,' he prompted her. 'You know, to come and look at your stuffed bear.' He handed her a business card from his jacket pocket. It read: GL Taxidermy.

Laurel clapped a hand over her mouth. 'Of course. You're the taxidermist.'

It was Graeme's turn to blush. 'Yes, well. Not the most romantic of professions, is it?'

'Well . . . no.'

'I also undertake restoration work,'

'Stupid me, I just didn't put two and two together when I called your office.' She emptied the last of the latte down her throat and stood up, feeling rather awash with hot milk. 'Tell you what, shall we go and have a look at that bear?'

'It's a sun bear,' declared Graeme Lillee, scrutinising the black furry thing from all angles.

'How can you tell?' asked Laurel.

'From its size and the patch on its chest.' He gave it an affectionate pat on the head and one of its canines fell out. 'Good workmanship. Done by an expert.'

'But its teeth are falling out!' protested Laurel.

'Quick spot of remedial work, soon have the little chap looking good as new.'

Laurel's face fell. 'What about health and safety? It must be a health hazard, surely!'

'Nope.'

'So I can't get rid of it?'

'Absolutely no reason to.'

'Oh, knickers!' Laurel sat down on the corner of her desk and aimed a kick at the bear's leg. She missed.

Graeme looked at her, head on one side. 'Why do I get the feeling the bear isn't really the problem?'

Laurel avoided his gaze. 'I don't know. Why do you?'

He folded his arms and scratched his chin. 'Well, let's see . . . I'm not much of a psychologist, but maybe you wanted an excuse to check up on me.'

'Check up on you?'

'To work out why I've been such a failure on my dates.'

'Oh,' said Laurel, who hadn't expected the conversation to take this turn. 'I, um, didn't know you had been.'

Mr Lillee wagged a reproving finger. 'You're a very bad liar, Laurel Page. So – why *am* I a failure in matters of the heart? What's the cause of it? Go on, tell me. I can take it.'

Normally she'd have come out with one of the soothing platitudes D&M loved to dispense to its clients. For D&M inhabited a world in which no one was unlovely or unlovable, and if you were on your own it was simply that you hadn't yet met That Special Someone. But Laurel felt distinctly glum. Talking about misfortune in love made her think about herself and Gabriel, and that was definitely not an aid to positivity.

'Maybe it's predestination,' she suggested bleakly.

178

'Maybe some people are just fated never to have anyone, and there's not a damn thing they can do about it.'

'You mean –we're all helpless? And it's not worth even trying?'

She shrugged. 'Maybe.'

For a split second, Graeme Lillee looked as gloomy as she felt; then he took a step back and smiled broadly. 'You're a genius!'

She blinked. 'What?'

'A genius! That's perfect – reverse psychology! Stop jollying me along, tell me there's nothing I can do about it, and bingo! Suddenly I feel ... I don't know ... refreshed. Like I can get out there and do anything if I really want to.'

'You do?' Laurel was frankly baffled.

He seized her hand and pumped it vigorously up and down. 'Thank you, Laurel, that was just what I needed to hear. Can you guess where I'm going now? I'm off to tell Stacey I'm ready for my next date whenever she wants to arrange it – and it's going to be a good one!'

'Glad I could be of help,' Laurel murmured as Mr Lillee slung his jacket over his shoulder and whisked himself out of her office, leaving the sun bear grinning gummily in his wake.

It was distinctly weird, the positive effect a few ill-chosen words had had on Mr Lillee. But what was even weirder was the effect they'd had on herself.

Graeme Lillee wasn't the only one who was going to give it his best shot.

Ravi was in a reflective mood.

179

Comfortably slumped on a chair in his favourite greasy spoon café, he moved one foot in time to the Mos Def album booming out of his personal stereo. His extra-large banana milkshake was leaving a moustache of yellow foam across his top lip, but he was too lost in contemplation to notice much or, still less, care. Outside the café windows, the last of the evening sunshine was turning the dimming light an orangey red.

Across Ravi's lap lay the *Evening Courant*, open at the local job listings.

He worked his way through them all in turn, giving each one a critical review. Nightclub doorman: great if you were six feet wide with a reinforced concrete head. Postman (strictly for insomniacs), kennel worker (spend all day shovelling up dog poo), Latin teacher (perfect if you liked talking to dead people), lifeguard . . . Hmm, not the greatest selection in the world.

Casually he wondered if he ought to ask for his job back – a thought that made him snigger. Which job? Had he left *any* of them under happy circumstances?

That thought hit him in the face like a wet flannel, and the snigger dwindled away into a silence that was louder than the music. A silence which seemed to yell the same words over and over again into his ear, until finally he gave in and spoke them out loud: 'Know what you are, Ravi? You're a twat.'

Ravi willed himself deeper into the music, but the final 't' kept echoing on in every repetitive bass-beat. He might have stayed sitting there, unmoving, until the café closed for the night and threw him out; but suddenly something prodded him in the shoulder. It gave him such a turn that he started and the chair fell over sideways, taking him – and a plastic ketchup bottle – with it.

By the time he had picked himself up and everyone else in the café had stopped laughing, it was pretty obvious who had done the prodding.

'Hello,' mouthed Stacey.

He took off his earphones and turned off the music. 'What are you doing here?'

She looked embarrassed. 'I'm ever so sorry, I thought you'd seen me.'

'That's OK, no broken bones.' A thought occurred. 'How did you know I was here?'

'Your brother said you might be.'

A head framed by spiky blue hair popped round the side of Stacey's ginger curls. 'Is that him?'

'Yes, this is him. Ravi, this is Alex, my sister's girl; she's staying with me at the moment.'

'Hi, Alex.'

'Couldn't get a sitter,' explained Stacey.

'I don't need a sitter!' protested Alex.

'Well I don't need to be taken to court for being an unfit foster mother!' replied Stacey. Taking out her purse, she handed Alex a five-pound note. 'Go and get some drinks, eh?'

'Can I have a Wagon Wheel?'

'Oh, go on then.'

She and Ravi looked at each other awkwardly, wanting and yet not wanting to make eye contact.

'Would it be OK if we joined you?' asked Stacey.

Chapter 14

Laurel took a step back, and gave a start as the arm of the old-fashioned guillotine jabbed her in the bottom. Another six inches to the right, and the aspidistra would be poking her in the ear. This was really quite unnerving.

She edged away from the guillotine and barked her shin on a chair-leg. It was exactly as if her office had shrunk in the wash. No, on second thoughts it was more like the furniture was advancing on her millimetre by millimetre, its dovetailed joints flexed and ready to pounce. She was glad she had that monolithic mahogany desk between her and the hatstand; it looked as if it might be handy in a fight.

In retrospect, she rather wished she hadn't decided to accommodate Ravi's files by hiding them behind the furniture, but it was the best compromise she'd come up with. At least this way she didn't have to sit at his desk whenever she wanted to work on something, and it kept the place looking reasonable – albeit a bit claustrophobic.

'Oi.' She glared at the coffee table. 'You looking at me?' Its air of practised nonchalance didn't convince her. Face it though, she told herself: you're talking to furniture. You're probably not the best judge of behaviour.

Laurel forced her mind back onto the job in hand. 'Focus!'

She dragged out her chair as far as it would go, pulled in her stomach till it met her backbone, and squeezed into the tiny gap between chair and desk. The settee made like it hadn't noticed as she picked up the letter-opener, but she knew she had it worried. Good. That's what this office needed, a bit of discipline. Come to think of it, it was most likely what she needed too.

A Mont Blanc of unopened envelopes dominated the desktop, towering majestically over the faded rattan in-tray. That stack of post was a miracle of engineering; if you'd tried to build one like that on purpose, it'd have taken eighteen months and an Arts Council grant.

As she made a start on her mail, the office sighed and relaxed around her. In fact the whole process was comfortably hypnotic. Things quickly sorted them-selves quite naturally into three distinct piles. First the inevitable bills: phone, electricity, gas, brochures, flowers, fresh pork chops for Killer (how much!); then a smaller pile of correspondence: letter from satisfied customer, letter from dissatisfied customer, letter containing large cheque, letter containing even larger invoice.

By far the most imposing pile was the one that had already half-filled the waste-paper basket. Laurel

184

hummed to herself as she weeded it out: junk, more junk, expensively produced junk, junk disguised as bills, junk disguised as bank statements.

Quite near the bottom of the heap lay one small, brown padded envelope. Intrigued, she held it to her ear and shook it, but it didn't rattle, and it was the wrong shape for a CD or a data cartridge – not that Dovecote & Marsh had much use for such things. She turned it over, but there was no return address. She even sniffed it, the way you sniff Christmas presents to find out if Grandma's sent you talcum powder again; but the little padded envelope wasn't giving anything away. Finally she gave it a thorough fondling, and felt it bend slightly in the middle. Aha, Inspector Page, a telltale clue.

The staples gave way with a satisfying pop, and sure enough, when she upended the envelope, a book slid out onto the desk. A small, black, slightly battered book with leather covers worn shiny from years of being slipped in and out of a handbag. Laurel recognised it instantly, and marvelled that it hadn't disintegrated from overuse years ago. Beside it on the desk lay an even smaller black card bearing Steph's flamboyant handwriting, in silver ink.

It's a start. S.

Laurel's eyes almost popped out of her head. Steph's little black book! She'd never even been allowed to touch it before, let alone look inside, not that she'd ever wanted to of course. With a swift glance to right and left she opened it gingerly and peeked furtively as though it might be booby-trapped. The yellowed pages were crammed full of names, numbers, addresses ... even

185

star-ratings from one to five! She flicked through and did a double-take. Good grief, eleven stars and a red exclamation mark?

Laurel snapped the book shut. Ugh, revolting. Like being shown a picture of your mum and dad having sex. She gave a prim, schoolmarmish sniff. What kind of person did Steph think she was, sending her second-hand pornography through the post? That was tanta-mount to implying that Laurel was desperate for her cast-offs, when she could quite easily get her own blokes, thank you very much.

Assuming she wanted any, which of course she didn't. Well, not Steph's second-hand ones anyway.

An electrical crackle of anger ran through Laurel, and she dropped the book into the bin with all the other junk.

By the time Laurel next saw Steph, the following evening, her anger had mutated into the hurt humili-ation of 'who-the-fuck-d'you-think-you-are-sending-me-a-list-of-your-hand-me-downs-you-snotty-cow?'

She was all fired up to give Steph both barrels, but when she stepped through the surfboard-shaped doors of the Sydney Vodka House, she realised to her dis-appointment that Steph wasn't actually there. Typical.

Ill-temperedly she hitched her bottom onto one of the bar stools, regretting the extreme tightness of her pants – not to mention the terrible itching under her T-shirt. It was so long since she'd been out on the pull that she'd quite forgotten how much effort it took to maintain the illusion of pertly braless breasts. Maybe parcel tape hadn't been such a good idea, though.

186

'G'day!' A double row of opalescent teeth loomed suddenly into view as the barman stood up from emptying the drip tray. The name badge on his vest read: Brent. 'What's it to be, then? Voddy on the rocks, or a nice cold tinny?'

'Oh. Hi.' Despite her determination not to play Steph's silly, adolescent game, Laurel found herself mentally awarding the barman marks out of ten. OK, so the sun-streaked root perm and the blond stubble were oh-so-eighties, plus she half expected those teeth to light up and play 'Tie Me Kangaroo Down, Sport', but on the plus side he was alive, male, and possessed of a nifty little set of pecs.

'Have you seen our new cocktail menu? I can recommend the Barbie on the Beach.'

The permatanned pecs tensed appetisingly as he leaned over and gave her the full benefit of his lime-green string vest.

'Really?' Laurel scanned the laminated card. 'OK then, what about the . . .' She giggled self-consciously, wrapping one ankle round the other and almost falling off the bar stool. Hell, but she was out of practice. 'One-Night Stand? Or the . . . er . . .' She felt her cheeks burn. 'Screaming Orgasm?'

He leaned a little closer, overwhelming her with the scent of fresh sweat and dolphin-friendly tuna. 'Well, if that's the kinda thing you're after, the sheilas tell me I do a very nice Long Slow Poke.'

At that moment, perhaps fortunately, Steph coughed behind her like a sixth-form drama queen. 'Well, well, Lozzie. I see you've started without me, you bad girl.'

187

She dropped her sequinned handbag on the bar and showed about half a mile of thigh as she slithered onto the stool next to Laurel's. 'Dry Martini, Brent,' she instructed. 'Hold the olive but I'll take a dash of Vegemite.'

The blond barman was aghast. 'Vegemite?'

'Believe me, it tastes better than it sounds.'

'I hope so,' commented Laurel, settling for a Barrier Reef, hold the prawns. ''Cause it sounds vomitous.'

Once the barman was out of earshot, Steph pulled Laurel towards her with the strap of her halter-top, half-throttling her in the process. 'Well, Lozzie, you learn something new every day! I'd never have had you down for a femme fatale.'

Laurel eased her windpipe clear. 'Pardon?'

'You.' Steph jerked her head towards the barman's back. 'And him. Five minutes later and you'd have ripped his pants off with your teeth.'

'Don't exaggerate!'

'Who's exaggerating?' Steph flipped a macadamia nut into her mouth. 'You're talking to the expert here, remember.' She crossed her arms and waved a finger in semi-serious reproach. 'I dunno, I leave you alone for five minutes and I find you making eyes at Surfer Boy! God help us Lozzie, have you no taste at all?'

More than you, thought Laurel. 'Are you telling me off for flirting?'

'Oh, absolutely,' grinned Steph.

'You've got a nerve! Specially since you were the one who started me off in the first place.'

'Me?' asked Steph innocently.

'You – and your damn book. Putting ideas into people's heads.'

'Ah yes, my little black book.' Steph's fingers fidgeted in the sun-dried eucalyptus chips. 'Actually, I might want it back.'

'You might?' Laurel felt something close to a pang of regret. Her drink arrived, and she drew a big turquoise mouthful up the silver straw. 'But I thought you sent it me to—'

'That's right Loz, I sent it to you to keep me . . . you know . . . on the straight and narrow.'

The end of the straw slipped from Laurel's lips. Surely she hadn't got the wrong end of the stick about Steph's little 'gift'? 'To keep you on the straight and narrow?'

'Mmm, why else? I mean, sending it to you I knew it'd be safe, and I needed to be kept away from temptation.' She sighed. 'But to tell you the truth . . .' She drummed her fingers on the bar. 'Lozzie . . .'

'Hmm?' Laurel was not sure whether to be less offended or more by the fact that Steph seemed to regard her as a safe bet and not a desperate one.

'If you were Gabriel, you'd have shagged me sense-less by now, wouldn't you?'

Laurel's jaw hinged slackly up and down as she thought of an appropriate answer.

'Yes, of course you would.' Steph flicked back an imaginary wisp of hair and preened herself in all thirty of the mirrors behind the bar. 'If I'd let you.'

'If!' snorted Laurel.

Steph threw her an old-fashioned look. 'Yeah, yeah,

189

all right, so maybe I'm sometimes a bit quick off the mark. But anyhow, you'd have tried it on, right?'

Laurel's eyes widened. 'You mean he hasn't?'

Steph slumped unhappily into the bar snacks. 'Mysterious is great, aloof is fab, enigmatic is drop-dead sexy, but – Gabriel? You know his problem? He's too fucking mysterious by half!'

'He is?' Laurel tried unsuccessfully to suppress a frisson of *schadenfreude*. 'You mean it's not perfect between you two after all?'

Steph leaned nearer, beyond the range of Brent's be-ringed ears. 'Wanna know something? I get more fun with a loofah, that's what. Oh Lozzie ...' Her head drooped until it was touching the bar top. 'Have I been getting it all wrong all this time?'

Laurel had never seen Steph wilt like this before. It was like looking at a blow-up doll with half the air missing. 'I'm not with you. Getting what wrong?'

'You know Loz, everything to do with—'

At that moment, Brent reappeared with a Martini on a tray. 'Sorry ladies, no Vegemite, we're fresh out. Will a chicken Oxo cube do?'

Steph considered for a moment. 'Oh what the hell, why not.' Grabbing a cocktail stick, she speared the brown stock cube and swilled it round her drink. Laurel wasn't sure whether to laugh or be sick.

'To do with what?' asked Laurel. But the veil had already fallen again and Steph waved the question aside.

'Nothing, just ignore me, I'm talking bollocks.' She wriggled on her stool. 'Listen, Lozzie, you have to help me.'

190

'Help you? How?'

'I want you to get Gabriel's file from the agency and give it to me. So I can do my homework.'

'I can't do that!' squeaked Laurel, abruptly lowering her voice as everyone in the bar turned to look at her. 'It's confidential.'

'But I'm your friend,' pouted Steph. 'Your bezzie mate in all the world, remember?'

'If you say so.' Despite their unspoken agreement not to talk any more about the past, Laurel very nearly pointed out that Steph's behaviour had flagrantly tarnished her best-mate status. 'And friends help each other, don't they? You did say you'd help me find the man of my dreams. In fact, you promised.'

Laurel might be a certified idiot, but she wasn't falling for that one. 'Uh-uh, sorry but no. You'll have to find out about Gabriel the old-fashioned way.'

'How?'

'By talking to him! If you want to know something, ask him straight out.'

'I can't do that! It's undignified.' Steph pouted big-time. 'You said you'd help.'

'Yes, and I will; but not like that.'

'All right then, you can help me another way. By coming on a date.'

Laurel looked Steph up and down. 'A threesome with you and Gabriel? Not bloody likely.'

'Don't be stupid! I meant a double date – me and Gabriel, you and your what's-his-name. Your new bloke.'

'Steph, I haven't got a bloke, remember?'

191

'But the last time we went out you had one right in your sights! You were practically drooling. Haven't you asked him out yet?'

Laurel squirmed inwardly; it was too embarrassing to reveal the truth. Her eyes dropped to the bar counter. 'I changed my mind.'

There was a long and meaningful silence. When she looked up again, Steph's expression had changed from disbelief to a kind of half-sneer. 'Changed your mind! Don't give me that, you were crazy about him.'

'So?' Oh shut up, Laurel willed Steph. 'Maybe I decided I didn't fancy him after all.'

Steph banged her glass down on the bar top. 'Laurel Guinevere Page, you're chicken! You are, aren't you? Come on, look me in the eye and tell me you're not.'

Laurel couldn't look Steph in the eye, but it wasn't because she was chicken. Or because Steph had just told the world her middle name was Guinevere. 'Ste-e-eph.'

'I don't believe this! Do you believe it, Brent? My mate Lozzie's too scared to ask a bloke she fancies out on a date!'

'I am not scared!' snapped Laurel, crimson-cheeked.

'OK then – prove it!'

'I don't want to.'

Brent leaned over the counter and scanned Laurel at close quarters. 'Looks scared to me.'

'Me too!' agreed Steph. 'Admit it Laurel, you're scared witless. You've completely lost your touch.'

That was just too much' the worm turned. Laurel picked up her drink, threw away the straw, quaffed the

192

whole lot in one gulp, cherry and all, and banged down the empty glass. 'All right then – I will prove it!'

Steph beamed. 'You'll ask him out?'

'Well . . . maybe not him, but someone.'

'Great! I knew you wouldn't let me down – not your bestest mate in the whole wide world.' She raised her glass high. 'Here's to our double date! Shall we say next Friday?'

Shit, thought Laurel. Then she ordered another drink. And another . . .

It was downright weird. By the time Laurel got home, well after one o'clock in the morning, she ought to have been dead on her feet; but she just couldn't go to sleep.

After the evening she'd just had, she could well have been too drunk to put her nightie on the right way up, or too hyped-up to lie still, or even too depressed to lift her head off the carpet. But she wasn't any of those. Nor was there any sense of foreboding about the cul-de-sac she'd recklessly driven herself down. She just took a look at her nice, soft bed and decided she didn't fancy sleeping – not yet, anyhow.

After a five-minute phone chat with her mum about lamb recipes, she snuggled down on the sofa with a pile of Jaffa Cakes, plunged into a really turgid Mexican novel and waited in vain for her eyelids to droop. When that failed to work she turned on the radio and tuned in to Chelt FM's late-night phone-in.

'So what am I going to do?' agonised Cheryl from Tewkesbury. 'I'm madly in love with Ricky but my big sister Danni got there first, like she always does, the cow, and I just don't know (sniff) how I'm ever going to get over him.'

Oh great, that was all she needed. Laurel turned off and tried a couple of experimental yawns, but that didn't work either. Two chapters and half a packet of biscuits later, she switched on the TV and braved the Channel 6 late-night soft porn flick.

Alas, forty minutes of suggestive breast-jiggling did nothing but remind her of the sticky tape still holding her boobs to attention. She peeled it off, put ointment on the rash, made an immense milky drink in a mixing bowl, drank the lot, went to the toilet three times . . . and finally concluded that she was still wide awake.

There was nothing for it. She might as well feed Neil and then go to work.

And there she stayed.

Sometime around dawn on Monday morning she groaned and told herself she was a grade A moron. Not only had she agreed to go on a double date with her best friend and her best friend's boyfriend, whose dark shaggability inhabited her every waking dream; worse still, she'd agreed to bring along her as-yet non-existent boyfriend.

It was one complication too far. Her brain seized up like a twenty-year-old car in the first cold snap of winter. Suddenly and inevitably, she felt weary. Resting her head on her folded arms, she let her eyes flick lazily around the office.

Hang on a minute.

She sat bolt upright. The answer was right in front of

194

her face. Her office was stuffed full of pink cardboard files; and inside those files were hundreds of men! She could so easily . . .

Oh no she couldn't.

But hey, why the hell not? Laurel stirred her near-cold tea and moved her chair a little closer to the window so that the morning sun could warm her face. You could, you know, she told herself. Go on, you know you want to.

That time she almost had herself convinced, but at the last moment reason stepped in, grabbed her by the throat and shouted in her face. You cannot do this! Not raid the office files just to find yourself a presentable date. Especially after coming over all ethical' with Steph.

She drew herself up like Joan of Arc at the stake, and resolved to banish the unworthy idea from her mind. No, it was the Lonely Hearts column in the local paper for her, or that weekly singles' club at Pittville church hall. She swallowed hard. Oh Steph, she groaned, why are you always leading me into trouble? You don't even have to try. All you do is walk back into my quiet, cosy little life, and suddenly everything's upside-down again.

Well, it was no good moaning about it, she might as well face facts. There was nothing else for it but Steph's little black book. After all, despite her problems with Gabriel, Steph hadn't yet got round to claiming it back.

Thank goodness she hadn't emptied her office bin – not that goodness had anything to do with it.

195

Chapter 15

Darcy wound his silver Persian haughtiness around Connie's bare legs, in what might just pass for a display of affection. It was well past his breakfast time and the service in this establishment was going right down the tubes.

Connie felt a delicious shiver as his silky fur trailed across her skin; the same kind of shiver she got whenever she keyed in a message to Joe. But she was completely unaware of the cat himself, and had even forgotten about Dad's bacon, sizzling noisily under the grill downstairs. Not even showered or dressed yet, she was sitting in front of the computer in her pyjamas, begging Joe to say yes.

Her fingers rattled across the keys. *Please call me.*

The cursor flashed a few times, then: *Sorry no can do.*

Then at least text me. Send me a picture maybe? ☺

The same answer. *Sorry.* ☹

But why? Why won't you?

This time he didn't reply at all. Connie bit her lip, trying not to be upset. He must have some good reason, she was sure he must. He wouldn't string her along or play games with her, not Joe. Not her lovely Joe. He just couldn't. Could he?

'Where's my bacon sandwich?' demanded a voice from downstairs. 'I'm not sitting here for the good of my health you know.'

'All right Dad, in a minute.' Her fingers tapped nervously beside the keyboard. Please answer, please.

'Half an hour I've been up and washed, and not even a cup of tea in the pot. If your sister was here . . .'

'Oh for God's sake put a sock in it,' she muttered. 'Or I will.' She raised her voice. 'I told you, I'll be down in a minute.' Just as she was despairing of ever getting any sensible answers out of Joe, another message popped up.

I could come and see you if you like.

At first she couldn't believe what she was seeing; she had to read the words three times over just to be sure. If she liked? If she liked!

Yes! When?!!

The smoke alarm went off downstairs as the bacon turned to charcoal, and Dad yelled something about some people being bone idle as well as stupid, but Connie didn't hear any of it. In sheer frustration, Darcy stole a slice of buttered bread and dragged it off behind the TV to kill and eat it. But all Connie did was lie back on her bed, hugging herself and grinning, until at last she couldn't keep it in any longer and let out a squeal of utter happiness.

On Wednesday afternoon, Stacey popped her un-

198

mistakeably ginger head round the door of Laurel's office.

'Problems?' enquired Laurel.

'Not really. I've done Stroud and I'm halfway through the Forest of Dean, and Bette's writing the answers for the *Courant*. Should I go down and see Kathy about the social now?'

Laurel glanced at the clock. 'Oh heck, I'd forgotten. Yes, you'd better. Let me know how you get on.'

Closing the door, Stacey walked lightly across the office, avoiding the faint shadow on the floor where Ravi's waste-paper bin had stood, and out onto the landing. At the top of the stairs she let out a long, deep breath and wrapped her fingers round the banister, feeling ever so slightly tipsy though she hadn't touched anything stronger than cranberry juice all week. Come on Stace, she urged herself: childminding, that's what you're supposed to be thinking about. Not Other Things You Don't Want Laurel To Know About.

She went downstairs and pushed open the door of the Happy Nappy. For once, it was almost an oasis of tranquillity compared to the bustle in the street outside.

'Where is everybody?' asked Stacey, blinking in surprise at the sight of just four well-behaved toddlers playing with Duplo bricks, and a row of sleeping babies in cots.

Kathy got up from the child-sized table, peeling a fruit gum out of her hair. 'Trip to the zoo with Frieda and Jaz,' she explained. 'Edward's mum doesn't approve of zoos, the twins are allergic and Poppy's got the sniffles.' She ruffled Edward's curly head. 'Shame

199

we missed out on the polar bears, but we're having our own fun here, aren't we?'

Edward looked up, round eyes shining. 'We're having blue swamp mud today,' he announced. 'And dinosaurs.'

Kathy smiled and interpreted. 'Blueberry yoghurt and dinosaur biscuits.'

'Lucky you!' enthused Stacey. 'I'm only having a banana and some colon cleanser.'

Kathy took a close look at Stacey. 'You OK?'

Stacey felt the spotlight turn on her and wriggled uncomfortably. 'Of course I am.'

'Sure?'

Stacey frogmarched the conversation smartly off in a different direction before Kathy started asking questions she didn't really want to answer. 'Laurel sent me down,' she said. 'To ask about the childminding. You know, on the evening when we have our big D&M get-together.'

'Everything's settled,' replied Kathy. 'I talked it through with my Regional Manager, and she's cool. They're sending two childcare assistants over from the Oxford branch, plus a nursery nurse from Swindon, and I'll be here as well so that's easily enough staff.'

'So it's OK for you to use this place then?'

'Yeah, she says as long as the mess is all cleared up afterwards and everything's ready for when the kids arrive the next morning, no problem. We'll make up the other room as a nursery, with cots and so on. Oh, and you'll need to tell me if you up the numbers, so we can arrange an extra childcare assistant.'

'Great.' Stacey sat down on the broad window ledge

and picked up a purple and yellow corduroy cat. 'Thanks.'

'I thought we might hire a man-eating tiger to throw the kids to if they play up,' commented Kathy.

'Sure, sounds fine.'

'And I'm going to paint myself green and pretend to be a spring onion.'

'Yeah? Whatever.'

Kathy sighed and shook her head. 'Wakey-wakey Stacey. And tell me what's wrong.'

Stacey looked up. 'What?'

'Something's obviously not right, so why don't you get it off your chest and tell Auntie Kath? It's not Alex's mum, is it? Or Alex?'

'No. No, everything's OK with Alex. She's doing well at school and everything.'

'What then?'

Stacey thought about saying 'nothing', but she knew Kathy well enough to be pretty certain she wouldn't be fobbed off that easily; and besides, there was a big part of her that wanted to tell someone all about it.

Her fingers waggled the cat's tail. 'I'm thinking about doing something.'

'Ri-ight.'

'Only I'm not sure how it would work out. And ... well.' She raised questioning eyes to Kathy's. 'Do you think you should do something if you think you might regret it later?'

Subconsciously, Kathy's arm hugged little Edward's shoulders. 'I think you ought to try.'

'Really?'

'Yes I do.' There was an odd, faraway sound to Kathy's voice. 'Otherwise while you're wondering whether you ought to do it, your chance to find out might walk out the door and never come back.'

It was quite a pleasant hotel room, but a hotel room nonetheless. Bette sat at the dressing table, reapplying her make-up and wishing this sort of thing could be dealt with more conveniently, in the comfort of her own home. Knowing Jack, he probably wouldn't even notice anyway. Not unless she dressed up as a donkey.

'So, how's it going at the old place?' Edwin Case fixed the back of her head with a steely gaze. Bette's eyes met his in the mirror. He might put the wind up his business competitors, but he didn't scare her. Besides, sitting up in bed wearing nothing but his spectacles, he looked more superannuated than superhuman.

Bette shrugged. 'I've already told you – absolutely fine. Completely hunky-dory.'

For a moment she thought she'd got away with it, but Edwin knew her too well. He folded his arms across an excess of greying chest hair. 'So it's true then.'

She glanced back at him over her shoulder. 'True?'

'What I've heard.'

'I don't know what you're on about.' Bette put away her make-up, zipped up the bag and picked up her hairbrush. It annoyed her to get caught up in his games, but she couldn't resist taking the bait. 'What things? Who from?'

'Just . . . people. Sources. You know I like to keep my ear to the ground.'

202

Bette said nothing. But she knew.

'So?' prompted Edwin.

'So I told you, everything's just fine. Your precious agency's as hidebound in stupid traditions as it ever was.' She swung round on the little pink stool and confronted him with a glare of her own. 'Which I'm sure pleases you no end.'

To her satisfaction, Edwin glanced away.

'You know that place was my great-grandmother's,' he reminded her. 'I'll not see one brick changed if I can help it.'

Bette sighed, packed away her things in her capacious handbag, and stood up. 'As if Miss Page could ever forget. Poor woman.'

'Now hold on a minute,' objected Edwin, 'since when am I public enemy number one? That girl knew the score.'

'Oh she did, did she?'

'And she agreed to it fair and square.'

'Huh.'

'I don't see what I'm supposed to have done wrong. It was all above board, you know.'

'If you say so.'

'Don't be angry with me, Bette,' Edwin coaxed. 'Come on.' He patted a still-warm dent in the rumpled sheets. 'Why don't you come back to bed and we can have fun making up?'

Bette picked up her handbag. 'Not now. Jack will be wanting his dinner, and I've got a colt needs worming.'

Edwin's brow furrowed at the mention of Bette's other half. 'But—' he protested.

'But nothing, end of conversation.' She reached for the door handle. 'I'll see you in a month's time, Edwin. If I feel like it.'

She stepped out briskly into the corridor, and the door closed behind her with a decisive click.

The way things were going, mused Laurel, Cheryl from Tewkesbury was going to be a nationwide phenomenon.

In the street below her open bedroom window, two taxi drivers were locked in animated conversation.

'Yes, but it's her fault, isn't it?'

'Her fault? Her sister's had every man she's ever fancied! Poor kid must be demented.'

'Still no reason to go trying to steal this bloke back off her though, is it?'

'You can't steal a bloke. Either he wants her or he wants her sister, it's up to him.'

Ah well, thought Laurel, at least I'm not alone. It struck her that there must be only so many problems in the world, and that right now there were probably hundreds of people all over Britain having hers. Thousands even. Funnily enough that wasn't much consolation; there was something to be said, after all, for feeling unique. Besides, all these thousands of other people were probably making a far better job of sorting out their – her – problem. Smug bastards.

Laurel sat down at the dressing table, drew herself up straight and forced herself to take a proper look in the mirror for the first time in three years. It was a genuine surprise to find that the person looking back at her appeared quite normal. OK, so some might say the nose was a bit big but at least it kept the rain off her chin. Plus, her new, wispier haircut really suited her heart-shaped face. And her dimples were almost cute. All things considered, she scrubbed up rather nicely.

Adjusting the straps on her new plunge bra from Gentle Incline to Great Rift Valley, she marvelled at hitherto-unknown acres of cleavage. After all this time, it felt really weird ditching her comfy jeans in favour of a slinky frock and heels that could puncture concrete. Why, she hadn't made this degree of effort since ... well, since.

Picking up Steph's little black book, she gave the pages a preparatory flick. At least you look presentable now, she told herself; let's hope some of Steph's sparkle wears off on you. And no chickening out, OK? You've promised yourself you're going to get out of this rut and you've told Steph you're going to come up with a sensational date; and no way are you raiding your own agency's books. There was a kind of delicious irony in the idea of turning up on Friday with one of Steph's gorgeous exes. All she had to do now was summon up enough courage to cold call a perfect stranger.

Chapter 16

L'Escargot Endormi had never seen anything quite like it since a rival planted earwigs in the bouillabaisse.

'I don't care if it is a foot long!' screamed Laurel, storming out of the restaurant and into the lobby. Heads turned, mouths gaped, and in the corner by the tree fern a prominent local dentist swore as he cracked a filling on an olive stone.

Crispin trailed behind Laurel, his white damask napkin still tucked into his trousers and fluttering like a half-mast flag of surrender. Stopping by the tank of live lobsters, he spread his arms wide, revealing armfuls of gold jewellery. 'Lau-rel,' he coaxed. 'Bay-bee!'

'Don't you "baby" me, you reptile!' Laurel wasn't sure which was more revolting: his line in conversation or his choice in ties. Every time he breathed in, the holographic lap dancer on his chest shed the top of her gold bikini. Laurel grabbed a stem of irises from the giant vase on the front desk and hurled it at him, javelin-style.

Crispin yelped as it hit him smack in the eye. 'What was that for?'

'Good shot, madame,' commented a voice behind her. She turned and almost fell over the maître d', a man so tall, thin and evenly tanned that he could have doubled as one of his own breadsticks. He raised a sardonic eyebrow, no doubt hoping it looked as cool as it did in the bathroom mirror.

'Thanks.'

'Taxi?' he enquired, as Crispin hopped all over the lobby, his hand still clapped to his eye. 'Lawyer? Perhaps Fat Tony with his sledgehammer and a few of the boys?'

Despite herself, Laurel smiled. 'Taxi please.' She glanced across at Crispin. 'I don't suppose you could . . .?'

'With pleasure, madame.'

'Hey!' protested Crispin as disdainful hands seized him by the collar and ejected him into Suffolk Square. 'You can't do that!'

'He just did,' replied Laurel.

'But you called me, you mad bitch!'

His parting shot about lesbians faded into the night like the ghost of an unpleasant fart. Laurel sank down onto one of the velvet-covered sofas in the lobby, let out a sigh of relief and opened her handbag to fetch out her credit card. Inside lay Steph's little black book.

Opening it, she flicked through the pages to Crispin's entry and gazed mutely at a row of five perfect stars. Well, it couldn't be intelligence, it couldn't be looks, and it definitely wasn't charm. One question demanded a rather urgent answer: what exactly earned a star in Steph's book?

Bette was a busy woman.

She really didn't have the time to nail her younger sister to the wall and give her a piece of her mind. Come to that, she had no appetite for yet another tiresome confrontation. She didn't even mind that much that Connie had ratted on Laurel – whom Bette rather liked – to her bit on the side.

No, it took something far more apocalyptic to blow the plug out of Bette's volcano: in this case, the conjunction of the last Jammie Dodger in the packet with Connie arriving extravagantly late, whistling 'Love Changes Everything'. With all the musicality of a rusty bed-spring.

It was more than the human frame could endure. As Connie strolled past, Bette stuck out a hand and grabbed her by the back of her sweater.

'So you've decided to honour us with your presence then?'

Connie attempted to free herself, like a fourth-former collared by the school bully. 'Here, get off my top, you'll stretch the neck out of shape.'

Bette's teeth clenched between curling lips. 'You can think yourself lucky I'm not stretching your neck out of shape, young lady!'

Connie blinked. 'Did you forget to take your HRT this morning?'

Her elder sister's lip drew back into a snarl. 'Shut up and come with me.' Bette's eyes loomed to within two

209

inches of Connie's. That seemed to have the desired effect. At any rate, Connie didn't protest much as she was frogmarched round the office, under the surprised gazes of Stacey and Killer the fish. In fact she remained inexplicably sunny, which only served to infuriate Bette even more.

'See this?' Bette's finger jabbed.

'It's a leaflet,' said Connie helpfully.

'Correction. It is the last leaflet.' Bette waggled her hand around inside the empty box. 'And why is it the last leaflet?'

'Because you've used them all up?'

'Because you didn't order any more from the printer! You had weeks to do it, it's your job, and did you do it?'

Connie shrugged but her smile didn't slip. 'You know how it is.'

'Yes,' growled Bette. 'I do.'

Next stop was the franking machine, at only fifteen years old one of D&M's more high-tech innovations. 'Whose job is it to top up the credit on this machine?'

'Er . . . mine?'

'Give the lady a prize. So why does Stacey have to keep going down the stamp machine for another ten books of second-class?'

'Oh,' said Connie. 'I must've forgotten.'

'For five consecutive weeks? Then it's just as well I'm here to remind you.' Bette poked her sister towards the two-foot-high stack of paper on top of the filing cabinet. 'See that?'

'Of course I can see it!'

'Then why haven't you done anything about it? And

while we're on the subject of paper, whose job is it to make sure the cleaning cupboard's well stocked with loo rolls?'

Connie giggled. 'Oh yes. Loo rolls. I knew there was something.'

'Oh you did, did you?' This was not working the way Bette had planned it. Where was the sweet cathartic buzz she was supposed to get from giving her sister hell? Seizing Connie by the shoulders, she sat her down forcibly on the bottom rung of a set of Georgian library steps. 'And you knew all about Laurel too, didn't you? All about what she was doing. So you just happened to pick up the phone and tell Edwin bloody Case all about it! Didn't you, you little sneak?'

Connie said nothing.

'When you know damn well the old bastard's dying to find fault with everything the poor woman does.'

Connie just went on smiling, even when Bette shook her till her teeth rattled.

'What the hell is wrong with you?' fumed Bette.

'Nothing,' replied Connie, not unreasonably for someone with a mile-wide smirk.

'Why aren't you being bolshie and offensive? Why aren't you swearing at me, like you always do?' A dreadful thought entered Bette's mind. 'Oh no, you've joined some stupid cult, haven't you? Macrobiotic rice and free love.'

Connie burst out laughing. 'Don't be silly!'

'Well something's up,' Bette declared. 'Otherwise, no way would you take all this from me. And you haven't had a go at me about Dad all day.' Her eyes narrowed. 'Come on, out with it. What are you hiding from me?'

Connie opened her mouth.

'And don't say "nothing", or I'll use your head for a toilet brush.'

Even that fearsome prospect only served to broaden Connie's smirk. 'All right then,' she announced, 'if you really want to know, Joe says he's coming to see me.'

'What!'

'You heard.' Connie pulled off a display of whole-body smugness. 'Joe. My Joe. The Joe you said didn't exist. He's coming to see me, and he's going to meet Dad, and everyone's going to be happy. And then,' she added with relish, 'you won't be able to put Dad in a home.'

'Come on Connie, you know it's the best place for him. And he makes your life a misery!'

Connie drew herself up like a cobra. 'We promised Mum we'd take care of him and some of us believe in keeping our promises.'

For a whole half-second, Bette was lost for words. Then the needle shot into her red zone and she erupted into full-on bile. 'Know what you are, Connie? You're not just pig-headed, you're even thicker than I thought you were. You and your so-called boyfriend.'

'You're just jealous! 'Cause your Jack's about as exciting as a pound of lard.'

'Jealous?' spluttered Bette. 'Of a stupid, empty-headed, gullible little girlie who thinks if a man wants her pants off he's in love with her?'

Connie's eyes grew rounder, but this time she was lost for words.

'My God girl, you really think he's coming, don't you? Well, d'you want to know something about your precious Joe? Do you?' Spittle flecked her lips. 'He's a man.'

This revelation had Connie baffled. 'Of course he's a man!'

'A filthy, stinking, cheating, low-life man!'

'My Joe's not like that!' Connie's head drew back into her neck, tortoise-like, as Bette advanced with all guns blazing.

'They're all like that, you idiot. Men are just slime. Promise you the moon but all they give you are stretch marks and a gin habit.'

'Just because your bloke's a dead loss and your kids are too busy making money to call you, that doesn't mean they're all like that.'

Bette was in no mood for discussion. She lowered her voice to a furious whisper. 'And this particular prize specimen hasn't even got the decency to show his face.'

Connie stared up at her sister in slack-jawed amazement. 'But he's coming to see me and—'

'Like hell he is.'

'He is!'

'Leave it.' Bette took a deep breath, straightened up and tried to slow the ferocious pounding in her chest. 'Just trust me on this one,' she pleaded; then turned and went back to her desk.

Laurel was having to do some radical rethinking.

She'd started out – not unreasonably – assuming that five stars in Steph's book meant good, and no stars

213

meant utterly crap. But she was beginning to suspect that the truth might be the other way round. After all, Steph's idea of male perfection did owe an awful lot to Black Lace novels. So perhaps the no-star 'no-ways' in Steph's little black book were actually paragons of old-style romance, dead wood by Steph's standards but at least guaranteed not to stick their tongue down your throat before the pudding course.

And besides, she'd made that stupid promise to Steph. She could only put off the Great Double Date for just so long.

That kind of reasoning had led Laurel to tonight's big mistake.

Tonight's big mistake was called Huw. He had big red hands, big bulging muscles, a big fast car, and a big thick neck that emerged from the collar of his shiny suit. The neck terminated in a bullet-shaped head, whose fuzzy sheen proclaimed 'I am not really bald, this is a stylish haircut. Honest.'

'Wha-hey!' he roared, whirling his racket around his head. The walls shook to cries of 'Who's the daddy?' as another sales rep bit the dust and Huw the alpha-twat strutted around the squash court like a rooster on Viagra. He looked across at Laurel, winked and gave her a double thumbs-up.

Laurel smiled feebly, waved back for politeness' sake, and sank a little deeper into the pool of sweat she'd been sitting in since Huw whitewashed her and moved on to bigger prey. The sales rep slunk past her on his way to the showers, pausing only to throw her a pitying look and a mouthed 'wanker'.

Spot on, thought Laurel. Evidently no stars really did mean no stars, even in Steph's book.

Connie sat at her desk, chewing her pencil and trying not to dwell on the thought that just would not go away.

Four whole days had elapsed, but she still couldn't get it out of her mind. Bette had never spoken to her like that before; Bette just wasn't like that. The nearest she ever got to passionate was swearing from the stands in Gold Cup week. And that, perhaps, was why her words had clung, insinuating a worm of doubt into Connie's thoughts.

Especially after Joe e-mailed to say he was really sorry, but something had come up and he couldn't come and see her after all.

With each day that passed, Connie was forced to accept some new uncomfortable element of truth in what Bette had said. Yes, it was her fault that they'd run out of leaflets. Yes, it was her job to top up the franking machine and she hadn't. Yes, the tea money hadn't been collected for weeks, and hidden under her desk there was a pile of unopened post so old she hardly dared look at it. Bette was right: her work had been slipping for ages. Clients were starting to notice, phoning up with little niggles. Soon they'd be taking their custom elsewhere. D&M's competitors were probably throwing parties all over town.

And suddenly, unexpectedly, she cared.

She tapped the end of her pencil on the desk, lending her thoughts a leaden rhythm. If Bette had been right

215

about her work, maybe – just maybe – that wasn't the only thing she'd been right about.

On tiptoe, Connie stalked across the office to the far windows and stuck her head out. Nothing was moving in the little car park beneath. On her way back, she stopped off at the toilet, poked her head inside the door and cocked an ear for signs of life, but there were none. Finally she stepped out onto the landing and listened hard for a couple of minutes. Nothing but the distant sounds of traffic.

Alone. At last!

Relieved, she discarded her shoes and wriggled her toes into the time-flattened pile, loosened the collar of her smart work blouse, stripped off her uncomfortable jacket and flung it across the office. It landed smack on top of the office cheese plant and draped itself over the leaves like a lampshade. Pirouetting twice, she skipped down the short corridor and entered Laurel's office.

The sight that met her eyes gave her quite a turn. However high the towers of paperwork in the main office might be, they were at least twice the size in here. A skyscraper of pink cardboard folders poked up loftily from behind one of the chintzy armchairs; client photographs lay in alphabetical piles all over the carpet; and a Giant's Causeway of overloaded boxes ran all the way from the coffee table to old Grandma Case's ancient roll-top desk.

She took a deep breath and allowed herself to feel properly guilty. Without Bette here to spank her bottom, she could stop being defensive and admit the ghastly truth. She really hadn't been pulling her weight these last weeks and months' and frankly, buying a nice box of biscuits for the kitchen was scarcely going to make up for it.

Slowly she circled the office, her fingers skimming gargantuan piles of correspondence and sheaves of client profiles. Could she? Her heart beat a little faster. Could she manage to get through some of this without Laurel noticing?

The sight of something unexpectedly familiar brought her up short. She recognised the smart blue cover instantly, even though the whole document was now almost obliterated by Post-It notes, paperclips and raggy-edged jottings.

It was the report she'd written. The one Laurel had welcomed like a plague of festering boils.

Feverishly, she flicked through the well-thumbed pages, trying to make out Laurel's scrawled comments. Can't do this. Not now. If only. Case won't let us. Huh? She read that one aloud, trying to figure it out: 'Case won't le—'

'Lost something?'

Connie jumped like a frog on a hotplate. Caught red-handed, she spun round. Laurel was standing in the doorway, damp and half-dressed in a shimmery evening top that showed off her shoulders. 'I was just . . . er . . . no, not really,' she admitted lamely. 'I thought you'd gone.'

Laurel's expression was inscrutable. 'So I see.'

Telling the truth was so hard, but anything else right now seemed pointless. She'd come this far, she might as well go for broke. Connie launched herself in. 'Miss Page, I—'

Laurel's right eye gave a warning twitch. Connie thought it best to start again.

'Laurel?' The eye stopped twitching. 'Laurel, I wanted to say . . . the thing is, I'm really sorry.'

For a moment all that registered on Laurel's face was puzzlement; then something seemed to click. 'I'm going out in an hour,' she told Connie, 'but I bet the two of us could get lots done before then, if we tried.'

'OK, let's try,' said Connie. And finally she smiled.

Chapter 17

When Laurel said she'd do something, she didn't mess about. That was one more thing Connie was beginning to learn about her boss.

Although she'd only promised to stay an hour, it was the best part of two before Laurel finally left the office, still applying her lipstick as she dashed down the stairs and out into the warm evening air. And then it was another two before Connie's arms started to ache from all the typing. She'd meant to leave far earlier, but somehow it didn't feel right, not after Laurel had been so nice to her.

Well, there was one thing to say for manual type-writers, she mused as she flopped down exhausted onto the sofa: at least they kept your upper arms from getting flabby. And at the extraordinarily advanced age of forty-three Connie was beginning to feel she needed all the help she could get.

As she watched the sky outside turn a deeper shade of blue, she mulled over the ways things were changing – not just around her, but inside her head. First Bette laying down the law, then Laurel being so friendly and helpful after all the systematic shittiness she'd had to put up with from Connie. Not to mention Joe's repeated failure to materialise like a genie from a bottle, and prove everybody wrong.

Suddenly lots of things didn't look quite so cut and dried any more.

Connie might have sat there all night if the sound of a distant siren hadn't jolted her out of her reverie. Oh shit – Dad! It was way past his teatime. If she didn't get home and feed him pronto, he'd be on the phone again, denouncing her to Social Services.

As she locked up the office, she promised herself that the mess of half-finished tasks wouldn't remain half-finished for long; first thing in the morning she'd be back to finish them off and tidy up.

She set the alarm, locked up the office and dropped the key into her handbag. And after I've sorted out the office, she told herself firmly, it'll be time to do something about Joe.

It was Friday evening. Already! One week today, Laurel was committed to going on that blasted double date; which was going to be hellishly difficult if she couldn't come up with a presentable escort. She fervently wished she could wriggle out of it, but Steph had insisted and in any case, a town the size of Cheltenham must be teeming with suitable candidates.

Take Marcus, for example. Despite the fact that she'd found him in Steph's black book, he was looking distinctly promising. Laurel had sensed that he had taste before she even met him: Eat the Tulips was one of Cheltenham's most chi-chi restaurants. Soft lighting, Chopin preludes on the piano, immaculate waiters gliding ghost-like from table to table ... Yes, his choice of rendezvous augured well, not to mention the fact that when she showed up almost a whole hour late, he was still there waiting patiently, with a smile on his face.

As he ordered the wild boar sauté with fresh truffle sauce and a bottle of excellent claret, Laurel observed her date with mounting optimism. Quite apart from a passing resemblance to George Clooney, he had a decent amount of hair (and none of it sprouting from his ears, nose or palms), impeccable table manners, an understated taste in clothes and an accent just the non-naff side of posh.

Admittedly Marcus was hardly the world's greatest conversationalist and Laurel had never had much of an interest in the finer breed points of the English springer spaniel; but then again she hadn't slept that well the last few nights and he didn't seem at all put out when her eyelids drooped over her prawn puttanesca.

Unfortunately, Laurel never really worked out whether or not Marcus was a good bet for the double date. When she fell asleep during dessert, he left the bill next to her slumbering head like some perverse tooth fairy.

And scarpered.

*

In an eaterie on the less rarefied side of Cheltenham, an extra-large stuffed-crust Meat Explosion was being carved up to the accompaniment of 'Arriverderci Roma' on a scratched CD.

'You're asking a lot of me, you know,' grumbled Ravi as he tore off another lump of garlic bread.

Stacey nibbled at her wedge of pizza. 'It's no more than I'm willing to do myself though, is it?' she pointed out, looking him straight in the eye.

Ravi squirmed a little. In the light from the wilting candle, stuffed in the neck of an empty Mateus Rosé bottle, Stacey's normally soft blue eyes looked hard and glittery as lumps of metal.

'Remember,' she went on, 'it's not just you, this is the two of us. Together.'

Although Stacey's feet were perfectly still under the table, Ravi fancied he could hear her foot tapping as she waited for his answer. Not that there was any point in wriggling; this could really only go one way.

'Oh all right,' he capitulated, popping the last piece of pepperoni into Stacey's open mouth. 'Let's do it.'

The following Monday evening saw Laurel going through the old routine.

Oh bum, she lamented as she struggled in vain with the fastenings on her hired dress. She knew she'd been a bit ambitious choosing the one with all the hooks and eyes and the boning, but she'd been so sure she could manage to do it up eventually. The question was, did she have time to rush home, grab her only other posh dress out of the laundry basket and hide the soup stain?

She was just wondering if a cabbage-sized corsage would do the trick when the door of her office opened and Connie staggered in, bow-legged under a stack of box files. When she caught sight of her boss, apparently practising a contortionist routine, the bunch of keys slipped from her teeth, bounced off the top file and ricocheted into the aspidistra.

'Oh,' said Laurel, blushing redder than her lipstick. 'It's you. I thought you'd gone home.'

'I did,' said Connie. 'Then I came back for these.' The corners of her mouth started twitching. 'You look very . . . um . . .'

'Stupid?' suggested Laurel.

'I was going to say dramatic. Great dress. Going somewhere special?'

'I might be,' Laurel replied, 'if I could figure out how to do up the back without double-jointed arms.' She craned her head back and made a fruitless grab for the middle section of her dress. 'I knew I should've gone for the boring sensible one with the zip.'

Dumping her pile of box files, Connie peeled off her jacket. 'Need a hand?'

A few days earlier, and Laurel would have been surprised by the offer. But lately the climate between her and Connie had definitely started to defrost. 'Thanks, that'd be great. I'm supposed to be somewhere by half-past, and I can hardly turn up like this!'

'No problem.' Connie eyed up the challenge. 'Wonder if I should start at the bottom or the top.'

223

'How about the middle?'

'I'd have to find it first! Have you any idea how many hooks there are here?'

'Too damn many.'

They chatted easily as Connie wrestled with the tiny hooks and eyes, stretching the bodice so tight that Laurel saw stars. Then Connie suddenly fell silent.

Laurel screwed her head round to look at her. 'Something wrong?'

'Not really.' She paused. 'I just wondered. Can I ask you something?'

'Sure, why not?'

'Why's Edwin Case trying to stop you doing things? Why does it matter what he thinks? You're supposed to be running things around here now, not him.'

'I'm only the manager,' Laurel reminded her. Then she realised what Connie had just said. 'How did you know about that?'

It was confession time. 'I saw my report,' admitted Connie. 'You left it lying on your desk. Yes, I know I shouldn't have looked, only I wanted to see what you'd written. I worked really hard on that report,' she added when Laurel didn't respond.

'I know you did,' sighed Laurel. She rubbed her chin and tried to decide. Was it better to have things out in the open and to hell with the consequences? 'Connie,' she began, 'can you keep a secret?'

'What sort of secret?'

'Put it this way. If you breathe a word to anyone I'll have your giblets for Sunday lunch.'

'Oh, that kind of secret. Yes, of course I can.'

'Cross your heart?'

'Cross my heart.' Connie drew a big X across her chest. 'But why?'

'Because if things work out I just might get a chance to run D&M the way I want to, that's why. Only nobody else is supposed to know.'

Connie's brow furrowed. 'I don't get it.'

'When I took over as manager, Mr Case inserted a special clause in the contract. If I can run Dovecote & Marsh for a complete year, exactly the way he used to run it, he'll sell the agency to me.'

'You mean, you want to buy D&M? You're mad!'

'Probably.'

'But if he's thinking of selling up anyway, why's Case insisting you don't change anything?'

Laurel shrugged. 'You tell me. But that was the agreement. Run it his way, or no deal.'

'Run it?' snorted Connie. 'Yeah, right into the ground! How are you supposed to get anything done with him breathing over your shoulder the whole time? Let alone make a profit.'

'Yeah, well, when I started I thought he was going to give me a bit of leeway, but obviously I was wrong.'

Connie thought for a moment. 'You do realise what's going to happen, don't you? You'll run the place for a year on crap wages, completely knacker yourself, and at the end of it all he'll just give you the boot and say he's changed his mind.'

Laurel pulled a face. It wasn't that she hadn't thought

225

of that possibility; she just didn't like being reminded of it.

'Yeah, well, maybe I'm hoping even Edwin Case won't be that stupid.'

Laurel was glad she'd made the effort for her date with Richard. True, all these meals out meant that her hired dress was more like a straitjacket, but she knew she looked good, and Richard was so stylishly turned out that anything less would have seemed like an insult.

The ultra-cool Balti Banzai (Gloucestershire's first-ever Indian sushi restaurant) was quiet on this particular Monday night, which gave them plenty of opportunity to chat about everything from world politics to the price of a decent moisturiser. A little tingle of excitement ran through Laurel as he topped up her wine glass without having to be asked, quoted a Ronsard sonnet in flawless Renaissance French, and complimented her on the way her dress enhanced her grey-green eyes. Mentally she punched the air and did a little victory dance. This was the one! At last Steph's book had yielded one man presentable enough to escort her on the double date. And how hilarious it would be to see the look on Steph's face when Laurel showed up with one of her exes . . .

There was just one question that remained un-answered. 'So, I've told you all about me. What about you? What do you do for a living?'

Richard gazed deep into her eyes, took her hand and pressed it to his lips. 'Normally I charge a thousand for the full night,' he said, 'but seeing as you've got such nice tits I'll do you half-price. Mind you, it's extra if you want anything kinky.'

Chapter 18

Connie sneaked her laptop into the office the next day, to check her e-mails. Spam, spam, Barry Manilow fanzine, more spam . . . and something from Joe! She'd hardly dared hope that he'd write again, not after the way she'd ripped into him last time.

Had he risen to the bait? Had he?

With trembling fingers, she opened the message. Yes! They had a date! And this time he swore he'd turn up. She was so busy forcing herself not to jump up and down with excitement that she very nearly didn't notice Graeme Lillee heading for the door to Laurel's office struggling with a stuffed bear.

Just in time, Connie bounded across the room and caught him by the arm. 'Sorry, Mr Lillee.' She steered him away and closed the door. 'You'll have to wait out here, she has a client in with her at the moment.'

Glenda Bates sat opposite Laurel, toying nervously with her teaspoon.

'Is something wrong?' asked Laurel gently.

Glenda put down her spoon and tucked a greying

strand of hair behind her ear. 'No, not really,' she said. 'It's just that I've never been in one of ... you know, these places before.' She darted glances around Laurel's office as though half-expecting the Vice Squad to burst in at any moment.

Laurel smiled. 'It's OK,' she assured her newest client, 'everyone feels nervous at first, but there's really nothing to worry about. We're here to help.'

'I can't help it, I just feel such a failure. You know, I keep thinking I ought to be able to find a partner without having to pay somebody to do it for me.' Her faded brown eyes searched Laurel's face for extra reassurance. 'Do you think I'm inadequate? My ex says I am.'

Laurel felt an immediate urge to have serious words with Glenda's ex. 'Of course you're not inadequate! Or if you are, half the population of Cheltenham are too. All kinds of people come to us. We just help them to meet more of the kinds of people they might like, that's all.'

Glenda relaxed a little and drank some of her tea. 'Is that everything then?'

'Well, that's all your personal details on file,' replied Laurel. 'Next, I allocate you your own personal match-maker, who works through all the gentlemen on our files to find exactly the right match for you.'

Glenda Bates munched on a biscuit. 'You will make sure he's not weird, won't you?'

'Weird?' enquired Laurel.

Glenda shuffled her feet under the table. 'I told you I had a few problems with my ex, didn't I?'

Laurel glanced down at the form. 'You did say there

were some unresolved issues, yes. If you could be a little more specific about them, it would help us to avoid repeating the same problem.'

Glenda demolished another two biscuits in one voracious gulp, caught Laurel's eyes and explained, 'I always eat like a pig when I'm nervous, sorry.'

'Don't be, I do it too. Go on.'

'It started with the humming, you see.'

'Humming?'

Glenda leaned forward confidingly. 'Do you like *Star Wars*?'

'Sorry?'

'*Star Wars*. The films.'

Laurel was bemused. 'Well, I suppose they're all right. Apart from the second one.'

'Ah, but imagine you're in bed with your husband and well, having an intimate moment, and then – just when you think you're about to, you know, reach your peak – he starts humming the bloody *Star Wars* theme tune!'

Laurel stifled an inappropriate giggle by swallowing half a cup of Earl Grey. 'No!'

'Oh yes. Every flipping time. And then there was the dressing up. I mean, role playing's all very well and I realise that lots of men have Princess Leia fantasies but I kind of thought I'd be the one playing Carrier Fisher! I've had my fill of weirdness.'

'So I can see,' sympathised Laurel. 'And whilst we can't actually promise to find your ideal partner, I can assure you that all our gentlemen are very thoroughly interviewed before we register them with D&M.' Unlike Steph's, thought Laurel, remembering the appalling Richard. She was beginning to bitterly regret ever mining the murky depths of Steph's little black book. 'And dozens of our former clients are now permanently together. In fact, a very nice couple from Tewkesbury got married only last week.'

Glenda sat back in her chair and relaxed her face into a smile. 'Your secretary told me. A good old-fashioned business, with good old-fashioned values – that's what people want these days, isn't it?'

'It is?'

'Oh yes, that's why I came here. You can forget your computers and all that. You can't make people fall in love by computer, can you?'

'Hmm, no. I guess not.'

'Anyhow, what I'm after now is a nice ordinary, boring, normal man who wears saggy Y-fronts and thinks an Ewok's something you cook a stir-fry in.'

'Right,' said Laurel. 'I'll remember that.'

There was a knock at the door, and Connie stuck her head in. 'Laurel? Mr Lillee's here for his appointment. And he's brought the you-know-what with him?'

Glenda's eyebrows lifted questioningly. 'The you-know-what?'

Laurel grinned. 'Don't ask.'

Laurel offered Mr Lillee a seat. 'Wasn't that Glenda Bates?' he commented.

'You know her?'

'Once stuffed a couple of ferrets for her brother. Isn't she married to that Terry what's-his-name? Mad keen on collecting sci-fi memorabilia?'

232

'Sorry,' smiled Laurel. 'Can't talk about clients – you know, confidentiality.'

'Oh. Of course, silly me, say no more.' He raised a hand, halting the conversation in its tracks. 'Change of subject – I've brought your bear back and he's good as new.'

'How lovely,' said Laurel, hoping her enthusiasm sounded genuine.

'He's got a full set of teeth now, but I had to replace a couple of the canines with false ones – the old ones were very discoloured. I hope your Mr Case won't mind, only I do like my clients to look their best so to speak.'

Laurel looked at him and tried to suppress a giggle.

Graeme looked frankly bewildered. 'What did I say?'

'I'm sorry.' She laughed. 'It's just, you sounded like one of those Hollywood morticians – you know, pretty-ing up the corpses with wigs and make-up.'

He chuckled. 'I suppose there are a few similarities. Mind you, I like to think my art's a bit more enduring.'

'Yes, of course it is,' agreed Laurel. 'You'll have to forgive me,' she added. 'It's been a very peculiar week, one way and another.'

'Ah, but I bet you haven't glued the trunk back onto a woolly mammoth,' replied Graeme sagely. 'Or tried to stuff a wasp. Believe me, you don't know peculiar until you've ventured into taxidermy.' His face fell. 'Not that you'd want to of course. People seldom do.'

At that moment, there was a brisk knock at the door and Connie came in, bearing another tray of tea. 'Sorry there's only Bourbon creams,' she said, clearing away the empty cups and brushing the crumbs off Laurel's desk. 'Only somebody ate all the Hobnobs.'

233

She departed and the door closed, shutting out the sound of Bette booming down the telephone: 'Not parrots, carrots, you stupid man! What would I want with parrots? I'm a stud farm, not an aviary!'

Laurel gazed out of the window. But she wasn't looking at the big old horse chestnut trees, waving majestically in the summer breeze; all she could see was Steph's face, when she turned up for the date without a man in tow. Why had she let herself get into this stupid situation? Why hadn't she just stuck to matching other people up? At least she was getting vaguely good at that.

'Shall I pour?' repeated Graeme, pot poised above Laurel's cup.

She started. 'What? Oh! Yes, please. Sorry, I was miles away.'

He poured the tea expertly, she noticed, not spilling a drop despite the wonky spout. 'Are you all right?' he enquired.

She looked at him. There was genuine concern in his eyes, which was faintly disconcerting. There were times when she didn't want people to be concerned about her; in fact she didn't even want them to notice she existed. 'Yes, of course I am.' She grabbed a biscuit and dunked it in her tea.

'Are you sure? I mean, I know it's none of my business, but you do seem awfully distracted.'

The end fell off Laurel's biscuit and sank to the bottom of her cup. She tried fishing it out with her finger, but the tea was too hot.

'Here – use my spoon.'

'Thanks.' She scraped soggy brown biscuit mush out of her cup and onto her saucer. 'You're right,' she capitulated. 'I am distracted.'

Mr Lillee took a biscuit from the plate, bit into it and brushed the crumbs off his knees. 'I'm sorry, I shouldn't pry.'

'The thing is,' blurted out Laurel, 'I'm supposed to be going on a silly double date with my friend Steph and her boyfriend on Friday night, and I still haven't got anybody to go with.'

'Are you serious?' He looked astounded, which was quite comforting. 'I'd have thought men would be queuing up to take you out.'

'Well they're not. Not any nice ones, anyhow.'

Laurel offered Mr Lillee another Bourbon cream, and was pleased to see that he neither stuck the whole biscuit into his mouth sideways, nor separated the two halves and nibbled the cream off. Come to that, he didn't slurp or dribble his tea, and he could hold a conversation with proper verbs in it.

Maybe. Just maybe . . .

'Mr Lillee,' she began. 'Graeme. Can I ask you something?'

'Yes, of course.'

'I was just wondering. Are you doing anything on Friday night?'

In the saloon bar of the Merry Hind, Don and Gabriel were deep in conversation. To be more accurate Don was deep in monologue, but what he needed right now wasn't sparkling two-way repartee, it was advice.

235

He gazed deep into the amber depths of his single malt. 'I just can't make up my mind,' he agonised. 'Do I, like, go in with all guns blazing, or do I keep on with the softly-softly approach? The woman's drivin' me crazy, Gabe.'

Gabriel wiped the froth off his top lip. 'Aye.'

'But this time, I really think I've got it cracked.' Don gulped down a fiery half-inch of neat whisky. 'I've got this plan, see. This really foolproof plan.'

His eyes sought out Gabriel's for manly encouragement, but all Gabriel did was crunch down hard on a pork scratching.

'So what d'you reckon then, mate?' prompted Don.

With long, slow deliberation Gabriel put down his pint, finished chewing and inspected an elderly beer stain on the counter. 'I reckon you're a bloody fool, man.'

Cut to the quick, Don leapt to the defence of his beloved Connie. 'Hey come on, I know she's no Stephanie, but she's—' A dark look crossed Gabriel's face and Don's élan foundered on the rocks of curiosity. 'Something wrong, mate? Bad pint or somethin'?'

The dark look turned to a shifty one, and Gabriel muttered into his glass. 'The ale's fine.'

'But you've got some sort of a problem, huh? Say – it's not woman trouble is it?'

Gabriel's manly shoulders hunched., 'Kind of. She keeps hinting for me to take her home.'

The fact that this might be construed as a problem was frankly beyond Don's comprehension. 'She wants you to take her home?'

'Aye.'

'So take her home! You fancy her, don't you? Or are you still hankering after that Laurel?'

'No, I fancy Steph well enough.' Elbows resting on the bar counter, Gabriel's chin sank onto his hands. 'It's just . . . difficult.'

'Difficult? Why's it difficult?' Don scratched his head, suddenly realising how very little he knew about Gabriel's life, despite the fact that they had been drinking together at the Merry Hind three times a week for the past year.

'Because I don't live on my own. I share with someone.'

Don shrugged. 'Oh, I'm sure he won't mind.'

Gabriel lifted morose eyes to return Don's gaze. 'Actually, I know she will.'

Bette eyed up the door to the kitchenette, flaunting itself teasingly on the other side of the office. Was she thirsty, or wasn't she? Or rather, was she thirsty enough to risk the perilous journey between her desk and the kettle?

As she watched, Connie zipped back and forth at top speed, carrying ever-larger piles of pink folders. To make things even more interesting, Laurel was charging about the office as well, making phone calls, interviewing clients, getting lots of stuff done, and dodging around Connie's legs like a Jack Russell after a rat.

All this hustle and bustle was damned annoying, and very distracting when you were trying to do the monthly accounts; but Bette had only herself to blame for it. After all, she was the one who'd told Connie to get off her backside and do some work. Hmm. Could she get to the kettle, make herself a coffee and get back to her desk without becoming roadkill on Dovecote & Marsh's carpet? She wasn't at all sure she could be bothered.

Amid the chaos one small oasis of tranquillity remained. An oasis currently occupied by Stacey, the only normal thing left in the office. Or at least she looked normal – serene even. With a yawn, Bette hauled her carcass out of her chair and wandered over to Stacey's desk.

As Bette craned her neck to take a peek over Stacey's shoulder, she cast a shadow over the blotter and Stacey gave an involuntary jump.

'Good God,' said Bette. 'Is that what I think it is?'

Stacey flushed crimson and moved her arms off the desk.

But Bette just smiled and tapped the side of her nose. 'Good for you, kid. And don't worry – mum's the word.'

Chapter 19

'No table? What do mean, no table?' Steph's bosom quivered with unleashed indignation. 'I booked three days ago, Henriette, you must remember – table for four in my favourite corner by the jazz quintet!'

The head waiter of the Blue Nose Brasserie shook her head wearily. 'Unfortunately, madame's usual table is unavailable tonight.'

'That's all right,' cut in Laurel, anxious to head off a fist fight. 'We'll have another table, won't we, Steph?'

'I'm afraid all our tables are unexpectedly unavailable, madame. We're completely full tonight.'

Gabriel loomed impressively over the small Frenchwoman in the tailored trouser suit. 'What's that then?' He nodded towards an empty table spread with a crisp white cloth and gleaming silverware.

'That table is reserved too, sir. A last-minute booking.'

Graeme shrugged phlegmatically. 'Oh well. Plenty more restaurants to choose from, eh? I'm not that peckish yet anyway.'

But Steph's eyes flashed. She wasn't beaten yet. 'What do you mean, last-minute booking? I booked bloody ages ago, and you let someone just walk in and steal my table?'

Henriette mouthed some kind of empty platitude, but didn't budge an inch to let them through.

'What kind of customer service do you call this?' demanded Steph. 'I'm a regular here you know!'

'Yes, madame.'

'Leave it, Steph,' urged Laurel. Steph shook her off and advanced menacingly towards the imperturbable Henriette.

'All right then, tell me. Who's so goddam important that they can waltz off with my booking?'

This produced a world-weary sigh. 'People, madame.'

'People?'

She tapped the side of her nose meaningfully. 'The right people.'

'Oh,' said Gabriel. 'She means rich bastards.'

'But I'm a rich bastard!' protested Steph, without a trace of irony.

Laurel couldn't let this go any further, she really couldn't; entertaining though it might be to watch Steph making a prat of herself. Pity she hadn't brought a camera with her. Pulling Steph away, Laurel stepped in to act as referee.

'Don't worry Steph, I'm sure they'll make it up to us.' Her look was so pointed it was practically intravenous. 'Won't you?' Henriette gazed back impassively.

'Will they hell,' grunted Steph.

'Oh, I'm sure they will,' smiled Laurel. 'After all, we're not moving from this spot until they do.'

By the time she'd been stared at for five solid minutes, Henriette would probably have peeled off her own skin and made it into a handbag if Laurel had told her to; but even after they'd come away with the promise of a free dinner, Steph wasn't happy.

'You come in three nights in one week, never spend less than a couple of hundred quid, and what happens?' The door of the restaurant slammed shut behind her. 'At the drop of a hat they give some queue-jumping tosser your table, that's what.' She threw a disgruntled look at Gabriel. 'I told you you should've worn that nice black suit I bought you.'

Gabriel's shoulders squared defensively. 'They can take me as I am or not at all.'

'Give it a rest, Steph,' urged Laurel, who happened to think Gabriel looked very, very VERY presentable in that leather jacket. 'It's not the end of the world.'

Graeme turned up his collar and eyed the sky warily. The clouds were growing darker and a mist of fine drizzle was threatening to turn into a downpour. 'Do you think we ought to move on?'

'Happen,' nodded Gabriel wisely.

Steph directed a hefty kick at the restaurant's topiary box tree, got the heel of her Manolo Blahniks caught in the filigree pot-holder, and almost fell over. 'I'm hungry,' she scowled, wrenching her shoe free and slamming it back onto her foot. 'Bastard thing. Bastard bloody everything.'

241

'Well then.' Laurel looked to the others for inspiration. 'What shall we do now?'

'There's not much point just hanging around here getting wet,' pointed out Graeme as a big black cloud burst right over his head. 'Perhaps we should go and find somewhere else to eat.'

Steph swung round and glared at Graeme, then grabbed Gabriel by the arm and towed him off down the road. 'Don't just stand there,' she snarled. 'Come on!'

The four of them made a thoroughly downcast procession as they tramped wetly along, dodging the backwash from passing BMWs.

'Where shall we go then?' asked Laurel. Too late, she caught the reckless glint in Steph's eye.

'Let's ...' She swung a pissed-off arm, narrowly missing Graeme's nose. 'Oh, what do I care, let's eat in the first place we come to.'

'What – here?' asked Laurel two minutes later. 'Are you quite sure about this?'

Only elven magic could have sneaked that jolly neon sign past the planning committee, mused Laurel as she gazed up at the garish purple words: ELF BURGER: fast fantasy food for the fun vegetarian!

The four of them looked up at the sign, then at each other, then back at the sign again. Nobody said anything. Laurel wondered if she dared claim to be a committed carnivore on the grounds that she despised vegetables. Then Steph's stomach rumbled again; and this time it sounded like a juggernaut full of rocks driving off Beachy head.

242

'Look,' she jabbed a finger at the pictures in the window, 'they sell food.'

'That's not food,' objected Gabriel.

'Don't be silly, it can't be that bad,' Steph insisted, one hand on the door handle. 'Come on Gabriel, we're going in.'

Just as she opened the door, a pubescent girl ran out screaming obscenities, closely pursued by a smaller boy with pink hair, brandishing something wobbly and squishy. A moment later, the girl was ducking down and the squishy thing was flying through the air.

'Er, look out Steph,' advised Graeme rather belatedly. 'He's got a—'

Squelch!

'Water-bomb.'

Too late, Steph contemplated the ruination of her best beaded evening trousers, their seat now hanging – wet and semi-diaphanous – from her bottom.

'You little sods!' she screeched. But the kids were already well away, pulling faces and hurling four-letter insults from a safe distance.

'Oh God,' said Laurel, 'you're not wearing any pants.'

'Thank you, Lozzie, I had noticed.' She snapped her fingers. 'Gabriel, jacket. Now.'

'Hang on.'

'Do you want me showing my backside to the whole of this scummy little town?'

Reluctantly Gabriel peeled off his jacket and handed it to Steph, who promptly tied it round her waist like a mini-sarong, probably – mused Laurel – mangling the leather beyond recognition.

243

'Let's go home,' urged Laurel. 'I've got some micro-pizzas in the freezer.'

'Sounds good to me,' said Graeme, rubbing his hands together.

They all waited for Steph to see sense and call a halt to the whole ludicrous episode; but they'd counted without the perverse determination that had once seen Steph Mihailovic clinch last place in a knobbly knees competition.

'You lot can do what you like,' she announced. 'But I'm going in.' And she promptly did.

'Well,' commented Graeme, 'at least it's different.'

'It's that all right.' Steph squelched unhappily in her basket-weave chair. In the background, somebody dressed as an elf sang an interminable song about Dingly Dell and the joys of recycling. A curious smell of barbecued socks hung over the salad bar, where stuffed beetroot nestled appetisingly on a bed of dandelion leaves.

Gabriel drew thoughtfully on his troll-sized, non-dairy papaya shake. 'How did you manage that then? Back in the restaurant?'

Laurel jerked back to life from the beautiful, serene trance in which she had been contemplating the perfect outline of Gabriel's left shoulder. 'Sorry?'

'All that staring.' He put down his cup. 'Bloody impressive.'

Laurel smiled. 'Oh, that. Let's just say there are psychological skills a good manager has to develop.' She assumed her sternest expression and directed it at them all in turn. It was fun. 'So you'd better all behave yourselves, hadn't you?'

Deep in the Darkwood Forest, something stirred.

And that something was a living tide of small children, swarming in determined waves over the crest of the table, as if its four occupants and their dinner didn't exist.

'I say, excuse me,' said Graeme, extracting his flattened burger from under a juvenile knee. 'Couldn't you go round the other way? Only we're eating.'

'But we have to go this way!' protested the ring-leader. 'It's part of The Quest!'

'What Quest?'

'The Enchanted Tree Stump,' chimed in the ring-leader's younger brother, complete with matching pixie hat. He waved a paper place mat under Graeme's nose. 'See? Over the Enchanted Tree Stump to the Magic Bridge, colour in the Orc and get a free carob lolly.'

Far too decent to deprive a child of its free lolly, Graeme picked the bits of wax crayon out of his burger and went on eating it as if nothing had happened. The children disappeared into the distance, no doubt to trample on other people's meals.

'Go on,' urged Steph, chewing on a blue jelly goblin. 'You were saying?'

'Oh yes, where was I?' He swallowed. 'So then I said, "Actually, I think I'm standing on it"!'

'You what? Oh my God!' Laurel and Steph collapsed in fits of laughter; and a second or so later, so did Gabriel.

245

Steph nudged Laurel in the ribs. 'He's a scream, isn't he? Wherever did you find him?'

Graeme blushed. 'You really think it's funny then? Only I've never told anybody that story before.'

'Why on earth not?' asked Steph.

Graeme shuffled his feet under the table. 'Just. Because.' Almost as though he were afraid somebody else might pay him a compliment, he leapt straight in with a complete change of subject. 'We've had our dinner then. So what are we going to do with the rest of the evening?'

'Find an all-night trouser shop,' said Steph, wiping her mouth on a paper lily pad. 'And then get horribly drunk.'

'Whatever,' said Gabriel, gazing dolefully into the depths of his empty cup.

'Mmm?' said Laurel, who had been too busy breathing in Gabriel's aftershave to follow the conversation.

'How about a film?' suggested Graeme.

Everybody groaned.

'I want to get pissed!' protested Steph.

'All right Steph, scissors paper stone,' proposed Graeme, hiding his hand behind his back. 'Ha! Sorry, stone blunts scissors, I win. Pictures it is.'

'Boring,' sniffed Steph.

'It's a late-night showing of *There's Something About Mary*,' he coaxed. 'And I heard they've got a bar extension.'

Everybody cheered.

*

246

As they stood on the pavement outside Elf Burger, waiting for the taxi to arrive, Laurel noticed the way Graeme's eyes followed every single passer-by with neurotic attention.

'It's OK,' she whispered, drawing his ear down to her mouth. 'You don't smell.'

'Really?'

'Really really. You never do. Or at least, you do, but only of soap.'

Graeme's whole body seemed to un-tense, as though someone had let some of the air out of an over-inflated tyre. 'Thank goodness for that, I've been sniffing myself all evening. People must think I've got hay fever.'

Laurel returned his smile. 'That's better,' she said. 'You know, you can be fun when you relax.'

'Me? Fun? I don't think I've ever been accused of that before.'

'That's OK, I've never eaten curried lentils before. There's a first time for everything.'

As they piled into the taxi and headed off to the multiplex, Laurel glanced sideways at Graeme and realised how glad she was that she had asked him along tonight. He's a nice bloke, she told herself; plus it's doing him good, so this can be my good deed for the day. In fact . . .

But then Gabriel came into sight, and somehow Laurel's thought just sort of fizzled out.

They looked as if they'd turned up several years late for the premiere as they trooped into the foyer in all their

247

over-dressed glory and queued up for four Cokes and a family bag of Revels.

Several appreciative wolf-whistles rang out as Steph bent down to pick up a stray ten-pence piece – only to be swiftly curtailed as the blokes concerned remembered that they were with their girlfriends. Gracious as ever, even with a damp and diaphanous bottom, Steph smiled back at her adoring public; but inside she was far from happy.

Gabriel was standing what – two inches, three? – away from her. Two whole massive inches. Why wasn't he wrapped around her like a bloody jungle vine, having to be fended off with half-hearted slaps? It was downright unnatural, in fact it was completely freaking her out. If anything, he was standing closer to Lozzie than he was to her.

There was only one conclusion she could come to. Something was not quite right with this relationship.

Chapter 20

It was a very nice cucumber: everything, in fact, that a cucumber should be. Large, smooth, long, firm, thrusting . . .

Hastily, Laurel replaced it among the others on display and steered her trolley towards Instant Pot Snacks. Surely they wouldn't remind her of Gabriel Jouet. But even as she was trying to weigh up seventeen different flavours of monosodium glutamate, his face seemed to imprint itself on every label in sight, from powdered soup to boil-in-the-bag noodles.

As she made her way round the supermarket to the accompaniment of 'Can't Get You Out of My Head', Laurel reminded herself that she did not lust after Steph's boyfriend, never had done and never would, and that even if – for argument's sake – she did happen to harbour the odd lascivious thought, she certainly wasn't about to act on it. And that was assuming Gabriel would be in the least bit interested in her lascivious thoughts if she did. Which of course he wouldn't.

Anyway, going round stealing other people's boyfriends was Steph's MO, not hers. She smiled self-righteously as she stretched up to reach a bag of tagliatelle. Bitchy? As if.

Trundling past the mangetout, Laurel cast her mind back to the day, three years ago, when life had suddenly turned complicated; the day she'd had to break the news to Steph that the then love of her life Carlos was utterly crap at his job. So crap, in fact, that Laurel had had to sack him or face a walkout by the entire Marketing Department. If only Steph could have been just a little bit reasonable, conceded that her latest squeeze was better in the sack than he was with a spreadsheet, things could have worked out fine. But oh no, Steph had to take it as a challenge to go straight out and seduce Jason. Well, thought Laurel, revenge may be sweet but that's no excuse for me to follow suit.

Though it was tempting . . .

No, she'd made her mind up: Jason was firmly in the past and so was that stupid double date. No more thoughts about Gabriel, no more mulling over how exciting it had or hadn't been to sit so close to him in the darkened cinema and imagine his hand accidentally brushing her thigh as he aimed for the popcorn. She picked up milk, fish food, chocolate biscuits, a bottle of shampoo and a Twix, and headed for the checkout. Definitely time to grow up and put him out of her mind.

She'd done so for a good three and a half seconds when she rounded the corner of Pet Foods and Accessories, and slammed her trolley right into one coming in the opposite direction.

Sod's Law dictated that it had to be driven by Gabriel; and Sod's Law was right.

Connie stood in her bedroom, amid the chaos of her disembowelled wardrobe. Somehow, none of it was right. She had fourteen tops in every shade of pink from palest apple-blossom through to puce, and not one of them would do for her date with Joe. She needed something that made her look different.

Completely different.

Her palms were sweating, her head was aching, she was ten days late with her OU assignment, and through the bedroom floor she could feel the whole house shuddering as Dad cranked up the TV volume to an ear-bleeding maximum. Some evenings there was just no escape. It would have been nice to go for a walk or a drink or something, but she'd got out of the habit of having a social life and if she left Dad on his own for long, there was always the risk he'd burn the house down just to spite her.

Connie turned round and flopped down on the end of the bed, amid her spread-eagled clothes. She'd loved them all when she bought them, but now she wasn't sure she liked any of them any more. For that matter, she wasn't at all sure she liked herself.

Her mind was in turmoil. For starters, there was everything Bette had said about men in general and Joe in particular. Even allowing for the moribund state of Bette's marriage she had a point. And then there was the fact that Connie had been less than a hundred per cent honest with Joe.

It hadn't been a deception, not really; more a question of survival. After all, he was twenty-four and not long out of college, while she was forty-three, living with her aged father and had all the freshness and glamour of a month-old turnip. If she'd admitted her age, sent him photos of how she looked now, would he really have been interested in her? It had seemed like such a good idea, e-mailing him those ten-year-old photos, but now she wondered how she was ever going to be able to look Joe in the eye when he saw her as she was now, sexy new outfit or not.

It was a hot, sticky, oppressive evening. She swung her slippered feet against the end of the bed. Downstairs, Dad was heckling the TV. Outside in the street, some bored kids were half-heartedly vandalising the bus shelter. Connie hadn't even the energy to go down and tell them to cut it out.

The computer cursor winked at her from the other side of the room. Go on Connie, you know you want to.

What she wanted and what she was going to do were two entirely different things. She blinked back the faint prickle of something that might have been a tear or a trickle of sweat as she sat down at the keyboard and hammered in the words before she changed her mind.

Sorry Joe, gotta take rain check, can't make date. Some other time, C.

It just kept on happening.

First the uncomfortable encounter in the super-market, then literally bumping in to each other at that garage on London Road, and, five minutes ago, spotting him just in time to avoid an unplanned rendezvous by the lake in Pittville Park. Suddenly, Cheltenham was full of Gabriel Jouet.

Doubling back behind a conveniently parked ice-cream van, Laurel peeked out and was half-relieved, half-disappointed to see him striding off into the distance past Pets' Corner, hands in pockets, the very epitome of phwoarr.

It was a sticky, sultry Sunday afternoon, there were an awful lot of people about and too many of them were Gabriel Jouet. Of late it seemed almost as if he and she were bound together by an invisible elastic band that kept springing back every time they tried walking off in opposite directions. Ah well, she mused, if she was going to hide in this queue she might as well have the 99 she'd promised herself in the first place.

Her mobile rang just as she was pocketing the change.

'Yes?' she said through a mouthful of Mr Whippy.

'Hiya Lozzie, it's me!'

The lift that was Laurel's heart snapped its cables and plummeted down the shaft. 'Oh, Steph, hi.'

'It was fun, wasn't it?' enthused Steph.

'What was?'

'Our double date, silly!'

Laurel considered the proposition. Nerve-racking, yes. Awkward, yes. Sexually frustrating, definitely. But fun? 'I thought you looked a bit down in the mouth,' she said. 'Like you weren't enjoying yourself at all.' She lowered her voice. 'After all, you did wet your pants.'

Several people within earshot stopped what they

were doing and turned to look at Laurel, who stuck her tongue out at them and retreated behind a tree with her ice cream.

'Of course I was enjoying myself, it was great!' Steph's voice was so bright and breezy that Laurel wondered if she was putting it on. And if so, why. 'In fact I've been thinking – when are we going to do it again?'

A shard of chocolate flake caught in Laurel's throat and she coughed until her eyes watered. 'Again!'

'Why not? This time I thought we could all go away somewhere for the weekend; maybe a nice country house hotel, or something.'

'You have got to be kidding!' retorted Laurel, picturing the torment of an entire weekend breathing in Gabriel Jouet's pheromones. 'No bloody way.'

'Why not? You can bring that nice Graeme, it'll be brilliant.'

'No it won't, because I'm not doing it.'

'You two make such a lovely couple.'

'We do not! I told you, Graeme's just a friend, and besides—'

'But Loz—'

'But nothing! I said I'd do it once as a favour, and I did it and it was awful and that's the end of it. Anyway,' she added, 'what's with the sudden interest in cosy four-somes?' A little something twisted in her heart. 'The way you've been going on about him, I'd have thought you'd want Gabriel all to yourself so you can have your wicked way with him.'

There was a short but telling silence. When Steph

254

spoke again, some of the breeziness had gone. 'What do you think of Gabriel?'

'He's . . . all right.'

'You do like him, don't you?'

Something cold ran up Laurel's spine. 'What do you mean?'

'You don't think he's you know, weird or anything?'

'Weird?'

'I mean, I know he's a bit quiet and all that, but they say still rivers run deep don't they? And just 'cause he doesn't say much, that doesn't mean he doesn't have, you know, normal urges. Does it?'

Don't talk to me about urges, thought Laurel. 'What's this all about, Steph?'

Steph let out a sigh. 'Can I be honest with you?'

Laurel was tempted to say that'd make a change, but she just replied, 'Of course you can.'

'The truth is, I'm a bit worried about Gabriel – well, about me and Gabriel. And you and Graeme, well, you seemed to get on really well with him when we all went out and I thought if the four of us spent a bit more time together you might be able to draw him out.'

'Steph,' said Laurel firmly, 'I am not doing a Sigmund Freud on Gabriel. I told you, if you want to find out something, why don't you just ask him?'

There was something faintly forlorn about Steph's reply. 'It's never happened like this before,' she said. 'I don't know where to start. Please do it for me, Laurel; just this once.'

Laurel steeled herself. 'Steph I'm sorry, really I am, but the answer's a definite no.'

'Pretty please?'

'Oh all right, maybe.'

When Laurel got to work the following morning, she thought she was the first to arrive. But as she walked into her office carrying the usual stack of junk mail, she found someone sitting in her chair – and it definitely wasn't Goldilocks.

'It's nearly half-past eight,' grunted Edwin Case nodding towards the ormolu eagles.

'Yes, I know,' said Laurel, concealing her annoyance. 'I thought I'd come in early.'

'Early! When my widowed mother was running this place, she used to get here at seven and work right through without any lunch. And she never took Christmas Day off.'

And in her spare time she raised forty-six children and invented the pop-up toaster, thought Laurel. With one arm tied behind her back. Laurel was tempted to mention her own all-night stints, but frankly she couldn't be bothered. 'Was there something you wanted to see me about?' she asked sweetly.

Edwin Case's tufty grey eyebrows clashed together like warring caterpillars. 'I have a bone to pick with you, young lady.'

Laurel dropped the bundle of mail onto the desk. She thought about taking a seat in one of the arm-chairs, but didn't want to concede the height advantage. 'Oh yes?'

'Our agreement quite clearly stipulated no changes were to be made.'

Laurel sighed. 'I've painted the filing cabinet grey, just like you told me to.'

'I am not talking about filing cabinets, Miss Page. I am talking about valued members of staff. Who gave you permission to dispense with Mr Da Silva's services?'

'Ravi?' Oh shit, thought Laurel. 'I didn't. He resigned.'

The caterpillars were now trying to eat each other alive. 'Resigned! And why would he want to do a thing like that?'

'I'm not sure.' She fought back with something that wasn't quite a lie. 'I think he was unhappy with the way the agency was being run.'

'With the way you were running the agency, you mean? He never expressed any dissatisfaction when I was in charge.'

Laurel gave up trying to play the psychology game, and sat down. 'It's a great pity Ravi felt he had to leave,' she admitted, 'but after all, we were overstaffed.'

It was a brave attempt, but it cut no ice with Case. 'No changes, Miss Page; was our agreement clear or was it not?'

'I suppose so. But if we just had one compu—'

'There may be a place for computers, Miss Page. But that place is not at Dovecote & Marsh.' Edwin Case stood up, square and malevolent in his navy-blue pinstripe; probably the only man in Cheltenham wearing a three-piece suit on the hottest day of the year. 'You know my requirements, Miss Page. They are not negotiable. If you feel unable to meet my high standards, I am sure there are others who would be only too happy to comply.'

He departed, leaving an odour of stale cigar smoke behind him. Laurel stood glaring at the door for several minutes, running through all the clever ripostes she could have come up with if she'd had time to think of them.

So Case's requirements were non-negotiable, were they? Well surprise surprise, thought Laurel: so are mine. And I've just about had enough of all this shit.

I'm going to find myself a proper job. In the meantime, if I'm going to lose this one no matter what I do, I intend to go down fighting. And that means giving Dovecote & Marsh a right royal kick in the pants.

All day long, the phone rang. From time to time, Laurel emerged from her office but nobody had any time to talk about chocolate éclairs or swap tips on propagating dwarf azaleas. Connie was just a pink blob in the distance, hemmed in by boxes. Stacey and Bette were up to their eyes in telephone calls. It was ironic really: Edwin Case wanted to keep things old-fashioned and personal, but they had so much work on at the moment that nobody had time to do anything but fill in forms.

She felt a pang of regret. Case was right about one thing: it was a shame about Ravi leaving. He was good at his job, he was funny, and basically it was her fault that he'd left. But if there was one thing she'd learned, it was that regrets were no use to anybody.

As she walked back into her office, her own phone rang. Automatically she picked it up. 'Dovecote & Marsh, can I help you?'

'Laurel? Is that you?'

The voice sounded as if it was coming from inside a stainless steel bread bin, but it was instantly recognisable. Her own voice brightened several shades. 'Graeme!'

'I'm really sorry I didn't get back to you sooner,' he said, 'only I'm in Durham.'

'Durham! Why?'

'Work, unfortunately. Well, fortunately I suppose, only it means I probably won't make it back to Cheltenham for weeks.'

'Oh,' said Laurel.

'I'm at the museum,' he went on. 'Believe it or not, the rear end fell off their blue whale, and it's a really big job putting it back together.'

'Gosh,' said Laurel.

'I couldn't turn it down.'

'No. Of course you couldn't.'

'Are you OK?' There was concern in Graeme's voice. 'You've gone ever so quiet.'

'I'm fine,' she said. 'It was just something Steph suggested – another evening out with her and Gabriel. You probably wouldn't have wanted to come anyway.'

'Yes I would,' protested Graeme. 'I'm ever so sorry I can't.'

And to her surprise, Laurel realised that she was, too.

Chapter 21

Stacey froze outside the door to Laurel's office, one hand in mid-air. She'd been just about to knock and go in, but that was before she heard Edwin Case's voice drilling its way through two inches of solid mahogany.

OK, so she'd been hesitant before, but not now. Listening to Mr Case berating Laurel about silly things that didn't matter one jot was enough to make up anybody's mind. All that stuff about not changing things even if they needed changing, all that concentrated grumpiness; the way things were going, he was the one who was sending Dovecote & Marsh to hell in a handcart, not poor Laurel.

Ginger curls wilting, Stacey turned round and tiptoed away. All in all it was just as well she'd got a Plan B. And maybe now was the right time to put it into action.

Trying to avoid Gabriel was like doing one of those SAS initiative tests, where they dropped you in the middle of some unfamiliar town with fifty pence and no trousers. Over the last few days, Laurel had found herself going to the most ridiculous lengths to ensure that her path didn't cross with Mr Jouet's.

Take the case of the nutty bun loaf. Laurel had always shopped at the nice bright supermarket on Tewkesbury Road, mainly to get her weekly fix of bakery products. She loved that damned nutty bun loaf with the sticky icing and the flaked almonds. But now she knew that Gabriel shopped there, she'd taken to doing a weekly run to that gloomy twenty-four-hour place on the other side of town, where all the assistants had bad acne and the bun loaves were decidedly inferior. Even there, she found herself holding her breath as she rounded the end of each aisle, convinced that she was about to come upon Gabriel comparing the prices of fabric conditioners.

And that wasn't all. Without consciously realising it, she'd stopped going to the park, the cinema (except on nights when she knew he was out with Steph) and the video store, had abandoned her favourite sandwich place, and ducked into shop doorways whenever she saw a white decorator's van drive past.

Things were getting very silly indeed. After all, why on earth should she be worried about running into Steph's bloke? It wasn't as if there was anything between them.

It was in that spirit that Laurel glanced out of her office window, saw the August sun beating down on the creamy-white facades of the buildings opposite, and decided that – Gabriel or no Gabriel – she was going out.

Cheltenham looked quite continental in the summer sunshine, with its ice-cream-coloured buildings, hanging baskets, and fat, fluffy pigeons splashing about in the fountains. It was hotter than it looked, too; the pavements hazy with that particularly English heat that specialises in producing red noses and smelly armpits. Outside Top Shop, a *Big Issue*-seller's wolfhound was sprawled flat out and panting, a red spotted handkerchief spread over its grizzled head.

You're right, thought Laurel: it's a bit too hot. Gratefully, she turned off the High Street into the relative cool of the Regent Arcade, in search of a nice cold drink, only to find herself right in the middle of a heaving throng of mums with babies in buggies.

'Hello Laurel,' said a voice by her side as she squeezed herself to the front to see what was going on.

Laurel all but jumped out of her skin. Turning, she saw Kathy from the Happy Nappy. 'Oh, it's you! You nearly gave me a heart attack.'

Clearly transported to some higher plane of ecstasy, Kathy nodded towards the half-dozen infant morris dancers who were toddling along to a jaunty accordion jig. 'Aren't they adorable? Just look at the cute little bells on their trousers.'

Laurel tried hard to see the scene through Kathy's eyes, but she'd never really been a small-person person. It wasn't that she disliked them – she wouldn't dare, not with all the nieces and nephews her sister kept producing. She'd just never quite got the hang of the incomprehensible noises and unexpected smells.

'They're very . . . um . . . yes,' she agreed.

'See that little blond boy, the one who keeps dropping his stick?' Laurel nodded. 'That's Eric. He's one of mine.'

'I didn't know you were a mum.'

Kathy laughed, a little wistfully, thought Laurel. 'I'm not. I meant, he's one of mine from the nursery.'

'Oh. Right.'

'I've had him five days a week since he was six weeks old, poor little mite. His father walked out on him and his mum for some other woman, and his mum's been working all hours to support the pair of them.' Kathy shook her head angrily. 'Some people. It shouldn't be allowed.'

They watched for a while as the tots bounced through their routine, small round faces tense with concentration. It was, Laurel had to admit, pretty cute.

'Kathy.'

'Mm?'

'You got to get straight back?'

'Not really, this is my lunch break.'

'See that ice-cream parlour over there? I really, really fancy one of their Creamy Caramel Sundaes with extra Jelly Tots and sprinkles.'

Kathy grinned. 'Make mine a double.'

'You really love kids, don't you?' remarked Laurel as she licked caramel fudge sauce off her spoon.

'They're my life,' replied Kathy simply.

'Do you want some of your own?'

Kathy studied the hazelnut on the top of her whipped cream. 'Not yet. Maybe one day . . .'

Laurel had the feeling she'd just blundered right into a sore spot. 'I'm sorry, I didn't mean to pry.'

'You didn't.' Kathy swiped a Jelly Tot from Laurel's

264

sundae glass. 'If you'd been prying I'd have told you to back off and mind your own business.' She chewed vigorously. 'It's just, well, I've never met a bloke I'd trust enough to want to have kids with. That's all.'

Laurel cocked her head on one side, trying to weigh Kathy up. On the one hand she was all pink teddy bears and patchwork dungarees; on the other there was something darker, a deeper undercurrent.

'You don't trust men?'

'I've given up on them. Most of them are shits.'

Laurel knew she really ought to shut up and leave it there, but she could sense a kinship and Kathy fascinated her. 'You've been through a bad relationship then?'

Kathy laughed out loud. 'A few more than one!' She pushed her long-handled spoon right to the bottom of her glass and scooped out a strawberry coated in lots of sticky sauce. 'Oh, I guess it wasn't always their fault; they just didn't understand. They don't, do they?'

'About what?'

'Kids. Well, the way I feel about kids.' She swallowed the strawberry. 'The thing about kids is, they depend on you completely don't they? Trust you to do what's right for them and protect them from the bad stuff.'

'Yeah, I guess they do. I know that's how my sister feels about her two, not to mention the new baby.'

'Of course she does, that's because she's a proper parent. Not like some.' Her eyelids drooped. 'Not like mine.'

Ah, thought Laurel. So that's where it's leading. 'If you'd rather I changed the subject ...' she suggested,

265

not sure if she was being considerate or cowardly. These last couple of years, she'd been through a lot of talking about bad stuff.

Kathy's back straightened. 'No, no it's fine, I'm cool about it now. My mum killed herself with drink and my dad was too busy knocking seven bells out of me to notice. The usual story. It's just that, well, when you've been through it yourself you want to stop it ever happening to any other kids, don't you?'

Their eyes met.

'Not all men are a dead loss, you know,' said Laurel. And she realised how far she must have come to be able to say – and mean – it.

'I know that.'

'Some of them are almost human.'

Her remark raised a chuckle. 'That's pushing it a bit.'

Laurel pushed just a little harder; somehow it seemed important. 'You know, you could come to the D&M social evening. There'll be plenty of staff to cover the childcare without you.'

Kathy fiddled with her spoon and avoided eye contact. 'Yeah, well, I did say I might pop in for an hour. If we're not too busy.'

'Which is just another way of saying you've no intention of coming!' She tilted up Kathy's chin and pulled a silly face. 'Ve haff vays of making you talk, you know.'

Kathy's uncomfortable frown dissolved into a giggle. Taking a spoonful of strawberry sauce, she aimed it right at the middle of Laurel's forehead. 'You'll never take me alive!'

'Does that mean you'll come then?'

Kathy lowered the spoon and jammed it into Laurel's open mouth. 'Oh go on. But only if I can get very, very drunk.'

There was something sneaky about Saturdays, especially beautiful sunny ones that just cried out for a picnic. You hatched plans, made your mind up you were going to do something really nice with the day – and then cruel fate threw a spanner in the works.

Today's impediment was the toilet. Ah well, thought Laurel as she contemplated its murky depths; it's not everybody who can get a size seven trainer lodged in their U-bend. At least it would entertain the plumber – if he ever got round to arriving.

Things always went wrong whenever Laurel attempted DIY; yet she'd never learned to leave well alone. In her time she'd nailed through fuse boxes, punctured gas pipes with carpet tacks, flooded utility rooms and accidentally walled up next-door's hamster. All right, so maybe she shouldn't have stood on the toilet seat to put up the bathroom cabinet, but twenty-twenty hindsight was a wonderful thing.

Just as she was about to phone up Mr Radley for the third time, the doorbell rang. She glanced at the clock as she lunged at the entryphone. If he was quick, there might still be time to drive out to a nice country pub for lunch.

'What took you so long?' she demanded. 'You said eleven at the latest.'

'You what?' replied a voice that definitely didn't belong to Mr Radley. 'Is that you, Laurel?'

'Oh shit,' said Laurel. It wasn't Mr Radley at all; it was Gabriel Jouet.

Gabriel hovered in the middle of Laurel's living room like Heathcliff in a Parisian lingerie shop. 'I found this in the taxi,' he said, handing it over. 'I've got a job over in Leckhampton, so Steph said to drop it in on my way. It's an earring,' he added helpfully.

Laurel took it. 'Oh. Thanks. It must have fallen off when the four of us were, you know. Out.'

'At the pictures, yeah. Good evening that.'

'Not bad, yeah.'

Gabriel shuffled his feet. Laurel tried not to let her eyes dwell on his more erogenous zones.

'Would you . . . er . . . like some?'

A small muscle at the corner of his eye started twitching. 'Sorry?'

'Tea. Would you?'

'Best not, I'm due in, um, you know.'

'Leckhampton?'

'Yeah. Leckhampton.'

There was a silence so screamingly loud that Laurel was surprised all the windows in the flat didn't shatter. In the end she said the first words that came into her head.

'I've got a blocked toilet.'

'Oh.'

'I thought you were the plumber.'

'Oh, right.' Gabriel looked deep into her eyes and murmured the words every woman wants to hear: 'I could try and unblock it if you like.'

Oh God, thought Laurel; he looks like Heaven and now he tells me he does plumbing as well. This is too much for the human frame to bear. 'Oh no, I couldn't possibly ask you to do that.'

'That's OK, I'm in my work clothes. Besides, I like tinkering with things. Have you got a plunger?'

As he said the word 'plunger', their eyes met and an ice-cold, electric shudder ran right through Laurel from the soles of her feet to the top of her head. Ooh, forget the toilet and tinker with me, she pleaded silently.

'Well, if you're sure.'

'Oh, I'm sure.'

So am I, thought Laurel, and as his lips drew closer to hers she didn't even contemplate doing the decent thing and resisting. If something was meant to be, what was the point of fighting it?

And then the doorbell rang.

Chapter 22

Hollow-eyed, Laurel flopped down on the toilet seat and addressed the blue ceramic duck on the corner of the bath.

'I can't believe I just did that.'

Correction.

'Well OK, I can't believe I nearly did that.'

The duck didn't say anything, but she could tell from its constipated expression that it didn't approve. Frankly she didn't blame it. Nearly or really: it didn't make a whole lot of difference. The fact was, if Mr Radley hadn't turned up with his adjustable wrench just as the climactic moment, she and Gabriel would have . . . well, whatever they would have done, she was willing to bet it wouldn't have involved wearing many clothes.

Face the truth Laurel, she told herself: you're a sex-starved slut. And you're not even any good at it. Plungers indeed. Your erotic fantasies play out like bad seventies' porno flicks.

Standing up, she slipped a hand into her jeans pocket. The earring was still there. She took it out and rolled it around in the palm of her hand. If I'm a slut, she pondered, what does that make Gabriel? I could have sworn he was just as interested in kissing me as I was in kissing him. She wanted to say that it was entirely different for him; that he had simply been overcome by some noble, irresistible passion – but that was bullshit. There was nothing noble about nearly snogging your girlfriend's mate.

The ceramic duck scowled meaningfully. Or your mate's boyfriend.

The awful thing was, if Gabriel turned up again now Laurel had a horrible feeling she'd want to carry on exactly where they'd left off.

'What about my umbrella?' demanded Connie's father, wedging himself stubbornly in the doorway. 'It might rain.'

'No Dad, you don't need your umbrella. Or your overcoat.' With more than usual insistence, Connie practically pushed him out of the front door. 'It's ninety in the shade out there. Even the ants are wearing sunblock.'

He zipped up his beige golfing jacket and pulled his cap down over his ears. 'If I get a chill and die . . .' He glared.

'You won't.'

'It's blowing a gale out here.' Somewhere in the stillness of the garden, a single rose petal dropped off its bush and floated peacefully down to the ground. 'Your sister wouldn't send an old man out without his overcoat.'

Her mandibles aching with the effort of not foaming at the mouth, Connie snatched a scarf from the hall table. 'Here. If you get cold you can put this on. Now go on Dad, if you don't leave now you'll miss the start of the dominoes.'

'I want my tea on the table at half-past five sharp, and make sure there's no gristle in my mince.'

Even after she'd seen him disappear round the corner on his way to the Legion, Connie fancied she could still hear her father's voice, nagging away about nylon socks, dental fixative and the thousand and one ways in which Bette was better at everything than Connie could ever be.

She stood in the hallway for a little while, taking deep breaths and reminding herself that what had to be done, had to be done. She'd made her mind up now and there couldn't be any going back.

Slowly and unwillingly, her feet climbed the worn green stair-carpet that still bore the scars of the time she and Bette had fallen down the stairs in the throes of trying to kill each other. The carpet wasn't the only thing that hadn't changed in the last thirty-odd years, she thought as she pushed open her bedroom door.

Joe's printed-off e-mails sat in a neat plastic folder, tidily stashed away under the computer keyboard. Sitting down, she slid it out and started to read them through for the umpteenth time.

I really like you, Connie, I've never met anybody like you, not ever. Yeah, thought Connie, but you've never actually met me at all, have you? And if you did . . .

She turned the pages. *I can say things to you I'd never dare say to anybody else. Not anybody. I can't wait to meet you and hold you, I just know it's going to be great . . .*

Her eyes misted as she ran her fingers over the huge kisses he'd put at the bottom of his last message. *See you very soon, kisses all over, Joe XXXXX. PS Don't worry, won't let you down, not ever.*

She had a small, self-indulgent cry. Then she switched on the PC, dialled up the Internet and e-mailed Joe to tell him not to write to her any more.

Not ever.

By Wednesday lunchtime, Laurel was over the worst of the guilt. OK, so going out for a drink with Steph on Monday night had been a bit awkward, but she was pretty sure she'd got away without Steph suspecting anything. As long as she could avoid Gabriel – or indeed, talking about Gabriel – she sensed that things would be fine. The only really difficult thing was going to be if Steph kept insisting on another stupid double date.

But Gabriel and Steph were just side issues. There were more important things that needed sorting out; like Edwin Case and the future of Dovecote & Marsh.

As she ate a four-cheese panini in the Mean Bean, surrounded by empty coffee cups, she tried working out her thoughts on a paper napkin. Right in the middle, surrounded by a twirly doodle, was a single word: Ravi. And radiating from it like spokes from a wheel were lines leading to other, increasingly desperate words:

'client exodus'; 'paperwork overload'; 'antiquated'; 'Case'; 'bankruptcy'; and, underlined three times in red: "MELTDOWN!'

This was getting stupidly hysterical. Laurel struck a line through the whole lot and took another sip of coffee. She had to stop thinking like a frustrated teenager, stop letting Case get to her, and start thinking like a manager again. Just like the word on the napkin, Ravi was the key to this. Before he'd left, OK they'd been overstaffed but they'd been coping, even turning a small profit. People liked him; he worked hard even when he looked as if he wasn't doing anything; and he'd supplied the old-fashioned personal touch that Dovecote & Marsh was supposed to be a byword for.

Trouble was, the way things were going now, the only thing D&M was going to be a byword for was inefficiency. Too many customers, too much paper-work, not enough staff to provide the exclusive one-to-one service people were paying for. Consequently customers were getting pissed off and starting to leave – and once they spread the word that D&M was going down the tubes, the rest would inevitably follow.

What to do about it, that was the question. Build an android Ravi, complete with fully-customisable client interface? If only. Hire someone new? But surely it was pointless trying to replace Ravi. Even if she found someone good who was willing to work for the kind of wages Edwin Case was willing to pay, it would take far too long to train them up. See if she could persuade Bette or Connie to switch over to full-time? No, that wouldn't work either. Bette was more likely to scare clients off, and Connie had enough on her plate already.

Laurel tapped the end of her pencil on the table top. No, it wasn't a new Ravi she needed, it was something more radical. Something Edwin Case would absolutely, definitely, one-hundred-per-cent hate.

Technology.

She glanced across at a young woman reading *Business Computing*. That was the kind of person they'd attract if they went on line: young, single, short on opportunities to meet available members of the opposite sex. Yes, D&M Online: it had a ring to it, and she was sure it could work. But D&M Online wasn't D&M, was it? Nor was it the kind of gig Laurel had been hoping for when she took over as manager – let alone the kind of operation Edwin Case was determined she was going to run. Besides, if she'd wanted to run yet another dot com, she could have stayed in cyber-floristry and made a fat profit out of being bored rigid.

She stared down at the mess of biro on her napkin. Why did all roads seem to lead to the Internet? Surely there had to be another way; a way that was efficient, yet still treated people like people? A better way of making people happy?

Maybe it was the delayed effect of the caffeine, but a thought bounced into Laurel's brain and she clicked her fingers so loudly that people looked up to see where the sound was coming from.

Technology. People. Technology and people. There had to be a way to use both, to get the best out of the machines but not lose the people. She was sure there must be. And the people mattered, she realised that now. Little by little, she had grown to care about the silly pink doves and all who sheltered under their wings.

After all, everyone deserved to find their other half, didn't they? And Dovecote & Marsh had a real gift for making dreams come true. Laurel thought back to all the success stories she'd read while working through the files. The blind couple from Winchcombe; Sid and Nellie, the two eighty-year-olds who'd rediscovered each other after more than sixty years apart; the lonely single parents who were lonely no more. And who could forget the look on that nice Mary Brooks's face when she came into the office to deliver invitations to her wedding, five years after the terrible road accident that had robbed her of her first husband? Yes, D&M gave people more than just romance: it gave them hope.

Sitting back in her chair, Laurel drained her cup and let the tension ebb out of her shoulders. It felt good to have made a decision at last, even a fool-hardly one.

It was settled. Edwin Case or no, she'd made up her mind what she was going to do with Dovecote & Marsh.

It rained on Thursday evening; a fitting accompaniment to the way Stacey was feeling.

'Are you all right, Auntie Stacey?' asked Alex, drawing the curtains and sitting down next to her aunt at the kitchen table.

'No,' sighed Stacey, reaching out and putting an arm round her niece's shoulders. 'I'm not very all right at all.'

277

Alex peeked at the sheet of notepaper, lying amid a mess of crumpled paper balls. 'Are you still trying to write that letter?'

Stacey nodded forlornly. 'I wish I didn't have to.'

'Why do you?'

'Because . . . Just because.'

'But I thought you liked working at the agency.'

Stacey put down her pen. 'I do. Or I did. But I told you, Mr Case is being horrible to Laurel and stopping her doing things to modernise the place. And now Ravi's left I think the whole business is going to fall apart. So you see, I have to resign.'

'But then you won't have a job,' pointed out Alex.

'Yes I will,' said Stacey. 'Ravi and I are going to set up our own agency, remember?' She smiled reassuringly at Alex. 'Ravi's really good at computers, I'm sure it'll all work out.'

It'd better, she thought to herself. Alex had had a rough enough time already, with her mum in prison for killing her violent dad and the rest of the family having nothing to do with them. For all her natural buoyancy Stacey was deadly serious about her responsibilities; but better for them both that she jumped ship now, rather than wait to be thrown out on her ear.

Alex considered for a moment. 'Are you going to marry Ravi?' she asked.

Stacey turned salmon-pink beneath her ginger curls. 'Alex!'

'Only if you do, I think you should tell him to grow his hair back for the wedding. he's got a funny-shaped bump on the back of his head.' Leaning over, Alex planted a kiss on Stacey's cheek. 'Go on, Auntie Stacey,' she said. 'Sign the letter and put it in an envelope.'

'What if I'm doing the wrong thing?'

Alex smiled. 'You're my favourite auntie, you never do the wrong thing.'

Around ten o'clock, Steph finished her meal at diBorgia's (linguine with seared scallops, blanched spinach and a rather nice red), paid the bill and stepped out onto Prestbury Parade. Sometimes she enjoyed eating alone; it was nice to cosset yourself and have space to think, without having to put on a show for some present or future squeeze. Sometimes it was nice just to be Steph.

The last of the daylight had dwindled away to nothing, and the street lamps glowed fuzzily in the moist, slightly drizzly air. Steph stuck out a hand to feel for rain. Was it worth going back inside and calling a cab, or should she give her new designer umbrella an outing? It was rather chick after all, with its wild-animal stripes and handle carved from real tiger's-eye.

Steph smiled as she raised the umbrella and clicked it open. She'd always felt there was a little of the wild animal in everyone, and she could think of at least one person who brought it out in her every time. If only she could work out how to bring it out in him.

There was a pub on the other side of the street. Just as she was about to step out of the porch onto the pavement, the door to the lounge bar opened, and out walked Gabriel, swiftly followed by a woman.

Well not so much a woman, Steph reflected later, as a hideously deformed blow-up sex doll: Anthea Turner with Jordan's boob job and the whole ghastly ensemble poured into over-tight black leather. As if that wasn't bad enough, the two of them were laughing and, as Steph watched in horror, the woman reached down and gave Gabriel's bum a lascivious squeeze.

As the heavens opened and lightning flashed across the sky, illuminating the scene with sadistic clarity, they ran giggling across the car park, where Anthea bundled Gabriel into the passenger seat of a black Audi.

Then the two of them roared away into the night.

Chapter 23

Laurel was trying to find a match for a man with big ears and a pet lizard when the door of her office burst open.

'Steph!' she exclaimed, knocking half a can of lemonade over the files. 'Oh damn.'

Connie's breathless head appeared in the doorway, behind Steph's left shoulder. 'I'm sorry, Laurel, I did say you were busy, but she said it was an emergency.'

'It is an emergency!' insisted Steph.

Laurel grabbed a tissue from the box she kept for unrequited singletons and mopped at the sticky wet pool. 'It had better be,' she said. 'We're not all ladies of leisure, you know, some of us have got work to do.'

'Yes, yes, I know all that; look, can I sit down, only it's urgent.' Without waiting for Laurel's answer, Steph flung herself into an armchair. 'You couldn't get me two Nurofen, could you darling?' she beseeched Connie sweetly. 'I think I've got one of my heads coming on. Oh, and a large brandy if you've got it.'

'Tea will do,' said Laurel, catching the look on her secretary's face. 'Thanks Connie, you're a star.'

Connie duly eclipsed, leaving the door ajar. Steph promptly jumped up, shot a look outside, closed the door and then dragged her chair right up to the desk, so that she was nose to nose with Laurel. 'I've found out!' she announced dramatically.

'Found out what?'

'Why Gabriel won't take me home.' Her expression hardened. 'He's got another woman!'

'What!'

'It's true – I saw them together!'

For one horrible moment, it flashed through Laurel's mind that Gabriel's other woman might just possibly be her. After all, she'd bumped into him enough times lately that they'd probably been spotted by half of Cheltenham; besides she still had a guilty conscience about last Saturday, even if the only things that had happened had been in her imagination. 'You saw them? Where?' she enquired, just about managing to sound cool if not collected.

'Coming out of a pub last night. In Prestbury.' Steph's carefully glossed lip curled into a sneer of disdain. 'Cheap little tart she was too, all tits and bottle-blonde hair.'

Laurel couldn't suppress a small surge of relief. 'Just because you saw him coming out of a pub with a woman,' she pointed out, 'doesn't necessarily mean—'

'I'd like to know what else it means! She had her hands all over him, the bitch.'

'Oh dear,' said Laurel, caught somewhere between empathy and *schadenfreude*. If she'd been a bitch herself she might have suggested that Steph now knew what it felt like, but there wouldn't have been much point. Steph's memory was selective at the best of times. 'That's bad. I guess that means there's going to be a showdown.'

To her surprise, Steph replied, 'No. It means I'm going to get the truth. Well, we are.'

'I thought you'd already done that. And what do you mean, "we"?'

'There might be another explanation: an innocent one.'

'But you said—'

'I know I did, but you can't take everything at face value, can you? What if I bawled him out and he turned out not to have done anything wrong? So I've decided: you and I are going to find out what's really going on.'

Laurel put up a hand in protest. 'Hey, whoa, hang on a minute. Why can't you just ask him straight out what he's been up to?'

Steph looked at her as though she were very slightly retarded. 'Because that would mean I didn't trust him.'

'But you don't!'

'Well, no, but I don't want Gabriel to know that, do I? I mean, if he turns out to be innocent I'd have burned my boats.'

Laurel wondered just what terrible crimes she had committed in a past life, to have deserved Steph as a punishment. She saw a lifeline and grabbed it. 'Gabriel's a D&M client,' she reminded Steph. 'I really don't think I can interfere.'

'Of course you can.' Steph fixed Laurel with a steely smile. 'I'm a D&M client too, remember. And besides, I'm your best friend.'

The following Saturday, Stacey and Ravi pushed the boat out and lunched à la carte. OK, so Elf Burger hadn't yet been awarded its first Michelin star, but you'd go a long way to find better Crispy Orc Balls. Besides, it was Alex's belated birthday treat and Alex was going through one of her veggie phases.

'Can we have extra pudding?' she pleaded. 'Can we?'

Stacey laughed through a mouthful of Carob Swamp. 'You can't still be hungry, not after that huge ice cream.'

'Not hungry,' Alex admitted. 'Just greedy. Oh go on, I won't throw up, I promise!'

Ravi winked, thrust a hand into his pocket and took out a ten-pound note. 'Extra pudding sounds good to me. Go on then, get us seconds all round.'

'But my diet!' protested Stacey as Alex leapt up and headed for the counter.

'Stuff the diet.' Ravi licked a blob of carob sauce off the end of her nose. 'I like you just the way you are.'

'Really? Even with my big bum?'

'Really. I wouldn't care if it was the size of a . . . a troll's.'

There was a short silence. Stacey put down her spoon. 'You know what we were talking about? Well,

I've done it.' Reaching into her handbag, she took out her resignation letter. 'What do you think?' she asked as she watched him read it. 'Is it all right? It took me ages.'

Ravi hesitated for a moment before folding up the letter and handing it back. 'The letter's fine,' he said quietly, 'but I think it's a really bad idea.'

Her face fell. 'But we agreed!'

'I know we did.' Ravi fiddled with his earring. 'You were so keen on the idea, I didn't want to disappoint you by saying no. But that was before I really thought about it.' He looked into Stacey's eyes and took her hand. 'It's not just you and me, it's us now, remember.' Stacey blushed with pleasure. 'We've got to think about Alex too.'

'Alex thinks it's a great idea, we talked it over and she said—'

Ravi kissed her gently. 'Stacey love, Alex would say anything if she thought it'd make you happy.' He glanced over to the counter, where Alex was trying on a pair of cardboard wings for size. 'That kid idolises you.'

The thought that anybody could idolise her seemed to throw Stacey completely off-balance. She was still sitting staring at Ravi when Alex returned carrying three Whipped Mango Masalas.

'Is it all going ahead then?' asked Alex, setting the tray down on the table.

'No,' said Stacey. 'Ravi's had a better idea.'

This was news to Ravi. 'I have?'

'Yes,' smiled Stacey, 'you have.'

*

285

While Ravi was wondering what bright idea he'd just had, Laurel and Steph were sitting on a sunny bench on the Promenade, lobbing bits of sandwich at the pigeons. They were quite posh sandwiches, and the pigeons seemed particularly keen on the wild boar pâté, but Steph was too on edge to have much of an appetite and Laurel was too busy worrying about what Steph was going to come up with next.

'Bugs,' said Steph suddenly.

'Where?' Laurel looked down but there was nothing to see but a solitary arthritic ant, hobbling across the pavement under the weight of a giant crumb.

'Bugs! Electronic ones – you know, listening devices, all that stuff.' Steph waved her hands around excitedly. 'Yes that's it! There's got to be a shop some-where round here that sells them. All we need to do is somehow get inside Gabriel's house, slip a microphone into a—'

'Steph,' Laurel broke in gently, 'don't you think you're going a bit overboard?'

Halted in mid-flow, Steph seemed to wilt slightly. 'No.'

Laurel slid closer along the bench. 'Can I quote you something you once said to me?' She didn't wait for an answer. 'Quote: "He's only a man, Lozzie," unquote. Why on earth are you getting so steamed up about a bloke? You of all people!'

'I'm not.' Steph looked up. 'Am I?'

Laurel nodded. 'Uh-huh.'

'Oh.'

'I mean, it's not as if you're like the rest of us mortals, is it? You can have any bloke you want – you just wiggle your hips at them and they're queuing up to shag you . . .' Her voice tailed off as she saw the expression on Steph's face. 'Steph?'

'Only they're not queuing up, are they?' said Steph flatly. 'Or at least, Gabriel's not. And if he's not . . .'

In a flash of revelation, Laurel understood. Perhaps for the very first time in her entire life, Steph Mihailovic was feeling insecure.

'If he's not, you're afraid that other blokes won't either?' Steph didn't answer but Laurel could see she'd hit the spot. 'Oh Steph, don't be stupid. Everybody gets dumped on by men sometimes.'

'I don't. Didn't.' Steph crumbled a crust of bread between her fingers. 'It's all I've got, Laurel. I'm no good at anything else.'

'Don't talk rubbish!'

'I'm not, it's true. I never bothered learning other skills, I never needed to. I've always known I can get what I want from a man just by being me.' She swallowed down the lump in her throat. 'What do I do now, Lozzie? What if I'm past it?'

Laurel wasn't sure whether to laugh or cry. She settled for putting an arm round Steph's shoulders. 'You're not past it and you never will be. You'll be pulling blokes when you're a hundred.'

Steph grabbed her hand and squeezed it hard. 'Help me, Lozzie. Help me find out what's going on with Gabriel.'

And like the soft-hearted fool she was, Laurel gave in and said yes.

It didn't take Laurel long to regret her promise. At eight o'clock on Sunday morning, there was a mighty hammering on her front door.

Still in her pyjamas, she staggered out of bed, past the fish tank, down the hallway and fumbled with the chain. Through the spyhole, she saw Steph's face, distorted by the lens into something the shape of a watermelon.

'Wassgoin'on?' she slurred through a sleepy fug as Steph erupted into the flat, sending Neil darting for cover.

'Hurry up, get dressed! We're going out.' Steph thrust a cardboard box and a carrier bag at her. 'And put these on.'

Warily, Laurel peeked into the carrier bag. 'Ugh, it's all hairy! Is it alive?'

Steph chortled. 'Don't be silly, it's a wig! I got you a red one, seeing as you're blonde, and mine's long and black. He'll never recognise us once we've got them on. The rollerblades are in the box.'

'Rollerblades! But I can't!'

'Ten minutes in the park and you'll be skating like a pro. Get a move on, Lozzie, we don't want to miss him, do we?'

It took a full ten seconds for Laurel to come to her senses.

'Steph, you're not thinking straight.'

'What?' Steph was already lacing up one rollerblade. 'Don't be silly, of course I am.'

Laurel laid a restraining hand on her shoulder. 'No you're not, you're jealous. And jealousy makes people do stupid things. God help me, I should know.'

Steph stopped lacing and addressed Laurel with a hard stare. 'Are you calling me stupid?'

'No, but this is. This whole rollerskating, following-people-about thing is insane! Face it Steph, you've got it bad and this was the first thing that came into your head. Why don't you sit down?' she suggested. 'We could talk things over properly.'

For the first time in quite some while, it occurred to Laurel that there were other people besides herself who didn't always manage to keep their emotions – or their lives – under control. Other people who could use a little professional help. Though Steph would probably die rather than admit it.

'Talk! I don't want to talk, I want to get out there and find out what's going on. Are you coming or not?'

'Not.'

Steph's lip curled. 'Some friend you are!'

'Yes, the kind of friend who tells you when you're just avoiding the issue.'

'I am not avoiding anything!'

'Oh yes you are. You're so chicken you'd rather prat about in a stupid wig than ask your boyfriend if he's cheating on you.'

This definitely rubbed Steph up the wrong way. 'At least I didn't end up in the funny farm because I couldn't cope with my boyfriend getting a bit of R&R on the side!'

I might have guessed, thought Laurel. She doesn't mention the breakdown for weeks, but first sign of an argument, and she's dredging it up to use against me. And people wonder why I don't talk about it. 'That's right,' she stabbed back. 'R&R with a certain person who was supposed to be my best mate!'

'Like you were supposed to be mine – but you still sacked Carlos! You can't blame me if I wanted to get my own back, and besides, it's not like I went looking for it, Jason offered it to me on a plate.'

Laurel threw her stupid wig across the room. 'Well, maybe that's what this woman's offering Gabriel.' She knew it was a mean thing to say, but she didn't care. Years of resentment were exploding out of her and it felt cathartically good. 'Maybe what she's got on her plate tastes better than what you've got on yours. Maybe,' she added with a final sadistic rapier-thrust, 'hers is fresher.'

And with that parting shot, she stomped off into the kitchen, leaving Steph to let herself out.

The red wig squatted accusingly on the passenger seat as Laurel drove into Painswick that evening, a solid reminder that she had quite a lot of apologising to do.

Trust Steph to live here, she thought as she parked amid the chocolate-box clutter of flower-covered cottages; a Cotswold village so exclusive that even the sparrows had to take voice tests before they were let in.

Only a girl from an ugly pebble-dashed semi on the wrong side of Cheltenham could have taken so whole-heartedly to the high life.

Steph's house (well, one of her houses) stood at the end of a narrow lane, and boasted everything from oriel windows to an old water-pump and a horse-trough outside the front door, planted with peonies. Laurel walked up to the front door, raised a hand to knock, chickened out and tried to think of lots of good reasons for not knocking. Maybe if she just left the wig and the ice cream on the doorstep as a peace offering, and ran away? But it was coming on to rain and who'd want to find a waterlogged wig and half a litre of melted ice cream all over their doormat?

There was a light on somewhere at the back of the house. Taking a deep breath, Laurel turned and walked round the narrow side passageway to the back door. This time she did knock, but nobody answered. She tried lifting the latch; and the door swung open.

'Steph?'

There was no answer, but she could hear the television news playing in one of the downstairs rooms.

'Steph? It's me, Laurel.'

It was a beautiful kitchen, thought Laurel: old-fashioned with copper pans and dried herbs hanging from a ceiling rack, and a big polished cooking range, yet full of every modern gadget you could wish for, from a breadmaker to an electric juicer.

All of them looked brand-new, unused even. A single dirty coffee cup sat on the draining board, alongside the empty wrapper from a Mars Bar. And a sudden feeling of isolation washed over Laurel, as if this house was unaccustomed to guests, or very much in the way of life at all.

'Laurel.' Steph appeared in the doorway, wearing a big white bathrobe. For once in her life, thought Laurel, she looked positively dishevelled. 'What are you doing here?'

Laurel held out the ice cream and the video. 'I came to say I'm sorry.'

Steph looked at her warily. 'Why?'

'Because I am.'

Steph ran a hand through her hair. 'You've no need to be sorry, you were right. I am past my sell-by date.'

'No you're not! I didn't mean it, I was just being nasty.' The admission was uncomfortable, but it was what she'd come to say. 'I guess I thought I'd worked through all that Jason shit but I hadn't. I wanted to hurt you.'

'The way I hurt you?'

'I guess.'

'And I did hurt you, I know. What I did was horrible.'

'It's in the past now.'

'But you'll never forget, will you? And neither will I.'

'Maybe. But I'll never forget the good things either. And there were always a lot of those.'

They stood looking at each other as if expecting the other to explode. Then Steph's shoulders stopped trying to attach themselves to her ears, and relaxed an inch or two. 'What's the video?'

'*Sleeping Beauty*.'

'Sentimental crap.'

'Oh, absolutely. And the ice cream's strawberry cheesecake.'

Reaching out an arm, Steph picked up the red wig between finger and thumb and dropped it into the pedal bin. 'What are you waiting for?' she demanded. 'Grab us a couple of spoons and let's get that video on.'

Chapter 24

'Quick!' hissed Steph, grabbing Laurel by the arm and jerking her behind the lawnmowers. 'Before he sees you.'

Laurel rubbed her semi-dislocated shoulder. 'Ow.'

'Shh! He'll hear.'

Laurel thought that highly unlikely, since the PA system was pumping out S Club 7 at full throttle, but she'd resolved to humour Steph after their last little contretemps, so she shut up and made like a mouse.

Steph advanced her nose beyond the Flymos and beckoned to Laurel. 'There he is,' she whispered, 'over by Stylish Outdoor Dining. Come on!'

'So Gabriel's thinking of buying a barbecue, so what?' muttered Laurel as she followed Steph down the aisle, their advance screened by a trolley-full of South American tree ferns. 'It hardly proves he's the Cotswold Casanova.'

'Ah, but *why* does he want a barbecue?' demanded Steph, slinking to the end of Mowers (Electric) and pretending to take an interest in a display of lawn-sprinklers.

'Because he likes his chicken half-raw?'

'Because he likes entertaining.' She sniffed. 'Entertaining *women*.'

'If you say so.'

The thought of Gabriel suavely seducing the laydeez with a charred drumstick and a barbecued banana was so bizarre that Laurel had to remind herself that this was Deadly Serious. Even though it was Monday night, the DIY superstore was thronged and for once Laurel was glad to have to push her way through the crowds. The anonymity made following Gabriel marginally less embarrassing. And at least it was less so than Steph's hare-brained rollerblading idea.

Cautiously, Steph craned her neck round the last of the lawn-sprinklers.

'Well?' said Laurel, her line of sight blocked by Steph's baseball cap. All she could make out was the back of Gabriel's black denim jeans. That was the trouble with following people: all you ever got to see were their backs, not that Gabriel's back was anything less than worth seeing.

'He's looking at the gas-fired one now. No he's not, he's . . . hang on a minute, he's scratching his bum.'

I could do that, thought Laurel; and promptly chased the thought from her mind.

'Now he's looking at the big flat double hibachi with the hostess trolley attachment,' Steph went on.

'Is it big enough to seduce anybody on?'

'Oh ha ha.'

Steph swung round to give her a disapproving glare.

'Are you going to take this seriously?' she demanded. 'Because if you're not careful I'm going to punch you.'

Laurel did her best to look rueful. 'Sorry.'

The next minute, Steph's whole body stiffened. 'I don't believe it – he's got another one!'

'Another what?'

'Blonde!'

'What – a completely different one?'

'That's what I said, cloth-ears – look!'

'Where?' Laurel fought her way through the tree ferns to see. And sure enough, standing right next to Gabriel with her arm linked through his was a tall, willowy woman with a trendy ash-blonde crop and a blue denim skirt that could have doubled as a hairband.

'Right!' Steph's eyes flashed brighter than the half-price halogen patio lamps. 'Now I've caught him red-handed, I'm going to sort out the cheating bastard once and for all!'

Before Laurel could offer any words of caution, Steph launched herself full-tilt at the barbecue section. 'So, Gabriel *darling* – aren't you going to introduce me to your little *friend*?'

He didn't turn to look at her, so she grabbed him by the shoulder and wheeled him round. 'Don't pretend you can't hear me, you—'

'Are you talking to me?' he enquired, gently freeing his arm.

'Who the hell is *she*?' demanded the tall blonde woman.

It wasn't Gabriel.

*

Laurel yawned, rubbed her eyes and consulted the ormolu eagles. Almost six o'clock, and everybody else had gone home. Maybe she should follow suit. It had been a pretty hectic week, and it was only Tuesday.

She was wondering whether to risk asking Steph round for pasta when the door of her office opened an inch and an eye appeared in the gap.

'Laurel?' The owner of the eye gave a belated knock. 'Have you got a minute?'

'Sure Stacey, come in.' The prospect of nice cheesy pasta with a crispy pancetta salad receded to a tantalising daydream. Still, she wasn't sure she could cope with another evening of Steph in her current reckless state of mind. 'I thought you'd gone home.'

The door opened and Stacey came in, looking pink-cheeked and ruffled; the long white envelope in her hands displaying definite signs of nervous mangling.

There was an uneasy shuffling of feet. 'I did. But then I came back.'

'Oh,' said Laurel, peering at the envelope. 'What've you got there?'

Stacey took a deep breath and laid it on the desk. 'My resignation.'

Laurel could not have been more startled if the Pope had given birth to triplets. 'You're leaving?'

'Yes – well, no. I don't know, maybe. It all depends.'

'On what?'

'You.'

Laurel stared at the envelope, and then at Stacey. 'I knew you were disappointed about a few things I hadn't got round to doing, but I never thought …'

298

'It's not you *personally*, really it isn't,' said Stacey earnestly. 'And I know it's not your fault. It's just that I, well, we . . .'

'We?'

'Me and Ravi. We sort of thought, if Mr Case is never going to let Laurel do what she wants with the agency, maybe we should set up an agency of our own; you know, run it the way we think it ought to be run.'

'Oh,' said Laurel, her heart sinking. 'I see.' But she couldn't blame them; they were right. If the D&M ship was headed for the rocks, there was no point in going down with it.

A second figure appeared in the doorway. 'Is it all right if I come in too?'

'Ravi!' exclaimed Laurel. 'Yes, of course it is. But why are you here?'

He drew up a chair. 'Stacey doesn't want to leave,' he explained, 'and the thing is, I never really did either. We've always liked working here.'

'And we like you, too,' added Stacey.

'But when you came here, we thought Mr Case had seen sense at last and there were going to be changes.'

'Only there haven't been.'

'No,' agreed Laurel, 'there haven't. It's not that I haven't tried, but he won't listen – not to me, anyway. All he cares about is keeping everything exactly the way it's always been.'

'Like no computers,' said Stacey. 'And the silly Bakelite telephones.'

'It can't be just about money,' sighed Laurel. 'He won't even let me bring in my own laptop.'

'Things can't stay this way,' said Ravi. 'Not for ever and ever. The agency will just die.'

'I know.'

He warmed to his theme. 'There's so much you could do with a business like this. Take the younger clients – they love the idea of the personal service, but they want modern facilities too, like an interactive website, and keeping in touch with their personal matchmaker by e-mail. And think how much extra time you'd free up for personal contact if all the client details could be held in one big computer database.'

'You're completely right,' nodded Laurel.

'You could link up with similar agencies in other parts of the country,' added Stacey, 'so people could find partners and friends in new areas. And lots of the clients want more lively social events and trips out, plus you could set up a proper friendship service for the older people – that's something you could develop from the penfriend scheme. Lots of older people are getting really interested in the Net, too, so we could launch it online.'

'And these are all things you're planning to do in your new agency?' asked Laurel.

Ravi and Stacey exchanged looks. 'We were,' said Stacey. 'Ravi's really good with computers, and I think I'm quite good with the clients. We thought we'd set it up in my spare room.'

'But?' ventured Laurel.

'But we'd rather do it here,' said Ravi. 'As part of D&M. Only I don't suppose . . .'

'What?'

300

'I don't suppose you'd want me back even if you could make the changes you'd like to make.'

'Which she can't,' interjected Stacey, fingering the envelope on the desk. ''Cause Mr Case won't let her. Not in a month of Sundays.'

'You know something?' Laurel took the envelope from Stacey's hand, threw it at the waste-paper basket and scored a direct hit. 'That's just where you're wrong.'

Stacey's eyes widened. 'What do you mean?'

'You'll have to trust me,' replied Laurel. 'That's all I can say right now. But I promise you, things around here are going to change.'

'These pigeons are getting awfully fat,' commented Laurel as she and Steph sat on the Promenade, throwing lumps of fruit cake. 'That one over there looks as if it's about to have a coronary.'

Steph grunted monosyllabically, and flicked a sultana across the pavement.

'You do realise this is getting to be a ritual?' Laurel went on. 'If we keep coming here every lunchtime the Council will put up a blue plaque and decorate us with hanging baskets.'

'Hmm.'

'Oh Steph,' groaned Laurel, 'this Gabriel thing is only making you miserable. Why don't you give it up?'

'Because I just can't,' replied Steph. 'Not yet. Not until I know for sure what's going on.'

Bette was no fool. What was more, she might be loud, overbearing and severely allergic to romance, but that didn't mean she was completely devoid of a sensitive side. And as soon as Stacey told her all about Ravi's imminent return to D&M, she put two and two together and realised what must be in Laurel's mind. Well, what Edwin didn't know about he couldn't mess up, could he?

Good on you Laurel, she thought to herself as she slipped out of bed, leaving Jack snoring like a fat hippo, sprawled across the sheets in his striped winceyette pyjamas. Good on you for being your own woman, and for putting two fingers up to the men who want to mess up your life. Good on you for not being like me. Married at sixteen, it had taken her six years and three kids to realise that Jack was not in fact strong and silent, but simply said nothing because he had nothing to say. It had been like that for over thirty years now, and she'd come to the bitter realisation that material comfort was the biggest trap of all. Sometimes she despised herself for it, but the unpalatable truth was, you could put up with an awful lot of Jack in return for a chance of your own Gold Cup winner.

Downstairs, the house was in semi-darkness, with dawn just coming up over the surrounding hills. Somewhere in the distance a horse whinnied. Bette padded into the kitchen in her slippers, picked her mobile off the worktop and dialled up Edwin's number.

He answered within seconds, just as she'd known he would. Men like Edwin Case didn't waste time sleeping when they could be out making money or evicting orphans.

'Case.'

302

She put on the special smiley voice that seemed to work wonders for Laurel on problem clients. 'Guess who.'

'Bette! Well well, to what do I owe the honour?'

'How'd you fancy a long weekend away – just the two of us?'

'You saucy little minx.' She heard an amused intake of breath on the other end of the line. 'You're not telling me that appalling husband of yours is actually letting you off the leash for a few days?'

Edwin's sneering tone irritated her. OK, so Jack might be a bloody useless husband but that was for her to say and nobody else. Nevertheless, she managed to keep smiling after all, this was for the agency's sake, not hers and certainly not Edwin's.

'How're you fixed for the weekend of the twentieth?'

'By Jove Bette, I thought you were having me on!'

Impatiently, Bette drummed her fingers on the worktop, hoping Jack didn't choose that morning to wake up early. 'The twentieth, Edwin: yes or no? Jack's got a donkey show in Wales.' He hadn't, but she'd make darned sure he had by the time the twentieth came round.

'Well, yes, I think that weekend's free. Hang on though – that's the weekend of the D&M social.'

'So?'

'I can't possibly miss one of our socials, I always go along. You know that. Got to keep an eye on the troops, what? Encourage the chaps, that kind of thing.'

'But Edwin,' purred Bette, dredging up everything she'd ever learned from Marilyn Monroe films, 'we might not get another chance like this for months – maybe even years. And I'm sure Miss Page can manage the social perfectly well.'

'Hmm. I don't know.'

'Anyhow, hardly anybody ever turns up, do they? Think about it – a discreet hotel somewhere, just the two of us.'

'It *is* tempting,' he admitted.

She sensed he was weakening, so she went in for the kill. 'I could bring along that kinky little leather bridle you bought me . . .'

How could he possibly resist an offer like that?

The Eviscerated Cow: now that was a proper Gloucestershire pub, and no mistake. Tucked away down a foetid alleyway behind the bus station, it boasted a lurid sign that drove tourists screaming to the nearest Irish theme bar, not to mention a death mask of Red Rum and a landlord with eleven fingers.

How Laurel and Steph had fetched up there on a Friday night was anybody's guess.

'All right,' announced Steph, picking the dried scum off the edge of her glass, 'I give up.'

A choir of angels sang hosannas in Laurel's head. 'You mean – you're actually going to stop following Gabriel all over Gloucestershire?'

Steph nodded.

Laurel beamed. 'You mean I can start putting blusher on again, instead of burnt cork?'

'Don't push it,' growled Steph. 'I'm only giving up because I've run out of ideas.'

304

'True, but we've been following him for days now,' pointed out Laurel, 'and he hasn't done anything interesting at all. Not even slightly less than dull.'

This was very true. There could be few less stimulating occupations than crouching in a car watching somebody buy twenty-five litres of white emulsion paint and a spanner.

'So what now?' asked Laurel brightly. 'Are you going to come straight out and ask him about his mystery blonde?'

Steph opened her mouth to answer, but just as the words were rising to her throat she caught sight of a small, curiously buoyant figure walking past the outside of the pub. 'That's her!' she exclaimed, scrambling to her feet and knocking over her chair. 'The tart with the boob job!'

'So what?' Laurel held her glass up to the light, marvelling at the sight of a beer so cloudy it was practically chewy. 'You've given up, remember?'

'Bollocks to that. I only said I'd given up following Gabriel; I never said anything about *her*.'

'But—'

'Come on Lozzie, get a move on or we'll never catch up with her!'

The blonde with the boob job wasn't an easy person to follow.

For a start she had the knack of walking fast in four-inch heels. To make matters worse, it had rained since they'd been in the pub, and the pavements were slippery.

'Come on Steph,' urged Laurel, barely keeping up as the blonde rounded the corner. 'She's getting away.'

'All right. I'm. Going as fast. (Gasp.) As. I. (Gasp.) Can.' Steph wheezed her way to the corner while Laurel bounced on the spot like Roobarb on acid.

'This was all your idea,' Laurel reminded her.

Steph threw her a look that said more than words ever could – well, polite ones anyway. 'Where'd. She. Go?'

'That way.' Laurel pointed at a receding figure heading along the High Street. 'Come on. My God, you're out of condition,' she added as she hauled Steph along. 'I thought sex was supposed to keep you fit.'

'Bits of me are very fit!' protested Steph.

'I won't ask which bits. Oh bugger.'

'What?'

'She's getting into that purple Porsche. I guess this is where we give up,' Laurel added hopefully.

'Not bloody likely!' retorted Steph. 'Look, there's a taxi rank over there.' Marching over to the first cab in the line, she wrenched open the door and uttered the words she'd always wanted to use: 'Driver – follow that car!'

Laurel and Steph had been standing outside in the drizzle for a good half-hour.

'Steph,' pleaded Laurel, 'can we please do something? Like go home?'

Steph scowled up at the first-floor window of the mews cottage, its oblong of yellowish light stark against the surrounding darkness. 'She's in there,' she spat. 'With him.'

'We don't know that for sure,' objected Laurel.

'Lozzie, he *lives* around here, he told me. And we saw her go in.' Her scowl deepened. 'He won't invite me back there, but she's got her own bloody key!'

'Yes, but we don't know for sure that they're living together.'

Steph looked at her pityingly. 'Oh come on.'

Laurel had to admit it didn't look good. 'All right then,' she admitted, 'so she's probably in there with him and they're probably not playing Monopoly. But standing out here in the rain's not going to do anything except give us pneumonia. So why don't we just—'

'You're right,' cut in Steph, shaking the limp tendrils of hair out of her eyes.

'I am?' Thank the Lord, thought Laurel; and reached for her mobile to call a taxi. But Steph had other ideas.

'Yes, you are. Come on, Lozzie. We're going in.'

Steph shot straight across the road like a trouble-seeking missile, Laurel in reluctant pursuit. 'Steph, it's after midnight, you can't just barge in there.'

'Yes I can.'

'Why don't we come back in the morning?'

Steph shook off her restraining hand and dived for the front door. 'Come on, come on,' she muttered through clenched teeth as she played Morse code with the doorbell. 'Put her down and open up, you sonofa-bitch!'

A light clicked on in the hallway, and Laurel heard the safety chain rattling. As the door juddered open, she held her breath and waited for the sound of fist on nose.

In the event it was the chest that emerged first, followed several seconds later by the rest of the blonde, fully clothed and looking severely annoyed. 'Look, I've told you bloody kids before, if I—'

She stopped and stared at Steph. Steph glared back. Laurel cringed.

'Who the heck are you?' demanded the blonde.

Steph didn't bother with introductions. She just elbowed her way straight in past the owner of the chest. 'Where is he? Where's the bastard hiding?'

'Hey!' protested the blonde, pursuing Steph as she ran up the stairs. 'You can't go up there!'

But Steph already had.

Gabriel looked even better without any clothes on; though Laurel wished she'd arrived on the scene a couple of seconds earlier, before he'd had a chance to clutch that pillow to his groin.

'Steph!' he gasped, backing away until the bedroom window cut off his retreat and his bare buttocks were on display to the whole of Marriott Street.

'Whatever it is, Gabriel,' said Steph icily, 'it's not going to be good enough, so I wouldn't bother saying it if I were you.'

The blonde's breasts arrived at the gallop. 'What the *hell* do you mean, barging your way into my house?'

Steph wheeled round. '*Your* house?'

'Minette,' whimpered Gabriel, 'tell her to put that candlestick down.'

Minette looked at him despairingly. 'God, you're pathetic.' Stalking over to the CD player on the dressing table, she turned off 'In the Navy', which struck Laurel as an odd soundtrack for a seduction scene. Still, it took all sorts. 'Yes ladies, *my* house. And if you'll be good enough to put down my candlestick and get *out* of my house, I won't have to call the police.'

In the sudden silence that ensued, Steph lowered her weapon with obvious reluctance. 'What's she on about?'

Gabriel slid along to the armchair and made a grab for his bathrobe, and Laurel couldn't help noticing that he was covered all over with oil. It didn't half show off his muscles, and what lovely muscles they were.

'It's her house, we share it,' he said. 'I'm her lodger.'

Steph's eyes narrowed. Clearly, she had heard that one before.

'Steph, she's my manager, for God's sake!' he blurted out; and he turned crimson under his all-over tan.

'And this is?' enquired Minette icily.

'My . . . er . . . girlfriend.'

Minette did not look best pleased. In fact her lip visibly curled. 'What – both of them? How energetic of you.'

'Don't be stupid! No, just Steph.'

'Your manager?' By now, Laurel was completely baffled. 'What do you need a manager for? You're a decorator.'

Minette laughed. 'Is that what you've told her?'

'I *am* a decorator!' protested Gabriel. 'Most of the time.'

'And when you're not?' demanded Steph.

'Gabriel's an exotic performance artiste,' purred Minette. 'And a very talented one at that. You should see his *Top Gun* routine.'

'He's a what!'

Gabriel's crimson complexion turned scarlet. 'A stripper,' he mumbled. 'I'm a male stripper, OK? That's what I was going when you barged in – practising my new routine.'

Steph looked suspiciously at Minette. Laurel gazed wonderingly at Gabriel. Minette stood with her arms folded, tapping her foot.

'So she's really your manager?' said Steph.

'Yes.'

'*Just* your manager?'

Gabriel and Minette exchanged looks. 'Yes,' said Gabriel emphatically, at the exact moment that Minette said, 'No.'

'Which?' demanded Steph.

'We did have a bit of a thing once,' Gabriel conceded, 'but it was over ages ago. And it was never anything serious anyway.'

'What!' protested Minette.

'Well it wasn't! We only went out twice, and it was a disaster.'

'What about the sacred bond between a manager and her protégé!'

'Sacred bond? Yeah, between you and your ten per cent. And while we're on the subject,' he added, knotting the belt on his robe much to Laurel's disappointment, 'accusing me of shagging every woman I look at isn't the greatest way to build up a stripper's career.'

'I'm just protecting you from sexual exploitation!'

Gabriel's head sank beneath his shoulders. 'You can see why I didn't tell her about you,' he said.

'I can see a lot of things,' replied Steph. Bending down, she picked up a crumpled scrap of fabric between finger and thumb. 'Oh my God, Lozzie, I've been going out with a man who wears faux-leopardskin thongs.'

'Only for work,' protested Gabriel.

Chapter 25

'Right', said Bette, marching into Laurel's office un-announced on Monday morning. 'I won't beat about the bush. I'm getting Edwin Case well out of the way for the weekend of the twentieth, so whatever it is you're planning on doing at the social, you won't have him poking his nose in.'

This took a few seconds for this to sink in. 'What do you mean, getting him out of the way?'

Bette thrust her hands into the pockets of her ubiquitous quilted waistcoat. 'Long weekend away, discreet hotel, him and me.'

Laurel's mind started boggling big-time. 'You. And *Edwin Case*?'

'We've got this . . . long-standing arrangement. Don't look at me like that,' added Bette combatively. 'I may be long in the tooth but I can still go the distance.'

'I never said you couldn't.'

'Besides, he may be an old bastard but at least he's not a gelding like my Jack.' Bette fixed Laurel with a purposeful stare. 'Anyhow, while I'm thinking of

England just you make the most of the opportunity, got that?'

Laurel pushed her teacup away from her. 'Why are you doing this?' she enquired, wonderingly. The thought that anyone could bear to go on a dirty weekend with Edwin Case had quite put her off her digestives.

'For the agency. And because if there's one thing I hate it's a cheat and a bad loser.' Bette dragged up a chair and sat down. 'You do realise he's only told you half the story, don't you?'

'What story?'

'All that rubbish about wanting to keep D&M exactly the way his mother ran it, for sentimental reasons.'

'I've always thought that was a bit weird,' admitted Laurel. 'I mean, he's never struck me as the sentimental type – but what other reason would he have?'

'The only one that matters to him: money. I take it he never bothered to tell you about his mother's will?' Bette could see from the look on Laurel's face that he hadn't. 'Well, when she died it turned out that if Edwin didn't keep D&M running just the way she'd run it for a full calendar year, he wouldn't inherit the rest of her estate. And believe me,' added Bette, 'when I say "estate", we're not talking three hundred quid in a biscuit tin.'

Laurel's eyebrows lifted. 'So that's why he's got this thing about computers and orange filing cabinets?'

'Exactly. All that guff about keeping his mother's spirit alive makes me sick.'

'So why doesn't he just run the place himself?'

'Because he can't be bothered, that's why. He's always hated D&M, and his mother knew it. Do you know what he calls the clients?' Bette leaned over the desk. '"Pathetic halfwits and losers"! And that's when he's being polite.'

'Good God!'

'So when he heard about this really good manager who was desperate to get out of the dot com industry and get into something where she could use the old-fashioned personal touch ...'

'He thought of me.'

'Exactly. And just to make sure you said yes to his crap salary, he promised to sell you the agency at a bargain price if you did what he wanted for a year.'

The penny had definitely dropped. 'But he had his fingers crossed behind his back, is that what you're saying?'

'After a year is up, if I know him at all, he'll just sell to the highest bidder. Did he put anything in writing?'

Laurel sighed and sat back in her chair. 'Of course he didn't. But we shook on it. Cheating git.'

Bette got up. 'Now you're learning.'

'Thank you Bette,' Laurel called after her as she strode out of the office, leaving behind the faint, erotic aroma of horse liniment. And Laurel added in the silence of her thoughts: Thanks for making up my mind.

There was more to life than Gabriel. Much more. All right, so it was difficult not to dwell on the enticing image of his rippling pecs, but now there was something even stronger surfacing through the muddle of her mind: a new focus. Even her mum had noticed a change of tone in her e-mails – and had started accusing her of having a secret sex life.

But it wasn't sex that was making her feel this good. It was the old killer business instinct she thought she'd lost long ago. Edwin Case wasn't going to know what had hit him.

Of course, you couldn't work on business strategies twenty-four hours a day. Which was why Laurel was doing power yoga on her living-room carpet, while Neil wiggled his fins in time to her whale music CD.

Empty your mind, she told herself. No, I said empty it, not think about Gabriel! But the floodgates were open now and she couldn't help wondering if he and Steph had sorted themselves out. Had Steph come to terms with Gabriel's 'artistic' sideline? Was he, even now, giving Steph her own private viewing?

Whether he was or not was frankly irrelevant. As far as she was concerned, Gabriel was history; no, not even that, since he'd never been anything but a fantasy in the first place. (A fantasy for most of the women of Cheltenham it would seem, given what they'd now discovered about his true profession.) I should get myself a man of my own, she decided. Hey, maybe I should stick a pin in Steph's black book and pick myself another blind date. Then again, maybe not.

Thoughtfully she wrapped one foot round the back of her neck. Her mind drifted but didn't get far off the image of Gabriel in his leopardskin thong gyrating and . . .

Ow!

316

Lifting up her second leg, she lost her balance, toppled sideways, knocked over the coffee table – and ricked her neck.

'Don't you dare laugh!' she warned Neil. But it was too late: the water in his tank was already quivering with mirth.

Fortunately Laurel's chiropractor did early-morning appointments, but even so it was almost ten by the time she got to work the next morning.

Head still painfully cocked to one side, she pushed open the office door and received a yellow beanbag duck smack on the nose.

'Oh heck, I'm really sorry.' Kathy rushed over and retrieved the duck from Ravi's in-tray. 'Is there something wrong with your neck?'

'No, I always walk around like this.' Slowly and painfully, Laurel creaked her head back into vertical. Things looked a little less wonky the right way up, but her eyes hadn't deceived her: the office was indeed aswarm with small children. When she did manage to comment, it was only to state the obvious. 'There are kids! Everywhere!'

'One of the toilets has flooded downstairs,' explained Kathy, deftly extracting a toddler's head from a wastepaper basket. 'Stacey said we could move some of the children up here.'

'It's only for an hour or so,' cut in Stacey, who was wiping mashed banana off her telephone receiver, 'till their mums and dads collect them. They won't be any trouble.'

317

Kathy was more of a realist. 'I know it's not ideal, and I'm really, really sorry. I mean, I know it wouldn't go down well with Mr Case if he found out about it.'

'No it wouldn't, would it?' mused Laurel. And her face broke into a broad grin. 'Carry on Kathy. No problem. Stay as long as you like.'

That afternoon, Laurel stopped by Stacey's desk. 'Busy?'

'Not too bad', replied Stacey. 'Me and Ravi have more or less caught up with that backlog of applications from last week.'

'That's good,' said Laurel, 'because I've got a little job for you. You remember that dance band Mr Case got you to book?'

Stacey's nose wrinkled in disgust. 'Those awful old men in sequinned straw boaters? He has them every time, it's no wonder nobody ever comes. The one on the tuba can't even play in tune. What about them?'

'I want you to ring up their manager and cancel.'

Stacey's jaw dropped. 'Cancel! But why?'

'Tell them ... tell them Mr Case has decided to go with something a little different this time around.'

'Mr Case has changed his mind?' Stacey was flabbergasted. 'But he never changes his mind!'

Laurel tapped the side of her nose knowingly. 'You know that, and I know that, but they don't. And as long as Mr Case doesn't find out we've cancelled his precious band it doesn't matter, does it?'

318

'But if we're not having the dance band, what are we going to have?'

Laurel beamed. 'Fun.'

Later that afternoon, while Stacey was phoning round clients telling them that the D&M social was going to be an Eighties Night, Laurel dug out her old address book. It didn't take her long to find the number she wanted.

'Dawn Fraser, *Cotswolds Today*.'

'Hi Dawn, it's Laurel. Laurel Page.'

'Laurel! My God, it's been *ages*! Where on earth have you been?'

It didn't seem like a good idea to say 'hiding from the world', so Laurel simply replied, 'Oh, round and about. You're still at the same magazine then?'

'Yeah, still writing business features for my sins. I tried contacting you through InterPosy, but they said you'd moved on.'

'You know what it's like, I just felt like a change. I'm running a dating agency now.'

'Wow, that's different! Any sexy blokes?'

'Oh, one or two. Actually, I was thinking – do you fancy lunch sometime? On me?'

'Blimey, the dating game pays well then does it?'

'Let's just say there's this upcoming event you might just be interested in covering . . .'

'Evening Stan, evening Jenna, evening Mark.'

All in all, it had been a busy old week, and by Friday night Laurel was definitely ready for a bit of downtime.

What better than a return darts match against the Feathers?

'Evening Laurel,' they all chorused back. 'Blimey Mark, you're not playing her tonight are you? She's lethal.'

'Had to, mate. Terry's broken down on the M40 and Lin's off having her varicose veins done.'

There was an audible hush as Laurel walked up to the oche. Frankly, it was hard to tell who was more worried: the Feathers team or her own. Heads ducked all round the public bar as she drew back her arm and let fly with the first dart.

When it flew smack into the bullseye, everyone put it down to pure luck. By the time she'd done the same thing three times in succession, they knew it had to be either black magic or something in the beer.

'Oi Alan,' said Len, plonking his half-empty pint glass on the bar. 'You can ditch the rest of this. I'll have whatever she's having.'

Chapter 26

It was a high-precision military operation, requiring split-second timing. A moment's hesitation and all could be lost – or if not all, the top of a finger at least.

Killer glared out from his tank in the D&M office, teeth glinting in the sunlight, defying all comers to take him alive. On one side stood Ravi, wearing leathers and a motorbike helmet, and holding a chunk of raw steak temptingly poised in a pair of barbecue tongs. On the other was Lothar, the man from the zoo: six and a half feet of Teutonic muscle armed with goggles, Teflon gauntlets and what looked like the reinforced wire basket from a chip pan.

'The ordinary fishing net is no good at all for ziss species,' explained Lothar. 'Their teeth are capable of penetrating steel plate, you know,' he added, and Ravi retreated a further foot, much to the displeasure of Killer, who was not at all happy to be seeing his lunch receding into the distance. 'Now, *mein* little fish, you come to papa, *ja*?'

'Should I be doing anything?' enquired Laurel, marvelling at the thought that anyone might want to be Killer's papa.

'You can have my job if you want,' said Ravi, his voice muffled by the visor.

'Please to wave ze steak about – *nein, nein*, closer to ze glass,' urged Lothar. 'We must drive him into a frenzy, so that he does not notice me sneaking up on him, *ja*?'

Ravi dutifully waggled his piece of steak; the fish eyed him up, then the steak, then went and skulked in the corner of his tank, there to chew on his big rock and make horrible rasping sounds.

'Well that went well,' commented Laurel.

'Do not worry,' replied Lothar. 'We have many scientific techniques.' He reached into a bag and handed a brown plastic fish to Ravi, 'Please to wiggle this in a seductive manner.'

The phone range. It's for you Laurel,' Stacey called out. 'Graeme Lillee. Shall I tell him you're too busy?'

Laurel felt a warm, pink rush of niceness. 'It's OK, I'll take it in my office.' As she went inside, she heard Ravi saying 'How the hell am I supposed to know what a sexy fish looks like?'; then she closed the door and picked up the receiver. 'Graeme?'

'Laurel, hi. Sorry I haven't been in touch sooner, but the blue whale turned out trickier than I expected. The state of the articulation was appaling, and you wouldn't believe what they'd stuffed the skin with.' He laughed. 'But you don't want to hear about my wonky whale.'

322

Yes I do, thought Laurel, surprising herself. 'Is it finished now then?'

'Almost. Only they liked what I did, and now they've got me working on a lopsided elk.'

'Oh,' said Laurel. 'So you're staying up there then?'

'For a little while.'

'Oh well.'

'But I'll definitely be back for the D&M social.'

'You will?'

He laughed. 'What's all this about an Eighties Night? I can't believe Mr Case is letting you do something so ... trendy!'

Just as Laurel was about to say, 'Don't tell anyone but actually he isn't,' there was a shout and a splash from the main office. With a hasty goodbye, Laurel put down the phone and stuck her head out to have a look. There on his back in the middle of the floor, thrashing about for all he was worth, was Ravi, a psychotic fish firmly attached to the visor of his helmet.

Ravi's muffled cries grew louder. 'Get him off! Get the bastard off me!'

'The little fellow jumped straight out of ze tank,' chuckled Lothar, unlocking Killer's teeth from the remains of the visor, scooping him into the wire basket and then into his new reinforced travelling tank. 'What a little rascal, *ja*? I think he is in love!'

'More pizza anybody?' Alex passed round the box and everybody helped themselves to a chunk.

It might not be the most sophisticated dinner party in the world, but the company was good and Stacey's sofas were soft and snuggly. Besides, this was supposed to be a working dinner.

Ravi tossed a crisp in the air and caught it in his teeth. 'I've been on to the caterers,' he said. 'They say can they have approximate numbers two days before.'

'Hmm, well, we can try,' replied Laurel. 'But we won't really know how many are turning up until they do.'

'Or don't,' pointed out Connie.

'Bad girl, Connie!' Stacey scolded her, wriggling into the tiny gap between Ravi and the arm of the sofa. 'Don't be such a pessimist.'

'It's not allowed,' agreed Alex, helping herself to the biggest piece of pepperoni on Ravi's slice of pizza.

'Quite right,' agreed Laurel. 'This social is going to be a success if it kills me.' Not that it'll have to try very hard, she reminded herself; 'cause Edwin Case will probably do the job himself. The main thing was that he didn't find out until it was too late. 'Now, what about the balloons?'

Stacey consulted her list. 'Pink and silver, six dozen, ready inflated. And they're throwing in a couple of glittery pink hearts free of charge.'

'Sound system?'

'There are people at the venue who'll set it up for us.' Ravi took another bite of pizza and tendrils of melted mozzarella dangled like tentacles from his munching jaws. 'But the new band might want to bring their own equipment.'

Ah yes, the all-important band. 'You're absolutely sure they're coming?'

'Definitely,' nodded Ravi. 'Their manager promised they'd be there.'

'As long as their flight down from Aberdeen isn't delayed,' remarked Connie glumly.

Laurel directed a hard stare at Connie across Stacey's glass topped coffee-table. 'Hey, you. Positive thinking, remember?'

'Sorry.' Connie straightened her slumping spine. 'Force of habit. It's all going so smoothly, I just keep thinking something's bound to go horribly wrong.'

'We won't let it!' declared Alex, raising her glass of sparkling apple juice. 'Will we, Auntie Stacey?'

'Not flipping likely,' laughed Stacey. And they all drank a toast to success.

Thursday night was usually Bette's bridge night, but on this particular Thursday she'd decided to make an exception. In any case, if she was brutally honest with herself she'd only taken up the bloody game as an excuse to get away from Jack for a few hours.

She was already waiting in the bar of the Merry Hind when Connie arrived, darting nervous glances to right and left. 'What on earth's the matter with you, girl?'

Connie slunk across to Bette's table and sat down. 'I don't know how you can come into pubs by yourself,' she said reprovingly. 'I mean it's not nice, is it? A woman on her own.'

'Oh for God's sake!' Bette tossed half a double gin down her throat. 'Stop living in the Dark Ages and relax.' She stood up. 'Gin? Martini? Bloody Mary?'

'I don't want a drink, I just want you to tell me what this is all about.'

'Double brandy is it then.' Connie's mouth opened. 'Shut up and listen to your big sister for once in your life.'

Bette returned a couple of minutes later with a large glass of brandy. 'Right. Drink that and listen carefully. One: I'm sorry I tore you off a strip that time in the office. Not about work, you deserved that, I mean about what's-his-name. Joe.'

Connie's eyes widened. 'You're *apologising*?'

'Yes, yes, all right, so I'm apologising. No need to make a song and dance about it.' For once in her life Bette looked genuinely uncomfortable. 'Two: I've brought you here to talk some sense into you about your love life.'

This was altogether laughable. '*You* of all people? Lecture me about that?' Connie sniggered. 'Now I've heard everything.'

Bette gritted her teeth. 'Just because I've made a hash of my own life, that doesn't mean I can't stop you doing the same. And the way you're heading, my girl, you're going to do exactly that.'

'What's that supposed to mean?'

'It means, stop dithering for once in your life. This man of yours. Joe—'

'Before you say anything. I've already told him not to write to me any more. So you've got what you wanted, haven't you?'

Bette sighed. 'Yes, well, maybe I was wrong about that. You're still hankering after him, aren't you? And

326

don't say no, you've been as miserable as sin ever since you kicked him into touch.'

'What are you saying?'

'Drink your brandy and be quiet. What I'm saying is, stop dithering and do something. If you want him, tell him. See him. Bed him if that's what you want. It'll either be the romance of the century or it won't. Either way you'll get him out of your system.'

'And then what?' demanded Connie.

'And then you can move on with your life.'

Don had been psyching himself up all week to do this. But now it was Friday afternoon, and he didn't feel any less petrified about it than he had on Monday morning, so he reckoned he might as well get it over with.

'Er, hi Connie.' He remembered to smile personably, and had been careful to wear plenty of deodorant to counteract the nervous sweating.

She looked up from her desk as he laid down the proofs of the new D&M brochures. 'You took your time,' she commented. 'I was expecting these on Monday.'

Normally this would have taken the wind out of Don's sails, but today he was determined to see this through. 'Well they're here now,' he pointed out. 'What do you reckon – nice, aren't they?'

She gave them the barest of glances. 'Not bad', she conceded, and went on sorting carbon copies into pink folders. 'What do you want, a prize?'

Don howled silently and longed to lope off with his tail between his legs, but no, that was not going to happen. This time he was going to succeed. 'Forecast's good for the weekend,' he commented, indicating the sun beaming through the office window.

'Is it?' replied Connie, rather vacantly.

'Got anything planned for Monday?' Don enquired.

'Monday?'

'It's a bank holiday, remember?'

'What?'

'Monday. It's a bank holiday on Monday.'

At least this time she looked up briefly. 'Is it? Oh yes, I suppose it is.' But her thoughts seemed somewhere else. Still, there was no point giving up when he'd got this far.

'I was wondering ...' Big deep breath, be brave, believe in yourself. 'I told you about my wee son Callum? His mother died a few years back, so I look after him on my own now.'

Connie grunted.

'Would you like to come out with us on Monday? I promised him we could go to the seaside for the day, maybe take a picnic. Or something.'

'That's nice.'

'He's a good wee boy, you'd like him I'm sure ...'

His voice tailed off as Connie wandered off mid-sentence and disappeared through the door into Laurel's office. Her voice floated back at him just before she vanished from sight. 'Leave the door open on your way out, it's really stifling in here.'

Maybe I should go in to the office and shift a bit of correspondent, mused Laurel as she sat at a pavement

328

café on the Promenade, toying with a hazelnut latte. Or water the plants or feed the fish or something.

But it was no good: the plants didn't need watering, the letters could wait, and Killer had gone off to his new triple-thickness tank at the Animal Experience. You're making excuses again Laurel, she scolded herself. It's August Bank Holiday for goodness sake! Chill out, have another strawberry tart, watch the world go by.

Mmm, he's nice. A thirty-something in cool blue casuals strolled past, jacket slung over his shoulder, and she automatically ticked everything off on her mental list. Tall, blond, slim, twinkly grey eyes: check. No visible wedding ring: check. Muscles to die for: check. No copy of *Gay Times* under his arm . . .

She lounged artistically in her chair, smiled and showed a bit more leg. But her heart wasn't in it and when he walked past without so much as a hello, she was almost relieved. Oh come on Loz, she urged herself: you're supposed to be getting yourself a man, remember? There are loads of them out there, and that last one was absolutely . . .

Perfect.

Only he wasn't, was he? None of them were. Oh, lots of them had all the things she *thought* she wanted in a man; but whenever she closed her eyes and thought 'sexy', the unwelcome image that still sprang into view every single time was that of Gabriel.

It was downright annoying, and worse, it didn't make any sense – she was over Gabriel. OVER him! Especially now she'd discovered his extremely tacky sideline. How could she still fancy a man who took more care over his appearance than she did? The trouble was, someone had forgotten to tell that to her libido. And until she could evict him once and for all from her thoughts, how on earth was anybody else going to get a look in?

'And that's another thing,' moaned Connie's dad as he stomped in from the front garden and slammed the door behind him, 'when are you going to redecorate my bedroom?'

'Soon,' replied Connie, counting to ten. 'Oh Dad, do you have to tread mud all over everywhere?'

'It's not mud, it's good clean compost. And you always say soon, it's all you ever say. You've been saying soon since Adam was a lad and does it ever get done? Does it hell.'

Ten became twenty. She didn't want another row with her dad, not now when she had something important to do and was afraid she'd bottle out if she didn't do it right away. 'I've been busy at work, Dad, you know I have. And there's the assignments for my OU course.'

Dad sniffed contemptuously. 'Dunno what you're bothering with that for, wasting money you could be spending on some decent wallpaper. You were thick as a child and you'll be thick till the day you die. Now your sister . . .'

'I'm sorry, Dad, it'll have to wait.' Connie forced herself not to point out to her father that all Bette's O levels had been a complete waste of time, seeing as she'd never had to support herself in her life. She only worked at Dovecote & Marsh because it gave her an excuse to get out of the house and away from her tedious husband. It would have been pointless arguing with Dad anyway: he had a blind spot about Bette and that was all there was to it. 'There's something I need to do on the computer.'

'Bloody computer,' he grumbled as she ran up the stairs, taking them two at a time. 'All the time you spend on that thing, you could have been out finding yourself a decent husband like your sister did.'

'Yes Dad.'

'So when am I getting my new wallpaper then?'

'Soon.'

She shut the door on his incessant complaints, switched on the computer and rehearsed what she was going to say. All the same, her fingers were still trembling as she typed the e-mail to Joe.

Hi Joe, miss you loads, think we should meet. How about the D&M 80s night on the 20th? See you there? C.

She waited a little while, and then the reply flashed up.

Miss you too. It's a date. J.

Chapter 27

'Yes, fine. Whatever. See ya.'

Laurel's end of the line went abruptly dead, and Steph snapped shut her mobile, deep in thought. Something definitely wasn't right with Lozzie again, that much was obvious even to her; the question was, what was it this time?

'More champagne, madame?' enquired the waiter, materialising at her side out of thin air.

'What? Oh yes, go on then. Why not.'

The pale gold liquid fizzed into the champagne flute, its extreme coldness forming a mist of condensation on the outside. Pondering the great Laurel enigma, Steph drew a ring of Xs around the rim of the glass. Love; ah yes, love. People said it made the world go round, and it had certainly featured prominently in Steph's life over the last twenty-odd years. True, it had struck her recently that that might have been lust rather than love – or perhaps a bit of both. At any rate she'd always found the whole thing rather confusing. Up to now.

She thought long and hard, drank a lot of champagne, and when realisation struck, she was so stunned that she quite forgot to flirt with the man two tables away who'd been giving her the eye for the last half-hour. Admittedly Steph wasn't noted for her intellectual swiftness, but she was far from dumb. It was just that sometimes he thought processes liked to travel by the scenic route. And she always, always got there in the end. Only this time, she rather wished she hadn't.

All those stilted conversations she'd had with Lozzie about Gabriel. All that business with the arguments in the wine bar, that time Steph had told her she was going out with him. Lozzie's reluctance to go on that double date, to help Steph follow him around, the fact that she'd blushed beetroot when they'd found him in the buff in his bedroom. Love. She chewed fitfully on the earpiece of her Fiorelli sunglasses. LOVE! Oh my God, she thought; that can't be it. Can it?

Surely Lozzie hadn't got the raging hots for Gabriel. No! Not Lozzie I've-given-up-men-forever Page and ... *Gabriel*? And yet all the signs were there. She'd even been avoiding eye contact with him, for goodness' sake.

Good grief, thought Steph, recalling Laurel's cast-iron willpower, this is serious. Because when Lozzie makes up her mind not to do something, she damned well doesn't do it. If she's allowing herself to fall for Gabriel even a teensy-weensy bit, she really must have it bad.

Maybe one and one wouldn't have added up to four for anybody else, but Steph had never been that good at maths. And suddenly everything started to make a kind of twisted sense.

Thursdays were late-night shopping in Cheltenham, and on these warm August evenings it felt quite daringly continental to be wandering around buying things after six pm.

Laurel's expensive tastes always drew her eventually to the lingerie department at Seuss & Goldsmith, Cheltenham's oldest and most exclusive department store. Whenever chocolate failed as an emotional prop, Laurel always found buying a new pair of pants worked wonders. It was a quiet afternoon in the store, and Laurel was so engrossed in choosing between the Nice Girl knickers, the Bad Girl scanties and the ones that promised a miracle bum-lift, that at first she didn't notice there were any other customers in the department. In fact it wasn't until an assistant asked 'Can I help you?' that she looked up and realised she was speaking to somebody else. And when Laurel realised just who that somebody was, she nearly dropped her Agent Provocateurs into the half-price bin.

'Have you got those in red?' asked Gabriel, holding up a pair of pink pants so tiny that the butterfly-shaped front panel looked barely out of its chrysalis. Laurel spied in fascination from behind a dangly jungle of Wonderbras. Knickers! Gabriel was buying Steph sexy knickers! So their sex life wasn't quite as non-existent as Laurel had been led to believe.

'Sorry, sir, I'm afraid these only come in Snowdrop, Pretty Peach or Sugar Plum. But our Séductrice range, over here, is available in crimson, scarlet and magenta. Does the lady prefer a brief or a thong?'

'A thong,' replied Gabriel.

That's news to me, thought Laurel, recollecting Steph's distaste at the sight of Gabriel's stripping gear. Still, maybe she just doesn't like them on men. And anyway, those aren't the sort of pants that stay on for very long.

'And will sir be buying madam the matching bra?'

'Oh aye, definitely. Have you got the scarlet one in a thirty-four double F?'

The small question mark in Laurel's brain grew to the size of the Eiffel Tower and toppled over. Thirty-four double F? Either Gabriel had a very bizarre idea of Steph's bust measurement, or else he was buying that bra for somebody else. And how many women in Cheltenham took a thirty-four double F? Offhand, Laurel could only think of one likely candidate . . .

'I think so, sir,' smiled the assistant. 'If you could just wait a moment I'll check in the stockroom.'

'Thanks,' said Gabriel, leaning up against the pay desk while the assistant vanished through a white swing door marked Staff Only.

He was gazing placidly into space when Laurel pounced. 'Hello Gabriel. Doing a spot of shopping are we?'

He jumped as though he had just been stung by something nasty. 'Laurel! I didn't see you there.'

336

'No, I know you didn't. But I saw you.'

'I was just—'

'Buying a present for Minette?' Laurel could see from the panic-stricken look on Gabriel's face that she had hit the mark. 'Like her in red underwear, do you?'

Gabriel went very pale under his outdoor-man tan. 'Oh shit. Look, it's her birthday, all right? I can buy her a birthday present, can't I?'

'Does Steph know what kind of birthday presents you buy your ... landlady?' enquired Laurel. It was obvious from Gabriel's tortured expression that she didn't.

'Now hang on a minute.'

'No, don't tell me this is none of my business, because Steph's my mate. And it's obvious there's a bit more than a rent book between you and Minette.' If she'd been more of a bitch, Laurel might have thought 'serve Steph right', but all she could think about was how hurt Steph would be. And no way did Laurel want anyone else to have to go through what she'd been through.

Gabriel sagged unhappily and dragged his fingers through his dark, glossy hair. 'If I tell you, will you keep it to yourself?'

'No promises.'

'All right, so maybe there was – is – something between us. I've been trying to end it for ages, but she won't have it.'

'I'm not surprised if you keep buying her red underwear.'

337

'No, you don't understand. Me and Minette, we've shared a house for years, ever since we were students, but for ages we were just good friends. Then it turned into more but when I wanted to knock it on the head she went all possessive on me.' His dark eyes pleaded with Laurel for sympathy but drew a blank. 'You don't know what it's like – the business is doing badly and I owe her money, so she pushes me into this stripping lark to make the rent. Then she gives me hell if I so much as look at another woman.'

Laurel could hardly believe her ears. 'You're a grown man, Gabriel! Why don't you just move out?'

He ignored the question. 'Any road, things are going bad with Minette. Then my mate Don persuades me to sign on with the agency, and I meet Steph, and I think, I can handle this, I'll find a way to sort things out.'

'Only you haven't, have you?'

He shook his head dolefully. 'Not yet. But I'm working on it.' The glint of panic returned to his eyes. 'Laurel . . . about this . . . You wouldn't go and tell Steph would you?'

'Because if she finds out she'll go ape? Sorry Gabriel, I'm not promising anything.'

Gabriel seized her arm. 'You've got to understand, Steph's really special to me.'

'Yeah, so special you've been cheating on her with Minette. And you're not being fair to Minette either.' She paused. 'Listen Gabriel, even if I did decide not to tell Steph, it'd only be on two conditions. First,

338

you make it clear to Minette once and for all that it's over.'

A glimmer of hope entered Gabriel's eyes. 'And what's the other one?'

'You grow yourself a spine.'

As she walked away she felt an overwhelming sense of relief, like she'd escaped from a fate worse than death. Yes, at last she'd been the real Gabriel Jouet. And the real Gabriel Jouet was a wimp.

At six o'clock in the evening, even the Sydney Vodka House was quiet; curiously in keeping with Steph's muted mood.

''Nother Bloody Mary?' ventured Brent. 'Or you could try our new Italian voddy with basil and oregano?'

'Just a straight vodka on the rocks.' Steph nudged her empty glass across the bar top.

'Man trouble?' Brent reached for the optic.

Steph nodded glumly. 'How can you tell?'

'With you it's always man trouble.'

'God, am I that much of a disaster?'

'Not a disaster.' He grinned as he dropped ice into the glass. 'I prefer to think of it as an adventure. Kind of a rollercoaster ride, know what I mean?'

Steph knew all right. And the way she was feeling, she'd have swapped it for a nice sedate pony ride along the beach. 'It's Gabriel,' she sighed. 'I think he and Laurel are, you know . . .'

Brent's highlighted eyebrows shot up under his straw-coloured fringe. 'What – you mean they're having a bit of the old in-out?'

Steph winced at Brent's turn of phrase. 'No, nothing like that. I just think they've got, you know, feelings for each other. I'm damn sure Laurel's got a thing for Gabriel,' she added, sinking most of the vodka in one. And the more she thought about it, Gabriel's lack of interest in developing a sexual relationship with her might also be down to him fancying her best mate more than her! 'Only she's too much of a mate to say so.'

'Ah, now I get you,' nodded Brent. 'The old eternal triangle.'

'Exactly. The thing is, I've got the feeling I'm, you know, coming between them. If it wasn't for me they could get it together, couldn't they?'

'I suppose they could.' Brent munched on a handful of complimentary macadamia nuts. 'Only – correct me if I'm wrong,' he patted Steph's hand, 'but you don't want to get out of their way, do you? 'Cause you're stuck on Gabriel.'

Steph nodded miserably. Even the revelation about Gabriel's line of work had not deterred her. 'I've got it bad,' she admitted. 'Oh Brent, you're a man. Tell me why I have to fall for the only bloke who's not totally besotted with me.'

Brent shrugged. 'Maybe that's the reason. 'Cause he's not. Maybe it's the challenge.'

Or maybe it's his bum, mused Steph. At any rate, Gabriel had touched something in her that she'd pretty much forgotten existed. And now this. 'What am I going to do, Brent?' she lamented.

Brent polished a sticky mark off the bar top with the hem of his Barrier Reef T-shirt.

'I dunno,' he replied. 'But I guess you could start by working out what's more important to you – your bloke or your best mate.'

Chapter 28

Don drew up a chair and opened his art portfolio. 'This is what I've come up with for the press packs. What d'you reckon?'

Laurel was seriously impressed. 'Hey, brilliant. This all looks really professional.'

He coloured with pleasure. 'Just doing what you pay me for.'

Laurel leafed through the proofs. Press release, brochures, artwork that somehow managed to be traditional and fresh at the same time – and the whole lot enclosed in a natty pink and silver D&M wallet. It got exactly the right message across. Cuddly but efficient; old but new. Now all she had to hope was that the press would actually bother to turn up for her precious Eighties' Night . . .

'It's perfect, really it is.'

'So I'll go ahead and get them printed up then?'

'Oh definitely.' There was a quiet knock at the door. 'Yeah, come in. Oh Kathy, hi!'

Kathy took a couple of steps into the office, then saw

Don and retreated. 'Sorry Laurel, I didn't realise you had someone in. Shall I come back later?'

'No, don't be silly, we're only talking about leaflets and stuff. Don, this is Kathy – she runs the crèche downstairs. Kathy, this is Don, our graphic designer from across the road.'

'Pleased to meet you, Kathy.' The corners of Don's eyes crinkled into a friendly smile, making his face look more than ever like a crumpled paper bag.

'Hi. So you're the clever one who does all the posters and things?'

'Oh, there's nothing very clever about it. These days we've got computers that do everything for you. It's not a proper job like yours, it's more like mucking about!'

'Oh, we can do mucking about,' Kathy assured him. 'You should see the state of our place after we've been doing creative play in the sandpit. Isn't that right, Edward?'

A small blond head appeared from round the back of Kathy's yellow tabard.

'Come on out Edward,' Kathy smiled encouragingly, 'and say hello to Auntie Laurel.'

He looked warily at Laurel, then at Don, as though expecting a frozen placenta to materialise at any moment. 'Hello Auntie Lowwel,' he lisped.

'Hello Edward.'

'Now give her the flowers. That's it, good boy.'

'Lilies!' exclaimed Laurel. 'Thank you Edward! What on earth have I done to deserve these?'

'They're just a little thank-you for letting us take over your office when the loo flooded. Goodness knows how

344

long it took you to clean up afterwards.' Kathy lowered her voice. 'What did you-know-who have to say about it?'

Laurel grinned. 'Mr Case? He doesn't know and I wouldn't much care if he did.'

While Laurel and Kathy were talking, unbeknown to them Edward was busily exploring the adventure playground of Laurel's office. The first they knew about it was when Don suddenly rugby-tackled the aspidistra – just as it was about to fall on Edward's head.

'No!' gasped Kathy, rushing forward.

'It's OK, got it. No harm done. He's like my wee Callum, always into everything.' Don righted himself and the aspidistra, then turned to Edward, who promptly burst into tears. 'Hey, what's up with you big man?' he said gently, squatting down so that the two of them were eye to eye. 'Want to see a wee bit of magic?'

Edward nodded solemnly through his sniffles.

'Look – what's this behind your ear? Hey, it's a ten-pence piece! Wherever did that come from?'

Edward stopped sniffling and took a definite interest.

'And goodness me, what's this?' Don feigned immense surprise as a jelly baby appeared out of Edward's pocket, swiftly followed by a second and a third. Edward giggled with delight.

'Good grief,' said Kathy, with a huge smile in Don's direction. 'Is he freelance? We could do with him downstairs.'

Gabriel was up a ladder outside the Town Hall, scraping the rust off some municipal guttering, when he heard his name being shouted from below.

Peering down between the rungs, he saw Steph. She was wearing the same green silk suit and high heels she'd worn on their first date; the ones that made her look all sexy and dominant.

'Gabriel,' she repeated, 'we need to talk.'

He looked doubtfully at his watch. 'Can it wait?'

'No.'

Reluctantly he climbed down the ladder, shedding a kind of rusty dandruff as he went. 'What's up?' he asked. 'Only if it comes on to rain before I've got the primer on, I'll be in trouble.'

'This won't take long,' Steph promised him. She hoped her smile didn't look too brittle. 'It's been fun, Gabriel, hasn't it?'

'I'm not with you.'

'*Us*,' she said. 'You and me. We've had some fun.'

'We have that,' he agreed. 'In fact I was thinking about this weekend—'

She laid a hand on his. 'No. Not this weekend.'

'Next weekend then?'

'Not next weekend either.'

He frowned. 'What are you getting at, Steph?'

For once, she wished he could be a bit faster on the uptake. It would at least make this a little easier. 'It's over, Gabriel.'

'What!'

'Like I said, it was fun while it lasted, but that was all it was, wasn't it? A bit of fun?'

Gabriel swallowed. 'You're dumping me?'

'That's not a very nice way of putting it.'

346

'What's the point of putting it a nice way?' he retorted. 'Whichever way you put it I'm still dumped.' He sat down heavily on an upturned plastic crate and ran a hand through his hair. 'I don't believe this, it can't be happening.'

'I'm sorry Gabriel, but it had to be said.'

'But why?'

'You know what I'm like,' she breezed. 'I told you – here one day, there the next, never sticking with one man for more than five minutes. I get bored easily Gabriel, it's nothing personal, it's just the way I am.'

'And that's that?'

'That's that.'

'So what happens now?' he demanded.

'I get in that taxi over there,' she pointed, 'and I get on a train and I go ... somewhere. I haven't decided where yet, but it'll be fun.'

Then she turned and headed for the waiting taxi, got quickly inside and drove away without a backward glance.

Because if she hadn't, Gabriel might have noticed that she was crying.

Mercifully, the train was on time; and as she stretched out her legs in first class, Steph at last began to feel her heart rate slowing to something approaching normal.

That had been horrible. Just horrible. If it hadn't been for the dread suspicion that sooner or later Gabriel would have dumped her for Laurel, she'd almost have wondered why she'd put herself through it. But it was done now, and if she cried any more her eyes would go

347

all puffy. And at least she had the warm glow of self-righteousness to bask in. For once she'd done the right thing by Laurel. It reminded her of the time (aged six) when she'd donated her sweet money to the poor orphan children and told everybody she was going to be a nun. *The Sound of Music* had a lot to answer for. And who'd want to end up like Maria von Trapp anyway? Seven million children and a wardrobe full of dirndls? No, the single life: that's the life for me, Steph told herself firmly. I'm going to take some time out just to be me.

She might have slept through the journey if it hadn't been for the strap on her Louis Vuitton bag, innocently trailing into the gangway. Ten minutes out of Kemble, just as they were going round a bend in the track, it snared the ankles of a tall man in a Paul Smith shirt and destiny flung him – quite literally – into her lap.

'Oh God, I'm so sorry, did I hurt you?' He picked himself up, dripping spilt coffee, and set about trying to pick up the bits of bacon and tomato roll off Steph's blouse.

'No, not at all.'

He surveyed his handiwork. 'I'm making this worse, aren't I?'

She gazed up into his eyes the colour of hazelnut syrup, and ran the tip of her tongue over her glossy lips. 'Oh, *much*.'

The hazelnut eyes met hers. 'I'll make it up to you – I'll, er, pay for the dry-cleaning.'

'Tell you what.' She picked up her handbag and stood

348

up. 'There's a bar at the end of this carriage. Why don't you start making it up to me now and buy me a drink?'

Steph was on her third Archer's when her mobile rang.

She excavated it from the bottom of her bag. 'Yeah?'

'Steph, it's me.'

Oh no, Gabriel, that was all she needed. 'Excuse me a minute, bad signal,' she said to her coffee-stained companion, and walked out of earshot. 'What is it?' she asked.

'I've got to know the real reason, Steph.'

'I told you the real reason!'

'No, I don't believe you, there's got to be more to it than that.'

'Well there isn't. Really. Look Gabriel, we've said all there is to say—'

'You mean you have, I've hardly got a word in edge-ways. I want to talk this through.'

'Well I don't.' In her pocket, Steph twisted a tissue round her fingers until it tore.

'But what am I going to do?'

That, at least, was easy. 'You mean you haven't worked that one out yet? For God's sake Gabriel, go and see Laurel.'

'Laurel?'

'Yes, Laurel. I think you two have got a lot to talk about.'

Chapter 29

When Laurel got home that night, the green light was flashing on her answering machine: ONE NEW MESSAGE.

She pressed 'play' and went to say hello to Neil. As she was attempting to coax him out of his plastic castle with some dried shrimps, Steph's voice filled the room.

'Lozzie: Hi, it's me. Forgot to mention, I'm going away for a bit.'

Going away? thought Laurel. Going away where? And why does her voice sound so high-pitched and weird?

'Thought I'd give you and ... and Gabriel a bit of space. It's for the best, you'll see. See ya, lots of love, byee.'

Laurel played back the message three times, but she still couldn't fathom out what was going on. So she called Steph's mobile, but all she got was her voicemail. And it stayed that way right through the whole of the next day.

It was almost as if Steph didn't want to be found.

*

351

Intrigued though she was by Steph's odd behaviour, Laurel had no time to dwell upon it. The night of the twentieth was only five days away, and there were pressing problems that needed attending to.

'Madonna or that girl out of Altered Images?' Stacey held up two blonde wigs for Laurel's inspection.

Laurel was beginning to regret making the Eighties' Night an optional fancy dress event. 'Neither,' she said. 'Your hair looks fine the way it is.'

Stacey looked disappointed. 'But dressing up's half the fun! Besides, it's all right for you, you look like Debbie Harry without even trying.'

Taken aback, Laurel inspected her reflection in the mirror over her office fireplace. 'I do?'

'Of course you do, you're dead glam. Me, I just look like a ginger poodle. So, which one shall I wear?'

Laurel was so taken aback at the thought of being mistaken for a sexual icon – albeit a superannuated one – that she was still trying to think of a reply when a very flustered-looking Connie stuck her head through the door.

'If it's bad new I don't want to know,' Laurel warned her.

'I'll go away then.'

'Go on, out with it,' groaned Laurel. They'd already had a clash with the local cricket club's annual dinner-dance to contend with, not to mention the cloak and dagger stuff of keeping everything from Edwin; what could possibly have gone wrong now?

'It's Mr Case,' said Connie. 'Bette says he's changed his mind about going away for the weekend.'

*

The days rushed past in a haze of panic; and before Laurel knew it, it was already Thursday afternoon.

Laurel never found out exactly what Bette did to persuade Edwin to change his mind back again, but it must be impressive because the next thing she heard, he'd splashed out on two tickets for a romantic weekend break in Prague. Rather you than me Bette, she mused as she rewrote her speech for the tenth time that day; sharing a duvet with Edwin Case was so enormously beyond the call of duty it probably had its own postcode.

Ah well, at least something was going right at last.

The phone rang and Laurel picked it up. 'Dovecote & Marsh, can I help you?'

A broad Scots accent rolled down the line. 'Hi, Milo McGee here – Diamond Ice's manager? I'm just calling up about Saturday night.'

Instinctively, Laurel held her breath. 'They are still coming, aren't they?'

'Oh aye, they're still coming. Well, four of them are.'

'But there's five in the band.'

'Aye, well, Lenny's got a wee problem.'

'What sort of problem?'

'He's broken his arm. Don't suppose you know a decent drummer?'

On Friday afternoon, Laurel stood in her office gazing at her wall-planner and forcing herself to take deep, calming breaths.

Everything was fine, absolutely fine; really it was. The Wellesley Suite at the Regency Imperial Hotel was booked, the balloons were arriving the next morning

353

with the chicken drumsticks, Edwin was safely on a plane to Prague, Laurel's speech was as ready as it would ever be and Ravi had even found a session drummer to stand in for Lenny. There truly was nothing left to worry about.

Well all right; maybe just one thing. What if nobody turned up? She tried to avoid looking at the pathetic pile of RSVP slips in her in-tray. Twelve definites and half a dozen maybes were hardly going to make for a sparkling night of entertainment and romance, particularly since fourteen of the eighteen were women and Laurel had ordered wine and food for a hundred.

Laurel was so deep in thought, she hadn't even noticed Connie coming into the room.

'Don't worry,' she said. 'People are just bad at filling in forms. They'll all turn up on the night.'

Laurel turned and looked at her. 'Promise?'

Connie gave a confident smile and hid her crossed fingers behind her back. 'Promise.'

Saturday evening arrived with the inevitability of a tax demand.

Oh my God, thought Connie as she walked into the hotel bar at the Regency Imperial. What have I done? What am I doing?

Her heart pounded against her ribs as she bought a dry white wine and took refuge in the darkest corner she could find. The clock on the wall said six fifteen. Really she ought to be helping Laurel and the others with last-minute preparations in the Wellesley Suite; perhaps she should abandon this ridiculous escapade and go and do her duty instead.

But no. Laurel didn't need her till seven, and anyway, that would be the easy way out. She'd bottled out too many times already; this time she and Joe were finally going to come face to face.

The thought that he was actually going to see her, albeit in the forgivingly dim lights of the Wellington Bar, made her stomach churn with alarm. Her fingers moved to the face she had spent hours making up; it seemed smooth enough, but Connie knew every microscopic crease, every crow's foot, every fine line that deepened whenever she talked or smiled. Maybe that's why she'd given up smiling much, these last few years.

What on earth is he going to think of me? she agonised, turning her glass round and round in her hands. He's expecting someone fifteen years younger, what if he doesn't even recognise me! And why on earth did I say I'd meet him at the social? If it all goes horribly wrong everyone I know from work will see, and I'll be completely, totally humiliated. She forced herself to be calm, to remember how lovely and considerate and sexy Joe's e-mails always were. Things would be fine; after all, he'd promised that they would. And besides, he'd be here in a minute. No point in getting herself all worked up; she'd had to look her best for her Joe.

Don had walked past the door to the Wellington Bar about fifty times in the last half-hour, but he still hadn't plucked up the courage to go in.

355

He didn't need to look at his watch to know that he was late; hideously late. Six fifteen, that was the time he'd agreed with Connie, and what was it now? Almost a quarter to seven. No wonder every time he'd glanced into the bar he'd seen her looking just a little sadder, just a fraction more despondent.

And it was all his fault.

Why he'd had the stupid idea in the first place was beyond him. What kind of thirty-five-year-old idiot with a kid and an ulcer subtracts a decade from his age and pretends to be fresh out of college? he wondered. An idiot like me. An idiot like Joe. But Connie was the first woman he'd really noticed since he'd lost his wife.

He walked past the door one more time and then he knew he had to go in. Once he'd crossed the threshold it was easier than he'd expected to walk across to Connie's table, but every step still felt like a stab in the heart.

'Hello,' he said.

She looked up at him, and he saw the hope fade from her eyes as she realised it was him. 'Don. Oh.'

'Enjoying the calm before the storm?'

'What?'

He jerked his head in the general direction of the Wellesley Suite. 'The Eighties' Night.'

'Oh. That.' Connie raised her glass and threw the rest of the wine down her throat. 'No, actually I was waiting for somebody. Only he didn't turn up.'

Time seemed to stand suspended in mid-air for just a fraction of a second. A second in which Don so very nearly confessed everything. But before the words had even formed in his brain he realised how pointless that would be. How cruel, even. And so he simply said, 'That's rough.'

She pushed back her chair and stood up. 'Yeah. Well. That's life, isn't it. I'd better go and help Laurel, I guess.'

'I guess.'

'You going tonight?'

He shrugged. 'Yeah, Laurel invited me. Hence the new shirt. Like it?'

Connie eyed its purple frilliness. 'It's horrible.'

'Oh.'

'Ah well, enjoy your evening.' There was a weary bitterness in Connie's voice, and Don realised that he had never in his whole life felt quite so guilty about anything.

He thrust his hands into his trouser pockets. 'I doubt it.'

Connie threw him a departing glance. 'Yeah, well, look on the bright side. At least you haven't been stood up.'

The phone rang at the Happy Nappy, and one of the girls from Oxford leapt to answer it. 'It's for you Kath,' she called. 'Someone called Laurel?'

Kathy looked up from changing a nappy. 'Oh heck, you'd better tell her I'm busy.'

'She says no you're not and you're not getting out of it that easily, whatever that means.'

'Tell her—'

'Tell her yourself.' The girl from Oxford thrust the phone into Kathy's hand. 'It's OK, I'll do the nappy.'

357

'Hi Laurel,' said Kathy.

The sounds of music and laughter forced Laurel to raise her voice. 'I've got a bone to pick with you, young lady. Why aren't you here?'

'Well, I know I did say I'd come but it's a bit mad here, I'm afraid. Don't think they can really spare me.'

'Oh yes we can!' retorted the other girl. 'Go off and enjoy yourself.'

'You heard,' said Laurel. 'If you're not here in half an hour I'm sending out a search party.'

Laurel put her mobile away and turned back to the party. And that's what it was turning into – a proper party, with people actually laughing, eating, talking, dancing! There were even couples out there who'd met and married through Dovecote & Marsh. By some miracle of muddling through, Laurel had managed to do what she'd always wanted to: she'd made people happy.

She could never have hoped for such a good response. The local media had turned out in respectable numbers, and Diamond Ice had even avoided playing their appaling novelty hit. 'I can't believe it, there must be over a hundred here,' she commented to Ravi.

'Nearer a hundred and fifty.' He patted her on the back in a brotherly sort of way. 'Well done, boss.'

'I haven't done anything yet.'

He eyed the speech she was clutching in her hand. 'You will in a minute though.'

She swallowed hard, but the lump in her throat wouldn't go away. 'You think I'm mad, don't you?'

'Completely.' He topped up her wine glass and raised

the bottle of lager in a toast. 'Here's to you – and us eh, Stace?'

Stacey's blue eyes twinkled with happiness. 'Oh look, Laurel – Mr Coxon's dancing with Gemma Brodie! They must be back together again. Isn't that romantic?'

The sight of people hand in hand, under two huge pink and silver doves, brought an unexpected pang of sadness to Laurel's heart. Bringing people together – that's what D&M was all about. About everyone having someone, going through life two by two just like the animals in the Ark. Stacey and Ravi, Mum and Dad, even Gemma Brodie and Mr Coxon.

All except me, she thought with just a twinge of self-pity. Because I don't do two by two, do I? I thought I didn't want that and now I know I do, I've probably left it too late.

For no particular reason, she thought of Graeme. He was so sure he'd be here, she recalled. And he's not. Funny how that matters when really he's nothing to me. Well, just a friend. No, not even that; I mean let's face it, I hardly know the man.

Funnier still how Gabriel's absence hadn't even registered until now. And now that it had, she couldn't have cared less.

Connie came over and laid a hand on Laurel's shoulder. 'It's nearly time,' she said. 'They're giving out the fancy dress prizes in a minute, then you can do you speech.'

Laurel looked at her. 'Are you OK? You're really pale.'

'I'm fine. Just nervous for you.'

Not half as nervous as I am, thought Laurel. But what the hell. She might as well go for it.

Chapter 30

So far, so good. At least nobody had thrown any tomatoes yet.

'I've not been part of the Dovecote & Marsh family for very long,' concluded Laurel, 'but it's come to mean a great deal to me, just as I know it means a lot to all of you.' A ripple of agreement ran round the assembled guests. 'And that's why we've decided to bring in these exciting changes – to make sure we're still here in another hundred years' time.'

Everyone clapped. A reporter from the *Cheltenham Courant* raised his hand. 'Aren't computers the opposite of what D&M stands for?'

'Not at all. We're not turning ourselves into an online dating agency,' she stressed, 'we're staying strictly traditional in spirit. We'll still be the same D&M we've always been – just much more efficient.'

'Will I still have my own personal matchmaker?' asked one elderly lady anxiously.

'Of course you will. The only change you'll notice is

that our services are better than ever. In fact, we're planning to introduce a new—'

'Are these changes Mr Case's idea?' enquired a man in a diamond-patterned Pringle sweater.

Laurel smiled fit to split her head in two. 'Mr Case is one hundred per cent behind anything that makes the business stronger.'

'That's interesting,' said the man. 'Because I'm one of the trustees of his mother's estate, and according to her will—'

Before Laurel had a chance to think 'now talk yourself out of that one', there was a disturbance in the crowd.

'Hey, watch who you're pushing, mate.'

'Get out the bloody road then.' A tall, dark figure pushed its way to the front, elbowed Ravi in the guts and stormed right up to the microphone. 'You told her, didn't you?'

Shock hit Laurel like a bucket of iced water. 'Gabriel!'

The crowd subsided into hushed expectation.

'You told her, you bitch.'

'Told who what?'

'Steph!' he growled, eyes bright with rage. 'Who do you think? After all that crap you sold me about promising to keep quiet, you went and told her all about me and Minette.'

Laurel was completely aghast. 'I never said a word to her about anything!'

'Oh, and you expect me to believe that do you? Well if you didn't tell her, who did? And how come she

362

dumps me and then when I ask her why, she tells me to come and see you?'

He advanced on her, and for the first time Laurel felt afraid. He was big, tall, and very, very angry. 'Wait a minute, Gabriel.' She backed away but found her retreat halted by the edge of the stage. 'Can't we just sit down and talk about this?'

In the audience, a battery of cameras flashed. Oh no, this was all she needed. AGENCY BOSS EXPOSED IN LOVE TANGLE SHOCK, she could see the headline already. Her only comfort was the effect it would have on Edwin Case. 'Gabriel, for goodness' sake!'

Another voice chimed in. 'Gabriel, you bloody idiot, calm down!' It was the seventh cavalry – in the shape of Don. Never had Laurel been more delighted to see someone she owed money to. He placed a restraining hand on Gabriel's shoulder. 'Come on mate, leave the lassie alone, whatever this is about it's not worth fighting about.'

'Don't touch me!' Gabriel swung round, fists flying, and caught Don smack between the eyes. Blood fountained out of his fractured nose, and Don doubled up with a howl of pain. A look of horror washed over Gabriel's face and he fumbled for a handkerchief to stem the bleeding. 'Oh God, Don mate, I didn't mean to.'

'Get away from him, you stupid lump!' Kathy sprang to Don's defence and slipped a protecting arm around his shoulders, oblivious to sticky red stains on her new white top. She snatched at the handkerchief. 'And give me that. Don love, are you all right?'

He moaned wordlessly and blew bloody bubbles. Kathy threw Gabriel a look that spelled 'murder'. 'You're pathetic, you are!' Gabriel shrunk at least six inches. 'Men like you only hit people 'cause they haven't got two brain cells to rub together.' The memory of her childhood surged up like a red tide, and suddenly Dad and Gabriel were one and the horrible same. 'Come here Don, let's get that nose seen to.'

'She lied to me,' protested Gabriel, pointing to Laurel.

Kathy pinched the top of Don's nose and gave him the folded handkerchief to staunch the crimson tide. 'Don't talk crap. If you think somebody like Laurel could be bothered to lie to a waste of space like you, it just shows you're even stupider than you look.'

'Thanks Kathy,' said Laurel. 'I couldn't have put it better myself.'

Unfortunately Laurel didn't have an opportunity to enjoy the look of mortification on Gabriel's face, because the press pack – who up till now had been more interested in eating sausage rolls – had caught the scent of blood and were moving in for the kill.

'Miss Page, would you like to make a comment on—'

'Is it true that you and Mr Case—?'

'What exactly is the nature of your relationship with this man?'

Laurel parried every question with a curt no, but the ladies and gentlemen of the press weren't giving up that easily. Cheltenham hadn't seen a fracas like this since the Guinness ran out in Gold Cup week. Well you've really done it now, she told herself as she backed away towards the door of the Wellesley Suite, the only weapon to hand a half-chewed pork pie. Case wouldn't just not sell her the agency, he'd probably sack her as well.

'We'll hold them back as long as we can,' hissed Stacey as Laurel slipped out of the door.

'Run for it,' urged Connie.

The trouble was, she hadn't a clue where to run to. In fact she wouldn't have stood a chance of escape if Graeme hadn't chosen that precise moment to step out of the lift.

'Graeme!' she panted.

'My train broke down. What's going on?'

'Need to hide, explain later.'

She headed for the lift but he shook his head. 'Got a better idea.' Reaching inside the lift he pressed the button for the eighth floor and the doors closed, leaving them outside. 'This way.'

Grabbing her by the hand, he dragged her round the corner, pulled open a door and pushed her inside. As he bolted it shut, she heard the sounds of feet in the corridor. 'Where's she gone?' 'Buggered if I know.' 'Must've take the lift – come on!'

The running feet retreated.

'Thank you,' whispered Laurel.

'Don't mention it.'

'Where are we?'

'The cupboard where the chambermaids keep all the cleaning stuff. I used to store my tools here when I was restoring their eagle owl.'

'Is there anything in Cheltenham you *haven't* stuffed?'

'Would you care to rephrase that?'

'It's awfully dark in here.'

'Do you want me to switch on the light?'

'No.'

Something really strange is happening to me, thought Laurel. Here I am, locked in a cupboard, missing my own party, I've got a crisis that needs sorting out and I'm probably about to get the sack, and what am I thinking about? Graeme.

OK, so maybe he's not my usual type, she conceded; but Jason and Gabriel were my usual type and look how they turned out. And Graeme's always been there when I needed him, always turned up to rescue me at just the right moment. If there's one thing Dovecote & Marsh has taught me, it's that not all heroes look like Brad Pitt.

Maybe it's time I took a chance on something. On someone . . .

'No,' she repeated, snuggling close to him in the warm, scented darkness. 'I'd really rather you didn't.'

In the distance, the band started playing 'Oops Upside Your Head'. 'What's been going on?' enquired Graeme.

'Nothing much.'

'So why are we hiding from a baying press pack in a broom cupboard?'

It was a good question. 'Well, if you put it that way . . .' Laurel managed a garbled explanation of recent developments. He must think I'm mad, she thought. Stark staring mad.

'I'll say one thing: life's never dull around you, Laurel Page.'

'No,' she agreed.

'I've missed that.' The words hung in the air for a fraction of a second, and then he added. 'I've missed *you*.'

'Really?'

'Truly.'

Laurel was glad he couldn't see her face; she was sure she was blushing. 'It's good to see you too,' she smiled. 'Not that I can actually see you at the moment but . . .' She sniffed the air. 'It smells in here.'

'Oh God, Laurel. I'm really sorry, I thought I'd washed all the—'

She drew his face down to hers. 'It smells of floor polish, Graeme. For the last time, you do not smell!'

'You're absolutely sure about that?'

'Oh shut up and kiss me.' And that was exactly what he did.

Epilogue: one year later, a cottage in Winchcombe

Steph picked another truffle out of the box on the coffee table, and turned the pages of the photograph album. 'This is one hell of a photo collection,' she commented. 'Makes my holiday snaps look dull, and that's saying something.'

'Well some of them are copies from the newspaper. It's not everyone who nearly starts a riot at a dating agency dance,' admitted Laurel, smiling at the one of Kathy delivering a vicious kick to Gabriel's ankle. 'Oh look, there's one of Stacey and Ravi on the day Alex's mum's appeal came through. Don't they look happy?'

Steph sniffed. 'They always look happy, they're like the bloody Tweenies, those two. Even worse than Kathy and Don, and they've been walking around with smiles on their faces for months.' It was amazing how two people could bond in the A&E department. It helped of course that Kathy was such a natural with Don's little boy. She had the family she'd always craved and Don had – at long last – got over his older woman fixation.

'You're just jealous.'

'Of Kathy and Stacey? Darling, I *don't* think so. And as for Connie . . .'

Ah yes, thought Laurel. Connie. On the next page of the album was a picture of Connie and her dad standing outside their house: their immaculately painted and decorated house, with its state-of-the-art kitchen and brand-new conservatory. Laurel still found herself rather surprised by the way Connie and Gabriel had come together, all as a result of her dad's advert for a 'good painter and decorator, must come cheap'. But with a woman of Connie's determination in the picture, Gabriel had finally managed to call time on his relationship with Minette.

Even allowing for the fact that Gabriel and Dad had hit it off like wildfire, Laurel found Connie's choice of life partner bizarre. Still, she supposed even Gabriel deserved to have somebody to love, although that somebody did have a temper and a father who could whinge for Britain. Maybe that's the attraction, she mused: he obviously *likes* being whinged at.

'Connie's done well for herself,' commented Laurel.

Steph's mouth fell open in mid-chew. 'What – Gabriel, you mean?'

'Good grief no! Well . . . yes, I suppose she has in a way. Anyway, he seems to like her bossing him about and her dad thinks the sun shines out of his backside.' She shook her head. 'I still can't believe you dumped him because you thought he and I—'

'Well, you did fancy him,' Steph reminded her.

'Yes, well, that was before I realised what he was really like. Anyway, what I meant to say was, Connie's done well since she stepped in as a temporary manager of D&M. She's a natural organiser.'

Steph wriggled her shoes off and put her feet up on the coffee table. 'You still haven't told me *exactly* what happened with you and old man Case. I mean, how come one minute he's threatening to go to the police and the next D&M's got a brand new owner and a computer system to match?'

'Bette,' Laurel replied simply. 'That's what happened to him. She didn't tell me the whole story, but it had something to do with some dodgy bedroom photos he'd rather not have splashed over the front page of the *Courant*.'

'You mean Bette blackmailed him into selling the agency to you?' Steph raised a glass in salute. 'Good for her.'

'And besides, it wasn't as if I'd really dropped him in it. He knew the changes made good business sense and he quite fancied taking the credit for thinking them up. All we had to do was defer for a few months, till the year was up, and then he could inherit his mother's millions and offload D&M on to me.'

'What a jammy git,' said Steph. 'Sounds like my kind of man.'

Laurel turned to her. 'Steph, practically *every* man's your kind of man.' At least it was if the last year was anything to go by: Steph had been pulling for Britain halfway across the world and back again, and was looking disgustingly happy on it.

'True. I wouldn't want to deprive the poor darlings by restricting myself to just one, now would I? Young, free and single, that's me. Well, as young as Botox can keep me anyhow.'

'Ah, but you'd better watch out,' Laurel patted her swelling stomach. 'This is what happens when you get involved with men – twins! And to think I swore I'd never end up like my sister.'

'You're nothing like Jools! None of that barefoot and pregnant crap for you, Lozzie, you're a pillar of the local business community. The day after the birth you'll be straight back to the D&M office, just like Edwin Case's widowed mother.'

'Ha ha,' snorted Laurel. 'Not bloody likely. Anyway, I think I know somebody who'd have a few objections.'

Steph turned and shouted towards the kitchen. 'Oi, Significant Other, where's that cup of tea you promised us half an hour ago? You've not got him very well trained, Lozzie,' she quipped.

Graeme entered the living room carrying a tray of tea. 'Tea up. Sorry it took so long, I had a call on my mobile from Lord Ryecroft.'

'What now?' marvelled Laurel, balancing a mug of PG on her gargantuan tummy. Ever since he'd worked on *Moths and Mammoths*, that big TV docu-soap at the Natural History Museum, it seemed like everybody in the world wanted Graeme to stuff something.

'Looks like his Tasmanian tiger needs refurbishing. All its hair's started falling out. Don't worry, I can be there and back in a weekend.'

Laurel looked up at him and a huge warm wave of happiness and pride washed over her. Even now, she found it hard to believe that things had moved so quickly between them; that an impetuous kiss between two dysfunctional people locked in a broom cupboard could have opened the door to something so life-changingly right.

They were neither of them perfect, that went without saying. But maybe that was the key; their insecurities were mirror images, their weaknesses and strengths, hopes and fears the perfect complement to each other. Like two slightly battered jigsaw pieces, they fitted together as though they had never been apart. And if Laurel had her way, they never would be ever again.

Mind you, thought Laurel, God knows what we'll be like when the twins are keeping us awake all night.

'Here's to us.' Graeme squeezed himself onto the sofa between Laurel and Steph, raised his tea mug in a toast – and promptly sneezed most of the contents halfway across the room, almost blasting poor Neil out of his plastic castle.

'Bless him, he's been a bit under the weather,' said Laurel, mopping up tea with a crumpled tissue. 'Some kind of bug I think.'

Graeme laughed and kissed his brand-new wife on the forehead. 'That's right, a nasty attack of the love bug. And one thing's for sure: I've no intention of ever getting better.'